PRAISE FO
BILLION.

Ms. Dearen's prose ensnares the reader from paragraph one and keeps up the pace with admirable dexterity... Stephanie and Bran are layered characters who develop throughout the book, and Bran's disability is sympathetically and realistically portrayed.

— JANICE MATIN, IND'TALE MAGAZINE

Rarely do I become emotional to tears. In this book, I started with tears and ended with tears. So many great elements in this book.

— RANDY TRAMP, AUTHOR OF NIGHT TO KNIGHT

I loved the new twist on the billionaire love story idea. Can't wait to see how the whole series turns out!

— LIA LONDON, AUTHOR OF THE NORTHWEST ROMANTIC COMEDY SERIES

There are wonderful characters, deep issues, humor, intrigue, and great chemistry! There's raw honesty in the character of Bran, the blind billionaire.

— TINA MORLEY, AMANDA'S BOOKS AND MORE

THE BILLIONAIRE'S TEMPORARY MARRIAGE

BOOK THREE OF THE LIMITLESS CLEAN BILLIONAIRE ROMANCE SERIES

TAMIE DEAREN

Copyright © 2019 by Tamie Dearen

All rights reserved.

No part of this book may be reproduced in any form or by any electronic or mechanical means, including information storage and retrieval systems, without written permission from the author, except for the use of brief quotations in a book review.

This is a work of fiction. Names, characters, places, and incidents are a product of the author's imagination. Locales and public names are sometimes used for atmospheric purposes. Any resemblance to actual people, living or dead, or to businesses, companies, events, institutions, or locales is completely coincidental.

Cover designed by Tamie Dearen Arts.

ISBN 9781691563319

The Billionaire's Temporary Marriage

*To all the parents of special-needs children,
who tirelessly pour out their hearts on a daily basis*

CHAPTER 1

Two vertical pink lines.

Brooklyn squeezed her eyes closed tight, hoping one of the lines might disappear. She looked again, but it was unmistakable. The second line remained. The line that spelled the end of her dreams.

I'm pregnant!

With a bitter laugh at the irony, she considered texting a picture of the positive test to Nathan. She'd deleted his contact information from her cell phone when the final divorce papers arrived in the mail yesterday. But she still knew his number by heart... though he'd torn that heart to shreds.

The moment replayed in her mind, as it had every day since the morning he handed her the divorce petition while she was still lying in bed.

"Just because my periods only come every three months doesn't mean I can't get pregnant." In shock, Brooke had attempted to make sense of the stack of papers in her trembling hands. "What about the fertility specialist?"

"I'm not giving a sample of my sperm to some laboratory just to prove what I already know. *You're* the problem. There's nothing wrong with me." He'd lifted his chin in pride as he destroyed her with his next words. "Otherwise, Wendy wouldn't be pregnant with my kid right now."

She flipped through the pages of the divorce petition, her eyes refusing to focus on the words. The room spun as her voice came out in a wobbly tone, bile rising in her throat. "You had this last night. Why didn't you give it to me then? Why did you sleep with me?"

"Just something for you to remember me by, baby."

As it had that morning, his laughter still rang in her ears.

Brooke flung the pregnancy test into the metal trashcan with a satisfying clang. Anger rising, she grabbed the two matching ones from the counter and gave them the same treatment.

"I guess the last laugh is on you, Nathan," she muttered under her breath, though she wasn't laughing. At least she wasn't crying. Not yet. But when reality sank in, she probably would be.

How could she possibly keep her job now? She'd already been worried the board would let her go when they discovered she was divorced. But this sealed her fate. There was no way the strict, religious-based facility would want an unwed, pregnant woman counseling their troubled teenaged girls. She might've been able to hide the divorce for the next five months until she'd accumulated the therapy hours she needed to get her counseling license. But she wasn't going to be able to hide her growing stomach for long.

Her hands slid down to rest on her belly, noting the roundness she'd attributed to water-weight.

A baby!

She could only hope the baby was okay, since she certainly hadn't been eating well. At least she didn't drink alcohol, having never acquired a taste for it. She'd written off her fatigue and upset stomach as stress, only this past week noting that the time between her menses was even longer than the usual three months. But this morning, when she'd lost her breakfast of dry cereal, she'd decided to use one of the pregnancy tests in her medicine cabinet, left over from the twelve-month period she and Nathan had purposefully attempted to have a baby.

She couldn't think about it, now. She had to get up and go to work. No one at Hayward Home had to know about the divorce, and she would hide the pregnancy as long as possible. But eventually, someone would discover the truth and she'd be out of a job.

Maybe, by some miracle, she would find another paying job that allowed her to get the counseling hours required for her license. Even if she did, what were the chances the benefits would include health insurance, like her present employment?

She hurried to her closet and flung the door open, groaning when she spied the only clean work polo, hanging there in all its offensive pink glory, laughing at her.

"I hate pink!"

She snatched the shirt, knocking the hanger to the floor in her haste. Just her luck! All the preferable polo shirts were in the bottom of the hamper. How could she have forgotten to do laundry, again? She'd have to be more organized if she was going to survive life with a baby.

I'm not ready to be a mother... especially not a single mom.

Sixty-six days... the sixty-day waiting period required in Texas, plus one day for her impatient ex-husband to schedule the final perfunctory hearing and five days for the papers to arrive in the mail. There could be no doubt how far along she was in her pregnancy. Maybe she would be more emotionally prepared by the time the baby was born.

TUCKING her purse strap over her shoulder, she grabbed a breakfast bar on the way out the door. With any luck, her stomach would settle and she could keep some food in it.

As she climbed into her aging two-door sedan, she tried to imagine maneuvering a baby seat into the back.

"Sorry, Andretti," she stroked her hand across the cracked vinyl seat beside her. "It's not that you haven't been a good car, but I really need four doors."

Yet she knew she didn't have the money to buy a vehicle, even if she traded for another used one. And how would she afford her medical co-payments, not to mention her fifteen-hundred-dollar deductible?

Coffee! Coffee would make everything better.

Even though it has to be decaf.

COLE STEADIED the disposable cup in his prosthetic hand, a task made more difficult by the lack of feeling. It was a delicate balance. Too loose and the coffee would slip from his grip. Too tight and the cup would crumple. He'd worn his favorite prosthesis, a lime-green mechanical arm that offered superior dexterity. Still, the lack of sensory feedback added major limitations. Soon he would have a state-of-the-art prosthesis that could actually *feel*, though this technology was still in the developmental stage.

He got the usual stares from the coffee shop patrons. Some were probably curious about his neon hand. But a few might've recognized him, despite his low-tucked cowboy hat.

Satisfied his coffee cup was secure, he used his "real" right hand to tuck a napkin in his pocket and retrieve his cell phone. He scanned his latest messages as he turned from the condiment counter and started toward an empty table next to the door.

Intent on his phone screen, he didn't notice the person entering the shop until he collided with her. While the coffee lid should've prevented any spills, it was no match for the reflex tightening of his mechanical hand. The cup collapsed, popping the lid off to send coffee splashing to the floor, splattering everything in its path.

Embarrassed, he put his phone away and surveyed the damage, an apology spilling from his mouth before he even got a good look at his victim. "So sorry about that. I wasn't watching where I was going."

He wondered how much money it would cost him to make up for his moment of carelessness. What was happening to him? He was losing his edge. His painstaking attention to detail had always been his trademark, but lately he'd made a number of serious and costly mistakes... enough to keep his attorney agitated.

"Could this day get any worse?"

His gaze jerked to the source of the feminine voice, a sight that set his emotions whirling. Glossy brunette hair fell in soft waves, framing a pair of deep-brown eyes and a pert nose. His pulse quickened with instant attraction. She held her arm forward at an awkward angle, her sleeve dripping with coffee that had drenched most of a once-white cardigan, parted to expose a garishly-bright pink shirt. Mouth gaping in a surprised O, she stared at him with her bottomless eyes, which appeared to grow larger by the second.

From this close proximity, she must've recognized him. He waited, with dread, for the fawning to begin. She was pretty—that much was for sure. Any other day, he'd have taken advantage of the situation, flirting and asking her out. She would know in advance it would be a single date, part of his one-and-done mantra. But today he wasn't in the mood to play the usual games. Especially since excited whispers were spreading around the coffee shop, every eye trained their direction. Phones came out as customers shared their celebrity spotting on social media.

"I'm very sorry, ma'am." He tipped his Stetson and handed her a business card, hoping to settle the matter before they drew any more attention. "I'll be glad to pay for your cleaning bill. Just call me at this number."

Her brows drew down, chin jutting forward, and the card was left dangling from his fingers.

"Is this your way of making a move on me? Because it's not going to work."

He blinked at her. "What?"

"Do I have a sign around my neck that says, 'Easy target?'"

A genuine smile slid onto his face for the first time that

morning. "I'm looking at your sign right now, and it clearly states, 'Don't mess with me until I've had my coffee.'"

Her cheeks flushed, a grin playing on her lips. He was pleased to have put it there.

"I'm sorry. I shouldn't have accused you of anything, but you won't believe what just happened." Her arms flailed with emotion, flinging coffee from her dripping sleeve. "Some guy in the parking lot just propositioned me. At eight o'clock in the morning! Can you believe that? All I did was say a polite hello. I guess I need a sign that says, 'Not interested!'"

She's feisty! I like it!

"If it's any consolation, the coffee stains ought to ward the creeps off for the rest of the day."

Her mouth tugged up at the corners. "That's a good point."

She seemed so genuine—a rarity in his experience, outside his close circle of friends. And more importantly, it seemed she didn't recognize him. He had to find out.

"I'm sorry about spilling on you. You see, I was holding my coffee in the wrong hand." He thrust his artificial arm forward, still holding the crumpled paper cup, confident she couldn't fake a lack of recognition when he pointed out the bright green prosthesis he was famous for.

"No, it was my fault. I was looking up at the menu when I came in." Her gaze skimmed past his arm without pausing, settling on her own soggy one.

It was hard to believe, but she seemed oblivious to his identity. He warmed inside, feeling a bit more inclined to flirt. "Perhaps, it was destiny."

"Probably so." She groaned, looking down at her clothes.

"I need to go home and change. But I can't, because I have a meeting at work in thirty minutes."

His hopes fell. *She recognized me, and now she's fishing for money.*

With a resigned sigh, he retrieved his wallet and pulled out some folded hundred-dollar bills. "Here's five hundred. Go buy some new clothes. There's bound to be a dress shop close by." His tone came out coarser than he meant.

"I'm not taking that." She backed away, staring at the money like it was a poisonous snake. "For goodness' sake, this sweater is ancient. And this is my least favorite work shirt. I'll be happy to throw it away."

She doesn't want money? Is it possible she really doesn't know who I am?

As the most well known of the four kingpins at Phantom Enterprises, Cole rarely went anywhere without being recognized. Generally, he flaunted his fame and fortune, an attempt to compensate for all those times his classmates had ridiculed him about his deformed left arm, which ended before it reached his elbow. Truth be told, his preference for the neon-green robot-like hand was in part to prove he was no longer ashamed of his defect. His efforts had made him as famous for his "fake" arm as for his wealth and success. And his recent appearance on the Millionaire Matchup finale, as the bachelor in the coming season preview, had gained him even more notoriety. Cole seldom met someone who hadn't heard of him, so he couldn't help being intrigued with this woman.

"You have to let me give you something for ruining your clothes." He drew the napkin from his pocket and dabbed futilely at her sodden sweater sleeve as a male employee arrived with a bucket and mop.

"I'm so sorry, Mr. Miller. We'll get this cleaned up right away."

"Mr. Miller, huh?" Brows drawn downward, her eyes darted from Cole to the employee and back. "You must come here a lot. Funny I've never seen you before."

"My first time to come in the morning," he said truthfully, as he stepped to the side, motioning for her to follow. "We should move out of the way."

"Mr. Miller!" A fiftyish man arrived and shoved a replacement coffee into his hand. "Here you go, Mr. Miller. Sorry about that cup. We should have had stronger ones. I brought you a souvenir mug, so you don't have to worry about that happening again. I'm Jack Winston, the manager."

Cole's victim cocked her head as she peeled off the sweater. "Who *are* you?"

"Don't you recognize him?" the twenty-something worker hissed, pointing with his mop handle. "He's Cole Miller! You know… Phantom Enterprises! The guy with the…" He made an awkward face, as people often did when the subject of Cole's prosthesis arose.

"Oh, no," she groaned, her cheeks glowing as pink as her shirt. "Can I just melt into the mop bucket? I can't believe I didn't recognize you."

"Not a big deal," said Cole. "Actually, it's kind of nice."

"Par for the course, after the morning I had. I get the chance to meet somebody famous, and I look like *this*." She gestured to her coffee-spotted shirt. At least her pants were dark, matching the coffee.

"Actually, your sweater took the brunt of it. Your shirt only has a few little coffee splashes on it."

"I'm not talking about the coffee." She gave him an exasperated eye-roll. "I'm talking about this stupid pink polo shirt. I promise, I don't usually wear hot pink."

"You don't?" Cole suppressed a grin.

"I don't usually wear any shade of pink. I hate pink. But this was the only clean work shirt I had. That's why I was wearing this ratty sweater on top when it's going to be in the high eighties today." She moved to the condiment counter and grabbed a handful of napkins while she continued in a nervous chatter. "I'll just blot it a little, but I don't care if it's ruined forever. Actually, it looks better with brown spots on it. Tones down the pink."

As she dabbed the napkin or her shirt, Cole spied the logo on her pocket, the distinctive double-H he'd come to know so well in the last few months.

Hayward Home!

His breath left him. Stunned, he stood like a statue while his mind raced.

She had to be an employee at Hayward. The answer to his prayers. Surely, she had access to the information he needed. At the very least, she knew someone with access. After months of dead-end trails and closed doors, she was the "in" he'd been looking for. Maybe he could buy her a coffee and casually get to know her. He painted on his most ingratiating smile and turned to speak to her. But she was gone.

"Nice to meet you, Mr. Miller."

The voice came from behind him. He whipped around to see her, head tucked down, as she slipped out the door.

He couldn't let her escape. Not when he was so close to finding the answers.

"Wait!"

Heart racing, he handed his coffee back to the confused manager and hurried after her. When he got outside, she was running across the parking lot, the soiled sweater hanging from her arm.

"Hey! Stop! I don't even know your name!"

She reached her car—a small, dated sedan—and jumped inside. Cole ran toward the parking lot entrance, intending to block her way, but she pulled out of her parking place and exited behind the building, her tires spinning as she drove through a patch of gravel.

What just happened?

CHAPTER 2

Cole watched Finn's face disappear from the large video screen on his office wall, but Finn's laughter continued, even after he slid from his chair, presumably to roll on the floor. The conference call was doing nothing to improve Cole's mood. He'd hoped to get some encouragement from his three best friends and business partners. But Finn's antics had the other two laughing as well.

"There's nothing funny about this!" Cole crossed his arms and glared at the screen, waiting for Finn to reappear.

With a strong friendship forged at a computer camp for teens with disabilities, Cole knew Finn cared deeply, despite his teasing. Living with a limited lifespan from his sometimes-debilitating cystic fibrosis, Finn kept a lighthearted attitude, laced with droll wit. Cole usually found Finn's sense of humor entertaining, but was in no mood for it today.

Jarrett Alvarez, on the split screen from his office in

Denver, was the first to regain his composure. Like Cole, Jarrett also wore a prosthesis, having lost his leg as a young teen due to bone cancer. "Maybe she ran away because Hayward Home warned her about you. Haven't you been fighting with them about releasing information?"

"Hayward Home doesn't know I'm involved. Garner made all the inquiries without giving a hint to my identity. He's been very careful."

"What if they kept tabs on the babies after they were adopted? They might've figured it out." Jarrett leaned forward, his elbows on his desk, dark hair falling across his forehead.

"My adoptive parents only lived in Houston for three years before my father died. I don't even remember him." Cole ignored Finn as he crawled back up into his chair, instead addressing the other two, who were at least attempting to be supportive. "Mom moved to Kansas to live with her parents. She married Dad two years later, so my name was changed from Davis to Miller five years after the adoption, and I lived there until I graduated from high school. I can't believe Hayward could keep up with all that."

"But Garner's been asking questions about you. Surely their records show the baby had a deficient arm, and you're a celebrity with a missing hand," said Jarrett. "They might've put two and two together and warned their staff about you."

"I guess it's possible."

He almost hoped it was true, though it would mean his chances of gaining information were slim-to-none. The woman's rejection bothered him more than he cared to admit. She'd thrown down the gauntlet, and he was determined to win… whatever it took.

"What if she isn't single, and she thought you were trying to make a move on her?" Jarrett asked.

"It's possible she's in a relationship." Cole wasn't particularly happy about the idea. "The guy at the coffee shop said she had a ring but hadn't been wearing it lately."

With a gulp of water from his insulated cup, Finn regained enough composure to poke fun at him again. "Maybe the woman ran away because she hates city guys who dress up like cowboys." Somehow, the tease sounded even more irritating with Finn's slight British accent.

"I own a ranch with 200 head of cattle." Cole ground his teeth together, once again defending his preferred mode of dress to Finn. "I think that earns me the right to wear boots and a Stetson."

"But you've never been on a horse."

Finn grinned his challenge. Cole had no desire to ride a horse, and Finn knew it.

"I don't need a horse. I can cover my entire thousand acres with my pickup and a four-wheeler."

"Let's get back to the subject at hand," said Branson Knight, who was broadcasting from New York, along with Finn. "What do you know about this woman?"

"Her name is Brooke, and she comes in for coffee three or four mornings a week." Cole wiggled his jaw from side to side, trying to relax the tight muscles. "The kid at Lava Java confirmed that she works at Hayward Home. He said he'd asked her about the logo on her shirts."

"I haven't seen you this uptight about a girl since college." Despite having two sightless prosthetic eyes, Bran's piercing gaze seemed to read Cole's mind.

"You still can't see me," Cole joked, pulling at his suddenly-too-tight collar.

"I see plenty." Bran cocked his head. "You think Brooke might be different from all the other women, and you're afraid to find out. At some point, you have to give love a chance. Why can't you admit you like her?"

Ever since Bran had tied the knot, he'd been after the others to settle down and get married. Finn had already followed suit, but Cole and Jarrett were firm holdouts.

"Because I *don't* like her. She's just my only lead to find out about my birth mom. If I could get to know her, she might agree to do a little research for me." Cole let out a nervous chuckle, his pen tapping a machine gun rhythm on the table. "But it doesn't matter. She's obviously not attracted to me, so it's another dead end."

"I bet the real reason she wasn't interested was that she saw you on that Millionaire Matchup show." Finn waggled his brows. "She knows you'll be married to someone else in a few months, so why bother?"

Cole let out a low rumble from his throat. "I'm *not* getting married. Not now. Not ever."

"Didn't you say they had you trapped?" Jarrett lifted his eyebrows in question. "That the document you signed was legally binding, with a million-dollar penalty for reneging?"

"Yes, but Garner's going to find some way to get me out of it." He hoped and prayed his words were true.

"I still don't understand why you even considered being on the show," said Bran. "Unless you're not as opposed to marriage as you say you are."

"Alice McGowen, the show's producer, made it sound different. I told her I planned to be single for the rest of my life, and she bet me her matchmaker could find a woman who would change my mind. The show pays a huge donation to the charity of my choice, just for being on the show." Cole counted it off on his fingers. "Ten women... ten television dates... a huge payment to Limitless and a ton of publicity for Phantom Enterprises."

"At least we've already had some great publicity," Jarrett said. "The stock prices took a leap after that show aired with your interview."

Cole rolled his eyes. "That's a small comfort."

"It's called Millionaire Matchup," said Finn. "Just tell them you're a billionaire, not a millionaire."

In fact, their computer-media-information company, Phantom Enterprises, was a multi-billion-dollar business. Their gaming systems branch, alone, was worth more than a billion. But the four funneled a large part of their money into Limitless, their non-profit arm, which benefited children with disabilities.

"I imagine they've seen the public financials on Phantom Enterprises," Cole said between gritted teeth.

"Why not just do the show?" asked Jarrett. "You might actually meet a woman and fall in love. If not, surely you can meet one you could stand living with for six months. Isn't that how long you have to stay married to fulfill the contract?"

"I'm not sleeping with some woman I don't even love, married or not. What if she got pregnant?"

A shiver went down his spine. He didn't expand on his question, but his friends understood his fears. He had nightmares of losing a baby to an abortion over which he had no control. Rather than a futile search for a woman he could trust with absolute certainty, he'd chosen never to allow any woman to carry his child.

"She could have her own bedroom," Bran suggested.

"The contract specifies that we have to share a bedroom after we get married." Cole found himself gripping the edge of his desk. "And yes, I know I wouldn't have to sleep with her. But I have to assume she'd be doing everything possible to make it happen while pointing out that we were legally married. I don't want to depend on willpower, alone."

"How would they know what happens in your own home?" asked Bran.

"They follow the marriage for six months." Jarrett intercepted the question. "They have cameras in the home and catch the couple having fights or romantic moments. It makes for some great reality TV. Everyone wants to see how wealthy people live, and the drama just adds to the appeal. You're lucky they don't have cameras inside the bedroom."

"That's another reason I'm not doing the show," Cole said. "I'm not giving up privacy in my own house."

"Maybe you shouldn't have signed the contract before Garner looked it over," said Finn.

"Thanks so much for stating the obvious." Cole ladled on the sarcasm. "You're about as helpful as Garner."

"What's his advice?" Bran asked.

"Garner says the contract is tight. Only Millionaire Matchup can cancel without a financial penalty. So he suggested I do something to make myself undesirable." Cole gave a bitter laugh.

"Just wearing that Stetson might do the trick," Finn teased.

Cole aimed a menacing glare at Finn. "But committing *murder* would be a sure thing."

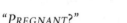

"Pregnant?"

Brooke winced at the shout in her ear, steeling herself for the rampage to come. Harper had inherited the family's fierce Italian temper.

"I can't believe this! You should've been more careful," Harper ranted. "Who's the father?"

It was Brooke's turn to be angry. "Nathan, of course! You know I would never sleep around."

Brooke walked to her office door and checked the empty hallway, before shutting it.

"Oh… you slept with him after he dumped you for Wendy?" Harper asked.

"The night before, when I had no idea what was coming."

"Ewww! You didn't tell me that. He's even more of a cow turd than I thought."

"I know you always hated Nathan. But there was a sweet side to him you never saw."

"You always believe the best about people, Brooke. You're just like Mom."

"You say that like it's a bad thing."

"I love Mom, but we both know she'd be in trouble if Dad weren't such a bulldog. Hang on a second. I need to pull onto the highway…" Harper's voice paused, and Brooke could hear the sound of her car's blinker and the motor accelerating. "Okay, I'm back. So what are you going to do?"

"I guess I'm going to have a baby. Should be easy for me.

After all, I've been counseling all these pregnant women at Hayward Home. I just need to listen to my own advice."

"You'd better not tell Nathan right away. If he found out, he might appeal the divorce."

"The divorce is final. I got the decree in the mail yesterday."

"But Texas has a thirty-day waiting period before it's really final. Aunt Patty told me all about it."

Aunt Patty was the proverbial black sheep of their mother's five sisters. She was on her fifth marriage. Or was it her sixth?

"Not us. We waived the waiting period in the divorce decree. Anyway, I would never take him back after what he did." Just because she still loved him didn't mean she was a dishrag.

"Good for you, sis. You've got the Ponzio backbone."

"So, I'll get to be a single mom." She said it with a *yippee* in her voice.

"I hope you don't give the baby up for adoption. Isn't that what most of the *Wayward* girls are doing?"

"*Hayward.*" Brooke wasn't sure why she went to the trouble to correct her sister. It wouldn't change anything. Harper loved to use substitute names for places and things. "Only about a third are giving up custody. The rest are going to be single mothers. We help them find jobs and childcare and such."

"I thought it was basically a private adoption agency."

"They started out that way, forty years ago. But now they provide these women with all the resources they need, so they won't feel abortion is their only choice. Adoption is one alternative, and they don't push it." Brooke shut down her computer and grabbed her tote bag, heading for the door. "Honestly, it's an awesome place, even if the board is a little on the strict side, as far as religion is concerned."

"A little?" Harper let out a harsh chuckle. "They won't even let you wear makeup to work. I'd say that's pretty strict. Didn't you say they might fire you if they find out about the divorce?"

"It's possible. And adding a baby to the picture isn't going to make it better." Brooke kept her voice down as she went down the hallway, even though she was probably the last to leave.

"Good grief! I hadn't even thought about that. *Hey!*" A horn sounded. "That idiot practically changed lanes right on top of me. Let's talk about your diet. What have you eaten today?"

"Well, I need to eat better, for sure. No time for lunch today. I'm on my way out, so I'm eating my sandwich." Juggling her bag and her phone, she found her lunch sack, hoping her nausea would settle with a bit of food.

"You brought a sandwich? What's on it?" Harper sounded alarmed, as if she'd said she was going to eat lead.

"Just a ham and cheese sandwich. Nothing weird."

"Don't eat it! Pregnant women can't eat deli meat. You could get a listeria infection!"

"Did you learn this at vet school? Are you sure this isn't something that's only true for dogs or cats?"

"No, it's for humans. I promise."

With a forlorn look at her enticing sandwich, she stuck it back in her bag, before punching the elevator button to open the doors. "Can I eat my grapes?"

"Yes, grapes should be fine."

As she plucked a grape off the stem and popped it in her mouth, a bone-tiredness swept over her. She wanted nothing more than to slide down to the elevator floor and hide her head in her arms. "Harper, I don't know if I can do this."

"Brooke, you *can* do this. I'll help you."

"Why did God let this happen? I tried to do everything right." Her voice croaked with climbing emotions, probably due to the pregnancy. At least she had an excuse for her mood swings now.

"I know the timing is awful, but I believe this baby is going to be a blessing from God. Just wait. When you hold it in your arms, you won't care who the father is." Harper cleared her throat. "Speaking of fathers, are you going to tell Nathan?"

"I guess I should, but not right now. I'll probably end up moving home."

"To *Nowhere*, Oklahoma?"

Brooke chuckled at her sister's joke. "*Bellaire's* not that bad."

"You'll never find a place to do counseling in Bellaire. You need to come live with me in Baton Rouge."

Brooke could almost see Harper give a sharp nod, like the matter was settled. A year older than Brooke's twenty-nine, her sister had always been bossy.

"I appreciate the offer, Harper, but you don't have time to help me with a baby. Not in your last year of vet school."

The elevator doors opened on the ground floor, and Brooke stepped out, glancing down the empty hallway. She turned down the long corridor that led through the downstairs of the residence hall toward the employee parking lot.

"We'll find a way to make it work," said Harper. "It could be fun."

As Brooke passed a water cooler, she stopped to gulp down a cup of water. Her stomach clenched in protest and she moaned. "I don't think this is going to be fun, no matter where I live. I've thrown up twice today."

"I thought you said you hadn't eaten."

"I haven't. Today my stomach doesn't even like water." The nausea subsided. "Okay, that's better. I think I can make it to my car. It's better when I'm sitting down."

"You need to find a doctor," said Harper.

"I'll have to find an ob-gyn here, at least for now. But if I move home, I'll have to see Dr. Kennedy." She shivered. "It would be so weird for him to be my doctor when I would see him at church every Sunday morning."

"Gross! No way I could do that. You can't have a baby in Bellaire, anyway," Harper said. "They don't even have a hospital."

"I plan to stay here as long as possible. But I have to make plans for when I lose my job."

"There must be some way you could stay in Houston. Can't you find another job? You have a college degree. If you aren't looking for a counseling gig, surely you could find something."

"Not too many jobs out there for a psychology major. And I need one with insurance. Even this job doesn't have paid maternity leave." Her head spun, and she stopped until she felt steady again. "I don't know how I can avoid moving home."

"How about a dating app? You could find another

husband, and get married before anybody at Hayward Home finds out about it."

"Sure. They're probably tons of guys who want to marry a pregnant woman. Anyway, I've sworn off men forever." Unbidden, Cole Miller's face passed through her mind. The humiliation of the morning flooded back, sending blood rushing to her face. "I haven't even told you the worst thing that happened this morning."

"Worse than being pregnant with your loser-ex-husband's baby and thinking you might be about to lose your job? I'm afraid to ask…"

"Guess who I ran into in the coffee shop this morning?"

"Who? Someone from the board of directors?"

"No. Your secret crush… Cole Miller."

"Oh my gosh! Are you kidding me? Did you talk to him? Did you mention you have a sister who's in love with him? I can't believe he's doing Millionaire Matchup. I'm going to lose him." She made a sad moaning sound. "Maybe he could pull some strings and get me on that TV show. I'd marry him in a heartbeat. Those other women don't love him like I do."

"Sorry. No chance of that happening. I was walking in the door, looking up at the wall menu for something with decaf, and I literally *ran into him*. His coffee spilled all over me. Then I babbled like an idiot and didn't even recognize him."

Brooke passed through the reception lobby and waved at the guard.

"How could you not recognize him? He isn't as good-looking in person as his pictures? No, don't tell me. Don't destroy my dream." Harper giggled.

"He's smoking hot in person." Brooke shoved her way out the exit door and onto the sidewalk that stretched alongside the row of dormitory style rooms. "I was just so flustered, thinking about the baby and all. I didn't really look at Cole until this employee was gushing all over him and called him Mr. Miller." Brooke fanned herself against another surge of nausea. "Then I saw people in Lava Java taking pictures of him and me. I'm probably all over social media, splattered with coffee, no makeup, wearing a horrid pink polo shirt."

"That totally stinks! Except for the part about meeting Cole Miller. And the part about the pink shirt. You know I love pink."

"I might like it, too, if I hadn't been forced to wear your hand-me-down shirts all through middle school. Every single one was *pink*."

"Ha! I did you a favor. With our coloring, we look great in pink." Harper didn't give her a chance to argue. "What happened after you collided with Cole?"

"I hightailed it out of there as fast as I could." Brooke stopped as she passed a trashcan, digging the sandwich from her bag and tossing it inside. "I can't believe I didn't even notice his hand. How could I miss a bright green robot-hand?"

"I wish I'd been there. I'd be perfect for him. I love cowboys. I could take care of his cattle and his dog… You know, he has a Blumastiff. That's a cool breed."

"Believe me, I wish it had been you instead of me."

"You have to go back there tomorrow and look for him. Show him my picture. Give him my number."

"Didn't you hear me? I was completely mortified! I'm never going back to that coffee shop, because I never want to see Cole Miller again."

She rounded the corner of the building and slammed into

a brick wall... a six-foot-one-inch, boot-clad wall whose hand reached out to steady her, sending a ripple of sparks to blow the circuits in her system.

"Sorry about that, Brooke." Cole grinned, flashing a dimple and somehow sucking every molecule of breathable oxygen from the air around them. "Seems like I have a habit of running into you today. *Literally.*"

With a mouth that felt like she'd gargled saltine crackers, Brooke rasped into the phone still glued to her ear, "Harper, I need to call you back."

CHAPTER 3

Cole whipped a bouquet of flowers from behind his back. "I got these for you, as an apology for spilling the coffee."

"Thanks," she said in a squeaky voice as she accepted the assortment of somewhat-wilted flowers. Her gaze flicked to the adjacent landscaping, whose nearby annuals were sparser than the rest, and she battled to keep a straight face. "You picked them out of the flower bed?"

His hand lifted as if to tip a hat, though the Stetson he'd worn earlier that morning was missing. On his forehead, an unruly lock of sandy-brown hair dared her to tuck it into position.

"It's the thought that counts, right?" he asked. "And notice, there are no pink flowers in this bunch."

A grin fought its way onto her face, but her pulse raced like a rabid dog was chasing her. He seemed to be flirting with her, but it felt all wrong. Her divorce had only been final for a few days. Anyway, it had to be her imagination.

There was no way Cole Miller could be interested in her. She held her breath, willing her heart to slow down.

"You're right—no pink. Thank you for the flowers." She drew her brows downward, attempting a stern look. "But what are you doing here? And how did you find me?"

"Shall we walk while we talk?"

With a way-too-innocent expression, he offered an elbow. She wanted to refuse. After all, he'd invaded her privacy by tracking her down. Unfortunately, she noted his bright green prosthetic hand protruding from the shirt sleeve jutted toward her. If she turned him down, he might be insulted, thinking she was balking at touching the prosthesis. She shoved the bedraggled flowers into her tote and set her hand in the crook of his arm, doing her best to ignore the strange lumps that might've been part of the prosthetic hardware.

"You can walk me to my car, but that's all." As they moved, a wave of vertigo hit, and she gripped a little tighter.

"It's a nice day, isn't it?"

"Don't change the subject," she said. "You've got a lot of explaining to do if you don't want me to think you're just like that creep who propositioned me this morning."

A sheepish smile exposed sparkling white teeth. "I just felt bad about the coffee mishap, and you ran off before I could make it right."

"But how did you find out my name and where I work? You have to admit, that's pretty high on the creepy scale."

"That's the first time anyone's ever accused me of being creepy." He cocked his head to the side. "Everyone knows who I am, so I'm usually above suspicion."

"Or maybe, everybody thinks you're creepy. Only no one says it, because you're rich."

Cole threw his head back and laughed. "Until you came along and felt obliged to let me know just how weird and disturbing I am."

"Exactly." She squinted at him, nausea swirling in her belly. "For instance, you're still avoiding my questions. How did you figure out who I am and who I work for?"

He shrugged his deliciously broad shoulders, and she wondered if he lifted weights with his prosthesis.

"It wasn't all that difficult, really. Lester told me all about you."

"Lester?"

"The guy at Lava Java." A wrinkle formed between Cole's eyebrows. "I think he has a thing for you."

She had only a vague remembrance of the coffee-shop employee she'd probably talked to at least a hundred times, but she wasn't about to admit how oblivious she normally was to her surroundings. "Oh, *that* Lester. Yeah. Nice guy."

Without prompting, Cole turned down the second row in the parking lot headed toward her sedan. "He said you used to wear a wedding ring..."

The unspoken question dangled in the air. She pretended not to notice. "Well, as long as you're here, I'd better inform you that my sister, Harper, is in love with you."

His gorgeous hazel eyes, with specks of dark green, crinkled at the corners. "Is that so?"

"Yes. I've been ordered to tell you that she would be the perfect wife for you. She loves cowboys. And she's in her last year of vet school, so she could take care of your cows and horses and dogs and such."

"I'll keep that in mind if I ever decide to get married."

"That's happening pretty soon, right? What with that matchmaker show coming—"

He groaned. "Don't talk to me about Millionaire Matchup. Biggest mistake of my life."

They reached her car and she fumbled for her keys in the bottom of her bag. His penetrating stare made her palms sweat, and she found herself prattling on and on. "Harper was hoping you could get her on that reality show. Seriously, I think you should consider it. If you have to marry someone, you couldn't find anyone better than my sister. She's not only super smart, she's also beautiful. Thick dark hair. Gorgeous complexion. The whole package."

"She can't be any more smart and beautiful than you."

His hoarse words caressed her, warming her from the inside out. Blood rushed to her cheeks while her heart performed a perfect double back-flip. So what if he was only flirting. His teasing comment was nicer than anything Nathan had said the entire time they were married. It helped that Cole had never laid eyes on Harper, who'd definitely inherited the best genes from their parents. In contrast to her sister, Brooke's nose was a little too pointed, her chin a bit too prominent, her lips too full. Harper had green eyes, while Brooke's were ordinary dark brown. Brooke found herself hoping the two would never meet and spoil his illusions.

With trembling fingers, she punched her key fob, re-locking the car door twice with a tell-tale honk, before finding the unlock button. He leaned against her car door, his arms folded, like he was planning to camp out.

"Uhmm... can I get in my car, please? And by the way,

you're probably getting dirt all over your jeans." Being single, she couldn't afford the luxury of washing the car.

He didn't budge. "Let's go grab a bite to eat. I'd like to know more about you. It won't even be a date, so you don't have to feel awkward. Just friends. I'll even let you pay for your own meal."

"Mr. Miller…"

"Call me Cole."

Long lashes blinked over those hopeful hazel eyes, and she felt like she was kicking a puppy.

"*Cole…* you've more than made up for the coffee spill that was as much my fault as yours. But you're better off not knowing any more than you already do."

"Why? Are you wanted by the FBI?" His eyes twinkled.

"No, it's just a waste of time. We have nothing in common to base a friendship on. Sure, I could use a rich friend, but I've got nothing to offer in return."

"Aren't you a counselor?"

The question caught her off guard. "Yes. Well, no. I don't have my license yet. But I have my master's in marriage and family counseling." *Fat lot of good it did me. I couldn't even save my own marriage.*

"I could use a little advice right now." Cole cleared his throat. "I'm willing to pay."

"Thanks, but I can't accept pay for private counseling until I get my license. I'm working under a licensed counselor right now. In fact, I have to go home and transcribe my notes for the day."

Saliva started flowing inside her mouth as her nausea returned with a vengeance. Desperate to sit down, she reached for the car door handle, expecting him to move out of the way. He didn't. Instead, his right hand came to rest on top of hers.

"Please, Brooke... I *need* to talk to you."

Before she could think of a response, her stomach heaved. She dropped her tote and turned, barely making it a few steps away before she threw up, right in front of him. At least there was nothing but water splatting onto the hot pavement.

His arm went around her waist. "Are you okay? Should I call an ambulance?"

"I'm fine." Eyes watering, she straightened, wiping her lips on the back of her hand. "I'm just pregnant."

"Pregnant?" He repeated the word in a strained voice.

"Yes, I'm a newly divorced woman, pregnant by my cheating ex-husband." She clenched her jaw, angry that her voice was trembling. "You see? I told you you'd be better off if you didn't know any more about me."

That ought to send him running.

His eyes narrowed, jaw hardening. "I'm driving you home."

COLE IGNORED Brooke as she let out yet another heavy sigh. Other than asking for her address, he'd barely spoken to her since helping her into the passenger seat. He knew he was acting like a boorish caveman, but it was all he could do to hold himself together while he drove. With his hands gripping the steering wheel so they wouldn't shake, he concentrated on the traffic and the navigation instructions from his phone.

"How are you going to get your car?" Brooke asked in an irritated tone.

"I'll take a taxi." His jaw was so tight he could barely squeeze the words out.

"You know, I drove myself to work this morning. I could've driven home."

He answered with a grunt. He couldn't possibly explain his compulsion to take care of her. Hopefully, his protectiveness wasn't ill-placed. Did he dare ask if she planned to keep the baby? If not, would she change her mind if he offered to provide financial help? He had to assume she needed money, or she wouldn't be driving this dilapidated car. Maybe her ex-husband wasn't paying child support.

"Tell me about your ex," he said.

After a moment of silence, she replied, "No."

"No?"

A glance at her face told him she'd progressed from irritated to angry.

"You don't have the right to know anything about me. Just like you didn't have the right to jerk my car keys out of my hand."

"I had to. You weren't in any condition to drive."

"That wasn't your call to make."

This probably wasn't the best time to offer help with her money problems.

"A gentleman doesn't desert a lady in distress." He turned onto her street, eyeing her complex—Park Avenue Apartments—with growing repugnance. The run-down buildings had nothing in common with the famous street in New York. He pulled the car in the driveway.

"Right over there." She pointed to the left. "Park in that spot."

He pulled to a stop and unfolded himself from the tiny car, racing around to open her door. With the strap of her bag over her shoulder, she climbed out, slicing him to pieces with her eyes.

"Thank you for hijacking my car." She held out her palm. "I'll take my keys, now."

"Please, Brooke…" His heart was doing the fight-or-flight thing. "I want to help you."

"I don't want your help." She snatched the keys from his hand.

"But, what are you going to do about the baby?"

"None of your business." As she stomped toward her apartment, he followed on her heels until she spat over her shoulder, "Leave me alone."

"Wait." He almost grabbed her arm but thought better of it. "I'm sorry I got so pushy. Please give me a chance to explain."

She reached the stairs and stopped, turning with crossed arms and narrowed eyes. "You've got sixty seconds." Her foot began to tap, counting off the time.

"You have to promise you won't tell a soul what I'm about to tell you. Don't you have to sign some sort of oath to protect a person's privacy when you're counseling?"

"Thirty seconds." The foot continued its steady beat.

He should leave now and keep his secret safe. He barely knew this woman. No doubt he'd already lost any chance of coercing her into pilfering information about his mother. Why did his shoes feel like they were full of concrete?

"I was adopted from Hayward Home." He wished his words back the moment they escaped.

"Are you kidding me?" The doubt in her expression was a relief.

"Yeah. I was just joking." He backed away and forced out an awkward chuckle, unable to meet her eyes. "I'm sorry I bothered you. Hope you feel better."

Her eyebrows lifted together, her hand flying to cover her mouth. "Holy crickets! You're telling the truth, aren't you?"

"No. Really. I was kidding. I'm actually from Kansas." He glanced at his watch. "I should get going."

He reached up to tip his hat, forgetting he'd left it in his truck. As he turned to make his escape, fingers gripped his arm.

"Cole…" Her hair fluttered as she blew a loose strand out of her face. "I know you're lying. You can't even look at me."

"I'm telling the truth, now. I was lying the first time." He locked eyes with her, hoping she didn't notice the sweat beading on his forehead.

She shook her head. "We can talk… but you have to be completely honest. Will you promise?"

Part of him wanted to run away as fast as he could, but the other part wavered, gluing his feet in place. Something in her deep brown eyes drew him like a magnet to steel. Was it possible he could trust her? Did he dare take a chance? If she told him she was going to have an abortion, he would probably lose his temper. Then she might retaliate by telling the world his secret.

When he didn't respond, her lips pressed in a tight line. She whipped around and clomped up the metal stairway, each step ringing her anger. With his chest so tight he could barely breathe, he hurried up behind her.

"Wait, Brooke… Can I ask you one question?"

She stopped, twisting to look over her shoulder. "You can ask. I may not answer."

"I know this is personal, but…" He swallowed a lump the size of Kansas. "Are you going to keep the baby?"

Her eyes went round, like a possum at night. "Why do you want to know?"

"Just curious. If funds are tight and you don't have enough money to take care of the baby—"

"Mr. Miller, I'm not giving up this baby for adoption, even if you offer me a million dollars. So if that's what you're looking for, this conversation is over."

Flooded with relief, his gut uncoiled. She obviously loved her unborn child, already. That alone made him determined to help her out. At the very least, she needed a new car.

"No, no, no." He stepped beside her, placing his hand on the small of her back, urging her upward. Obviously, she also needed a new place to live, something on the first floor and in a nicer neighborhood. "I don't want to adopt a baby. I want to help you keep him."

Her stiff posture drooped as she trudged upward. "Mr. Miller, I really don't understand why you would do that. But right now, I'm too exhausted to argue with you."

Two flights of stairs, followed by a long walk down and around the corner on the open balcony corridor, and they reached her apartment. The stairs seemed too far removed to be safe if there was ever a fire. He bit his tongue as she jiggled the key around to unlock the door, which didn't even have a deadbolt. He hated this place already.

The small apartment was clean and tidy, though sparsely furnished. The paint and flooring had certainly seen better days. Brooke dropped her bag and crossed to the well-worn couch, collapsing onto it with melted bones. He stepped into the compact kitchen area and located a glass in the cabinet. His attempt to use the refrigerator water dispenser was rewarded with only a loud buzzing sound.

"That thing doesn't work," Brooke said, from the couch, cracking one eye open. "You'll have to drink tap water. I'm sorry I can't offer you a soft drink."

He filled the glass at the sink and brought it to her. "This is for you."

"For me?" she asked, her eyes wide. "Thank you."

She must think he was a spoiled, inconsiderate brat if she was shocked that he would bring a pregnant woman a glass of water. As he moved the footstool and gently lifted her feet onto it, he heard a loud sniff.

"I wish you wouldn't do that." She snatched a tissue from the box on the end table and dabbed her eyes.

"Do what? Move the furniture?"

"No. I wish you wouldn't be nice to me." She wadded the tissue in her hand. "I'm trying to stay mad, and you're making it hard."

"Don't be mad." He gave her a pleading smile. It was worth a try, even though she seemed impervious to his charms. Perched beside her on the couch, he would've touched her arm, but he didn't dare touch her with his robot hand. It might freak her out. "I'm only trying to help."

Arms folded across her chest, her chin lifted. "And what do you want in return?"

He tried to say, "Absolutely nothing," but his lips refused.

If he lied to her now, he'd be no better than her cheating ex-husband. She'd been hurt enough.

"I'll be honest with you," he said, his throat so tight it was hard to breathe. "There is something I want from you. But you have to trust me when I say that's not why I'm helping you. And the real truth is I'm going to help you whether you help me or not."

Pupils dilated, her eyes bored into his. He blinked but didn't look away. After a short eternity of staring until his soul was laid bare, she gave a sharp nod.

"Talk to me. I'm listening."

CHAPTER 4

Brooke wasn't sure exactly when it happened. She'd been quite intimidated when he first started telling his story. In fact, the entire situation seemed rather surreal. But somehow, as he talked, she'd begun to think of Cole Miller not as rich and famous, but as an ordinary guy who'd had a tough childhood and come out of it with more than a few scars. Considering the cruelty of his schoolmates, it was amazing he hadn't succumbed to depression. It seemed his friendships with the teens who eventually became his business partners had sustained him through the years.

"If you really want to talk to your birth mom, you should try locating her through one of the DNA websites."

"Been there. Done that." He fell back against the couch cushions. "I've been on three of those sites for the last six years. No leads whatsoever."

"Listen, Cole. I wish I could help you. I really do." It was hard to disappoint him when he looked like a forlorn little boy. "But even if I could access the records, I can't disclose protected information about your birth mom."

"I know. But I thought..."

His voice trailed off as his fingers pushed his hair into adorable disarray. Lost in thought, he stared at something on the other side of the wall.

"You thought what?" she encouraged.

He leaned forward, elbows on his knees, his gaze aimed at the ratty carpet that never looked clean, no matter how many times she vacuumed. "See, I don't really care if I meet her or not. My parents love me, and I don't want another mother."

"Then why do you want her information? Are you concerned about your health history?"

"No." His head turned, and pain-filled eyes locked with hers. "I just need to know why she did it."

"You mean why she gave you up for adoption?" She laid her hand on his arm. "Most of the girls who come to Hayward Home are young, single, and destitute. Thirty-five years ago, when your birth mom was there, adoption was usually the only alternative. Now, we give financial support, so two-thirds of the women decide to keep their babies."

"But maybe..." His Adam's apple convulsed in his throat. "Maybe she was going to keep me until she saw what was wrong with me."

"Oh, Cole! Surely not!" Brooke put her hands on her slightly-rounded belly. "I can tell you right now I would love this baby no matter what. There's no way I would give him or her up just because there was a birth defect."

"I was two months old when my mother got me. I think my birth mother tried to love me, but couldn't."

She swallowed back her growing emotional response, tears stinging at the back of her eyes. "There has to be some other explanation."

"It could be even worse than that. I've been told it's possible…" His stare shifted to some place beyond the opposite wall. "…that my missing arm is the result of a botched abortion attempt."

Brooke's stomach lurched, and she clutched the couch cushion. "It's not impossible, but that has to be very rare. If that actually happened, it would've been at an illegal clinic by some unqualified abortionist."

"I'm aware of that." His tone was flat and emotionless, but his jaw muscles clenched. "I've done my research."

"But you should also know that thirty-five years ago, most of the women in Hayward Home were there because a parent brought them. So whatever happened with your birth mom probably wasn't even her decision."

His gaze snapped to hers. "Right there—that's all I would need. Even knowing she was underage and her parents signed her in. That would make all the difference. Can't you find out for me?"

"I'm sorry, but it wouldn't be ethical." Her chest hurt, watching his shoulders droop at her words. "Can't you just choose to believe that's what happened?"

"You think I'm screwed up, don't you?" His laugh was bitter. "Well, you're right. But usually I cover it up."

"You're not any more screwed up than I am." She shifted as her stomach protested its emptiness in a loud way.

He frowned and rose to his feet. "You need dinner. Let me cook something for you."

Seeing to her needs seemed to pop him out of his

melancholy, an encouraging sign that he wasn't clinically depressed.

"You can cook? I figured you had a private chef at your house."

His lips curved in a crooked grin as he walked into the kitchen and opened the refrigerator. "My mother would kill me if I wasted money like that. I even do my own laundry."

"That's amazing! Do you clean your own bathroom, too?"

He peeked around the refrigerator door. "No, but please don't tell Mom I hired someone to clean."

"So you don't have a chauffeur driving you around in a limo?"

"I drive my own Ford pickup, and it's even been mudding."

"That sounds fun. I've always wanted to go mudding."

"I'll take you mudding sometime on my ranch." He said it like it was nothing. *Cole Miller* offered to take her mudding. *The* Cole Miller. It was starting to feel like a weird dream again.

Harper was going to *die* when she heard about Cole's visit. Brooke had already ignored ten phone calls from her. No doubt, if she weren't living four hours away in Baton Rouge, she'd be knocking on Brooke's door.

He stuck his head back into the fridge. "You've got nothing in here."

"Yeah, I know. I'll go to the grocery store tomorrow after I get paid. I can eat some cereal for dinner tonight."

"You're pregnant. You need to eat healthy." His scolding tone struck her wrong.

"That's none of your business. You have to cut me some slack, anyway. I just found out this morning."

He slammed the refrigerator door closed and marched back. "You mean you haven't even been to the doctor? Should we go to the emergency clinic?"

"There's no hurry to see a doctor. Besides, I have to keep it a secret as long as possible, so I can't take off work."

"Why hide it? Was your ex abusive?" He perched on the edge of the couch, his expression so worried she forgave him for being intrusive.

"Nathan was a jerk at the end but not an abuser."

"Then why can't people know you're pregnant?"

She waffled for a moment between protecting her privacy or telling him the truth. But after he'd been so vulnerable, she felt obliged to do the same.

"The board at Hayward Home is really conservative. I had to be a married church-attender to even be considered for the job. They probably won't like having a divorced woman counseling their unwed mothers, much less a divorced *pregnant* woman." She cut him off before he could argue the point. "They're allowed to discriminate for things like that for professional employees. I'm technically employed by a church."

The furrow between his brows deepened. Then he smiled and reached over with his real hand to pat her knee. "You don't need that job. If they fire you, *I'll* take care of you."

"I don't want your money." She knocked the condescending hand away, refusing to admit his touch had sent a thrill to the tips of her toes. "After what happened with Nathan, I never want to be dependent on a man again. Anyway, I need that job to get my counseling hours in so I can get my license."

"But I need to make this right." Cole popped to his feet

and began to pace, his frenzied movements contrasting with the molasses in Brooke's veins. "That's what I do. I fix things. Obviously, I'm not that great with my hands, so I fix things with money."

"Some things can't be fixed with money." She could think of several ways a large amount of money could solve most of her problems, but it felt wrong. In her heart, she knew she'd regret accepting that kind of charity, no matter how tempting the money and its source.

Her stomach growled again. "There *is* something you can do for me. Two things."

He turned to face her. "Anything. What do you want?"

"First, can you grab a box of Cheerios out of the cabinet next to the stove?"

He practically sprinted into the kitchen. "Where are the bowls?"

"I don't need a bowl. Just bring me the box."

He returned with the cereal and a grimace. "Plain, dry Cheerios?"

She dug her hand into the half-empty box. "I never put milk on my cereal. Soggy cereal is gross."

His head gave a little shake. "What's the other thing?"

"This is a big one..." She knew he'd balk at her next request, but she had to try. "And it's probably impossible."

"I can't make independent decisions about Phantom Enterprises or Limitless, but other than that, I'll do my best. What is it?"

"I mentioned it before, but I'm serious about it. Can you try to get my sister on Millionaire Matchup?"

He made a face like he'd bitten into a piece of rotten fruit. "Brooke, I—"

"You don't have to promise to marry her. Just give her a chance."

"I would, but I'm not going to be on the show."

"You're not? But I saw you on the preview at the end of the last season."

"You heard my story." His eyes became narrow slits. "You understand why I can never get married. No offense, but I don't trust women. I'll never be able to, unless I get some answers from my birth mother."

Only her training kept her from blurting out, "That's dumb to judge all women by the actions of one." She knew that every person's perspectives were colored by their own experiences. And the more traumatic the experience, the more likely it would affect everything else a person perceived. Hadn't she already decided she would never trust another man?

"If that's how you feel, why let people believe you're going to be on the show?" she asked before shoving another handful of cereal into her mouth.

"It's a long story." His gaze went to the ceiling. "Basically, someone goaded me into it, and I was rash enough to sign a contract without reading it. I'm serious about avoiding marriage, so I have a one-date-per-woman policy. I thought I would be the show's lone rebel bachelor, who rejected every prospect. Didn't know the contract specified a huge financial penalty if I don't marry one of them."

"I have an idea." Brooke sat up straight, excited by her plan. "Hear me out. You could get my sister on the show and choose her at the end. Except the two of you could have a private contract that says the marriage isn't real and is going to end on such-and-such date."

"To fulfill the contract, we'd have to live together and that's not happening."

"Cole..." She made her voice gentle. "I honestly think you might have a chance to heal with my sister. Harper is the kindest soul you'll ever meet. She's probably taken in a dozen stray pets. Who knows? If you live with her for a couple of months, you might decide you trust her enough for a real marriage."

She took a sip of water, watching his reactions. His fingers stroked his broad jaw, shadowed with the day's growth of beard, and her hopes sprang to the surface. He was actually considering the idea. All her sister would have to do was postpone her senior year of vet school. Surely that was a possibility.

Cole's contemplative expression morphed into a smug grin.

"I think it's a great idea."

"You do?" Brooke was already anticipating giving Harper the news. She would have to record the phone call, somehow. This was going to be epic! She took another sip of water.

"Except, instead of your sister, it should be you."

She sucked in a stunned breath, and the water in her mouth went with it. A choke turned into a gag. Seconds later, she was racing for the bathroom, her stomach heaving.

CHAPTER 5

"Let me get this straight." Garner took off his glasses and massaged the bridge of his nose, his elbows resting on the gleaming mahogany desktop. "You asked a woman to marry you, hoping to get her on the show as one of the contestants, and now you want me to draw up a prenuptial agreement?"

"I just want to know if it violates the contract. I still have to talk her into it," Cole said as he paced in front of the desk, irritated at the previous evening's end.

"You mean she turned you down?"

"She did, but I'm sure she didn't mean it. Puking up Cheerios put her in a bad mood."

Garner's forehead wrinkled in question, but he muttered, "I'm not even going to ask."

"I'm positive I can persuade the producer to include Brooke in the show. Alice owes me that much, after she tricked me into signing on the dotted line."

"From what I remember, it might break the contract to

enter into a separate legal arrangement with one of the female contestants." Garner retrieved his glasses and thumbed through the twenty-something-page document on his desk, yellow highlights and red-inked notes littering every page. His finger landed on one particularly colorful spot. "Yes, I was right. And the contract definitely states you can't specify an end to the marriage in your official prenup. The courts would frown on that, anyway."

Cole leaned over the desk and glared at the upside-down document, tempted to light a match to it. He was running out of time and options. He had to make this plan work. Otherwise, he had no choice but to pay the million-dollar penalty to back out of the show. There was no one to blame but himself. He'd made an expensive mistake, disregarding the lesson he'd learned long ago, never to trust anyone who hadn't proven himself.

"But what if we had a *secret* prenuptial agreement?"

"Too risky. One slip of the tongue, and you'd be in breach of contract." Glasses off again, Garner pinched the bridge of his nose. "You know, I didn't have a single gray hair until I started working for you."

Cole chuckled as he sank into one of two chairs facing the desk. His attorney sported the same premature white hair he'd had six years ago when Cole had hired him.

"I don't think you can blame that hair on me."

"You're right. My father gets credit for it." Garner leaned back in his chair, an enigmatic smile on his face. "But I want to be frank, Cole. I'm worried about you."

"There's no need to worry. This mistake isn't going to break me. I'd just prefer not to lose a million dollars."

"It's not the money. You've always been the type who

examined every possible outcome before choosing a course of action. You were meticulous to a fault. What happened to make you so careless?"

"I've been thinking about that, myself." Cole gripped the arms of the chair. "Trying to track down my birth mother has thrown me off my game. The closer we got, the more distracted I was. The day I signed that contract with Millionaire Matchup was the day you gave me the news about Hayward Home."

Garner's dark eyebrows arched high on his forehead, contrasting against his white hair. "I shouldn't have told you until I knew we could access the information we needed. They still claim the existing records were lost between the time the old agency shut down and when it reopened with a new name."

"I don't believe that," Cole said, his throat strained.

"Neither do I. But the claim makes it virtually impossible to force their hand. We're beating a dead horse." Garner's expression softened. "I think we have to let it go, for now, and hope you get a lead from one of the DNA sites."

Cole still didn't mention Brooke's connection to Hayward Home. After spending time with her, he felt guilty that he'd initially pursued her simply to gain information. Last night, she'd included that as one of several reasons she refused to marry him. He wanted to believe his motives were more altruistic now. But were they? Not that it mattered, since Garner had shot down his idea.

"There's really no way out of this idiotic TV show without paying them off?"

"I've been working on it." Garner sat forward and typed on his computer keyboard. "It wasn't too hard to convince them that having a reluctant, surly bachelor might not be good for their ratings, but they don't have anyone to take your place. So I've got feelers out all over, although no one has responded yet. I'm hoping to locate a substitute."

"You mean I might not have to pay?"

His mouth twisted to one side. "You'll still have to pay, but I'm negotiating to reduce the amount."

Cole swallowed the curse word that came to mind. The one time he'd used foul language in front of his mother, she'd made him swish with vinegar. The lesson had stuck. Though he might think them, he never spoke a bad word aloud.

"It ought to be illegal for them to force me to marry someone, contract or not."

"Sorry. The contract is tight. Either you marry one of the contestants or you pay the penalty. Nothing illegal about that, unless you're already married."

"What?" Cole's heart leapt into his throat. "What are you saying? The contract is illegal if I'm already married?"

"Yes! That's it!" Garner clapped his hands like an excited child. With frenzied motions, he snatched the stack of pages and flipped through them, almost to the last one, and jabbed it with his finger. "Right here. Standard terminology. 'If one or more provisions of this agreement are held to be unenforceable under applicable law, such provision shall be excluded from this agreement.'"

"What does that mean, in plain English?"

"It means, we won!" Garner's smile split his face in two, as he waved the rumpled pages in the air. "They can make you do the show, but they can't force you to marry one of the contestants. Not if you're already married. That provision would be unenforceable, because it would be illegal."

"And there's no clause that says I have to pay them if I marry someone who isn't on the show."

"I don't think so." He scanned back a few pages, his finger tracing the lines, then he looked up, exultant. "It's not in here. They have every kind of provision to prevent marriage to a non-contestant *after* filming starts, but not *before*."

"Seems like an awfully big loophole."

"Heads are going to fly in their legal department." Garner laughed, tossing the pages on his desk. "I guarantee that loophole won't be in their next contract."

Cole knocked his palm against his head. "I can't believe we didn't think of this before."

Garner said a word that would've earned him a mouthful of vinegar from Cole's mom. "I never considered this option because you told me, and I quote, 'I will never get married. Not now. Not ever. No matter what the circumstances. End of discussion.'"

"I suppose I might've said that." Cole cleared his throat, his face heating. "But this won't be a real marriage, so it's not the same."

"What do you mean by *not real*?" An oh-no-not-again expression crept onto Garner's face. "If it's a fake marriage and Matchup can prove it, they can still sue for breach of contract."

"It'll be real enough. We'll live together and all that. But we'll have separate bedrooms." Cole's mind raced. "And we can write the prenuptial agreement any way we want. We could make the termination date… I was thinking five or six months, but we should make it longer. That way my insurance will cover when the baby's born."

"Baby? You got this girl pregnant?" Garner's forehead

dropped to his desk, but his voice continued, a muffled moan. "She's going to milk you for all you're worth. I swear, you've taken ten years off my life."

"Stop worrying. It's not even my kid. Her ex-husband is the father. I wanted to give her some money, anyway, so this works out great. We'll set her up with a couple hundred thousand. I guarantee, she won't want more than that. She's got a lot of pride."

"As your attorney, I have to warn you about this. Under Texas law, if a child is born to a married couple, the husband is presumed to be the father. Legally, you'll be that baby's father, despite knowing that's not true. That means, you'll be obligated to provide child support. And with your money, the court is going to order a hefty payment. You'll be on the hook until the child is grown, unless the mother remarries and her new husband wants to adopt the child."

"If her slimy ex does the math, he'll probably demand a DNA test."

"The courts won't demand a DNA test at his request." Garner pursed his lips. "Your safest option would be to divorce her before the child is born. But even then, the courts might order you to pay something. Hopefully, she can prove the ex is the father and get support from him instead. He's the one who ought to be paying it."

"I can't do that to her. Or the baby." Cole's stomach churned like he'd eaten something rotten. He imagined Brooke, forced to go after the cheating ex-husband in court and deal with him for the rest of her child's life. She was already brave enough to face motherhood on her own. She deserved better. "Look, I'm never going to have any kids of my own. I'm okay paying child support for this one."

"You don't understand." Garner's hand slammed onto the desk so hard it made Cole jump. "This is going to cost you way more than a million dollars. You'd be better off paying the penalty to get out of the contract with Matchup."

"It doesn't matter. I'm going to marry Brooke. I don't care what it costs me."

He knew he was being rash again, but he couldn't stop himself. What was it about Brooke that clouded his judgment? Maybe it was the way her eyes teared up when he'd bared his soul to her. Or that she'd already managed to soften his anger at his birth mother... helping him see from her perspective. If nothing else, he owed Brooke for that.

He didn't believe in coincidences. Clearly, God had brought her into his life for a reason. Marrying her was the right thing to do.

If only I can convince Brooke.

"I can't put a marriage termination date in the prenuptial agreement, anyway. Millionaire Matchup could use that to prove the marriage was fraudulent." Garner's sigh was louder than a gale-force wind. "If you're going to go through with this, you'll have to file for divorce the old-fashioned way. But my advice still stands... do it before the baby comes."

"I'll consider it."

"Great," said Garner, in a tone that implied it wasn't great at all. He stood and gestured toward the door. "Now, if you'll excuse me, I'm going to go and take some aspirin. It seems I've developed a pounding headache."

BROOKE HAD HALFWAY EXPECTED to see Cole when she ran

into Lava Java to get her decaf coffee. She made a point of calling Lester by name, which resulted in a great deal of blushing and stuttering. She squelched her disappointment at Cole's nonappearance with a glazed donut, thrilled that both treats rested peacefully in her stomach.

The morning had been uneventful, except for the dozens of text messages and voice mails from Harper, demanding an explanation. Brooke had finally silenced her with a text, truthfully reporting that she'd thrown up multiple times and gone to bed early. She wasn't ready to tell her sister about her evening with Cole. Besides, she reasoned that much of their conversation had been confidential, and she didn't have the right to share.

She didn't regret rejecting his "proposal." Or at least that's what she told herself. Though she had to admit the offer was tempting. If circumstances were different, she'd be picking out linens for her wedding registry.

Having lived through the heartbreak of divorce once, she had no desire to repeat it. Sure, they would both know up front that love wasn't a part of the relationship. But how could she spend time with Cole Miller and not fall for him?

Not that she'd used that argument in her conversation with Cole. Instead, she'd pointed out she would be big and pregnant by the end of filming. How did he intend to explain that to millions of viewers? Was he going to claim to be the baby's dad? She'd also argued that she couldn't film the show and keep her counseling job, which defeated the whole purpose.

"It's a generous offer," she'd told Cole, "especially considering you saw me throw up twice in one day. But I don't think we should ever see each other again."

And now, driving home from work at the end of a long day, with no communication from Cole, it appeared he'd taken her words to heart. Swallowing the inexplicable lump in her throat, she used voice commands to call her sister.

Harper answered on the first ring. "It's about time."

"Sorry. Yesterday was pretty traumatic. I even threw up in the parking lot."

"Uh-huh." Her tone said she wasn't buying it. "And who was that man?"

"Man? What man?"

"Don't play games with me, sister. I heard a man's voice right before you hung up on me."

She scrambled for something reasonable to say.

"Oh, *him*! He's just a friend. Actually, he's a client, and I really can't talk about him."

"Since when do you have male clients at the women's home?"

"Anyone at Hayward Home can make an appointment to talk to me," she said truthfully, "even the employees."

"Aww, nuts! I thought it might've been Cole Miller." Harper made a noise...something between a sigh and a moan. "I went back and watched the show where they announced him as the next millionaire bachelor. His eyes are sooooo dreamy."

"Yes, they are." *You ought to see them close up!*

"And I know he's probably a jerk in real life, but he seems so nice on TV. Did you know their company gives millions and millions to help kids with disabilities?"

"I'm sure he's a nice guy."

"You probably didn't even go to the coffee shop this morning," Harper accused.

"I'll have you know I went at my usual time and he wasn't there."

"Fooey! I really had my hopes up." Harper's sigh blasted her ear. "Tell me how you're feeling today?"

"Still nauseated, but at least I haven't thrown up, like yesterday. I ran by the grocery store on the way to work and picked up some saltines. Nibbling on them seems to do the trick."

"When are you going to tell Mom and Dad? I bet it'll make you feel better. Mom's going to be over-the-moon excited."

"I'm going to wait until I'm past the time when I'm likely to miscarry. I don't want to get her hopes up."

"How long is that? I'm bursting to tell somebody I'm going to be an aunt!"

"I wish I were happier about it." Brooke blinked her watery eyes to focus as she exited the freeway. "All I do is cry at the drop of a hat. I tried to get pregnant for a year. I ought to be ecstatic, but I'm not. Is that awful of me? Do you think I'm going to be a terrible mother?"

"Brooklyn Allegra Ponzio, you're going to be an amazing mother! Mom and Nonna have been training you for it since the day you were born."

"You really think so?"

"I know it. You're just hormonal and under a lot of stress. But everything's going to be fine. The worst that can happen is you go home to Bellaire and delay getting your license for a couple of years. Even that's not the end of the world."

Brooke took a deep breath and exhaled. "Harper, have I ever told you how lucky I am to have you as my sister?"

"Yes, but you can say it again."

Brooke laughed. "You crack me up!"

"No, really… say it again. I like to hear it."

"I'd better not. If your head gets any bigger, your neck will probably snap in two."

Brooke turned into her apartment parking lot, disappointed not to find an unfamiliar Ford pickup among the neighbors' cars. She ought to be glad he wasn't there. He was one of the most stubborn men she'd ever met, so she'd done well to persuade him to stay away.

"Hello? Brooke? Are you there?"

"Oh, sorry. I was parking the car and I got distracted."

"I was inviting you to come visit this weekend," said Harper.

"There's no way I have the energy to drive four hours there and back." Brooke gathered her things and climbed out of the car. "Why don't you come here?"

"Can't. I'm on call in the small animal emergency clinic. But at the end of May, I'll have a few days off before the summer semester starts."

"Text me the dates, and I'll put them on the calendar. Maybe I can ask off work."

"Will do," said Harper. "Call me if you run into Cole Miller again."

"Fat chance, but I'll let you know if it happens."

Brooke jammed her key into the door knob to start the delicate process of teasing the lock open. After only five tries, the lock released. She turned the knob and shoved, but the door didn't budge. She tried again, adding her shoulder for more weight. It was then that she noticed the deadbolt lock.

I don't have a deadbolt! Am I at the wrong door?

The door swung open and heavenly aromas assaulted her nostrils. Cole Miller's face greeted her.

"I saw your last name on the mailbox—Ponzio—so I made lasagna and garlic bread for dinner. Then I realized, that's probably your married name." He stuffed his hands in his pockets, looking adorably nervous. "Do you like Italian food?"

She managed a nod before her bag was lifted from her hands and a gentle tug on her arm pulled her inside. Her heart was beating so fast she felt faint. She must've swayed because Cole urged her toward the sofa.

"Are you dizzy? You'd better sit down."

She was suddenly mortified at the sad state of her apartment, though it hadn't occurred to her the night before. The threadbare couch and the side chair with a rip in the faux leather. The table with the peeling wood veneer. No wonder he was so solicitous. He pitied her.

At last, she untangled her tongue. "Cole, what are you doing here?"

He knelt on the ratty carpet in front of her and lifted her hand, cradling it between his mechanical hand on the bottom and his natural hand on top. She ought to pull away, but it might be awkward. She had no choice but to let him press his lips to the back of her fingers. Yet in spite of the platonic nature of his tender kiss, a shiver rippled through her body.

"I'm here to prove that it wouldn't be such a terrible thing to marry me."

CHAPTER 6

The shell-shocked expression on Brooke's face wasn't exactly what Cole was hoping for.

At least she didn't throw up... that's an improvement.

"Why don't we discuss it over dinner?" He scrambled to his feet and offered his hand. "Can you make it to the table? Or do I need to bring it to you?"

She didn't budge an inch. "Did you break into my apartment?"

"No, but it would've been easy to do." He stuffed his hands in his pockets. "That's why I installed that deadbolt. The key is on the table."

"How did you get inside?"

"Your apartment manager let me in when I told her we were friends, but I forgot my key." He cocked his head. "It probably helped that I agreed to take a selfie with her."

"She just took your word for it? She didn't even call me to confirm?" One eyebrow arched in a this-is-unbelievable look he was becoming familiar with.

"Like I told you, most people trust me because I'm famous. You, however, are a bit more challenging."

"I don't trust any man, right now, especially one I barely know. But, I'll make a deal with you." She pushed up from the couch without waiting for him to offer his assistance again. "The day you trust me is the day I'll do the same for you."

"What are you talking about? I already trust you. I confessed everything to you, didn't I?" He barely held his temper in check, but he knew she was simply being irrational. He'd heard that was a problem for pregnant women.

"You trust me professionally, but you don't trust me as a person." Her hands balled into fists and slid down to her hips. "I don't trust you, either, but at least I'm honest about it."

"I think offering to marry you proves I trust you quite a bit."

"If I agreed to be on Millionaire Matchup with you, I'd be giving up everything… my privacy, my job, potentially my career. And I wouldn't even have a guarantee you'd choose me."

"I have a different plan, now. If you marry me right away, it'll get me out of the contract, completely."

Her eyes practically bugged out of her head. Any second she might start throwing things around the room. Was that a common hormonal reaction?

"You don't know what you're saying."

"I do. I've already discussed it with my lawyer. He wrote a prenuptial agreement this afternoon. I think, if you read it—"

"No."

"But I'm offering to be the baby's legal father. That means I'll provide child support."

"No." She said it a little louder.

"Essentially, you stay married to me for the next nine months to a year, and you'll be able to raise your child in the lap of luxury."

"I told you before, Cole, you can't buy this baby."

"That's not fair! I'm being more than generous and asking for very little in return." He stomped to the table and grabbed one of the water glasses, which he'd already filled while preparing their dinner. Noting how his hand shook as he lifted it to his mouth, he willed himself to calm down.

"Then why do you want to claim to be my baby's father?" She followed behind him, shaking her finger in his face.

"So you won't have to deal with your ex to get child support," he said, his chest tight with righteous anger.

"I'd just be trading one ex for another." She turned her face away, her voice small. "I admit you're a lot nicer than Nathan, but you're also rich and powerful. If something happened and you wanted to take my baby away from me, I wouldn't be able to stop you."

"I would never do something like that." Though her suggestion hurt his pride, he understood why she said it. He knew exactly how it felt to be powerless.

She faced him, her eyes glistening. "I don't think you would, Cole. But I can't take that chance."

"I wish you could trust me."

"You don't trust me, either, or you wouldn't have a prenuptial agreement. And I think you'd be insane to trust me that much, when you don't even know me."

"I'm only trying to help you. And this would benefit both of us."

"I believe you're trying to be nice, but you're also naïve. Marriage isn't easy." In that moment, her entire body seemed to sag. She wobbled on her feet and grasped for the back of the dining chair beside her. "Nathan loved me when we got married and look what happened. How can you expect it to turn out better when we don't love each other?"

He moved to support her elbow and urged her to sit down. It seemed all the fight had gone out of her, because she didn't resist.

"Let's eat while we talk and you can think about it. There's no hurry to decide."

"How long can I think about it?"

He smiled. Maybe there was a chance she would change her mind. "Our appointment to get our marriage license isn't until three o'clock tomorrow."

Though he'd said nothing to warrant her scorching glare, the heat of it forced him back a step.

I sure hope this hormonal moodiness doesn't last the whole nine months.

BROOKE SWALLOWED another delectable bite of lasagna. She'd listened to her stomach rather than her head and agreed to postpone further discussion of the impossible marriage until they ate. She couldn't let that delicious-smelling dinner go to waste.

"You never answered my question about your last name —Ponzio." Cole helped himself to a piece of garlic bread and would've added another one to Brooke's plate if she hadn't waved him off. "Is that your maiden or married name?"

"It's my maiden name. I kept it to make Dad happy. He didn't have any sons to pass on the family name." She wiped her mouth with her napkin. "It turned out to be a good thing, when I got a divorce. Since I didn't have to change my name, no one at work knows it happened."

"You have a close family?" he asked, before taking a bite of garlic bread.

"Just me and my sister, Harper." She snapped her fingers. "Harper! She's the solution to this whole problem. You can marry her, instead of me, like I suggested in the first place. You get out of doing the Matchup show. I don't have to worry about my independence. Everybody's happy." *Especially Harper!*

Brooke didn't say what she was thinking because she didn't want to scare Cole away. She couldn't imagine him living with her sister for six months without falling head over heels in love. Every guy who'd ever met Harper was in love with her, though she'd been too focused on finishing vet school to pursue a serious relationship. But if Harper were going to make an exception to that rule for anyone, it would be Cole Miller.

He chewed thoughtfully and swallowed. "Two problems with that idea. First, I don't know or trust Harper. And second, that doesn't help you and the baby."

Brooke pushed her plate forward, her half-eaten dinner suddenly unappetizing. "I know you mean well, but you need to get this through your thick skull... I don't want your help."

"You may not want it, but you need it." Cole gestured

with a forkful of lasagna. "You don't want it, because you think there're strings attached. But there aren't any."

She gave a bitter laugh. "Everything has strings attached. Life is full of invisible strings. They get all tangled, and you have to cut them off if you ever want to be free."

Cole abandoned the last of his lasagna and shoved his plate away. "What would it take for you to feel safe?"

Brooke considered her answer carefully. Now was her chance to convince him this was a lost cause. "For one thing, we'd have to end the marriage before the baby came. I don't want you making a claim on him."

"You could file for divorce whenever you want. My attorney says we can't put an end date on the prenup, anyway. We could be married as short as a couple of months." Something resembling insecurity marred his usual swagger. "If you can stand me that long…"

"Don't pretend this is about me rejecting you." She used the scolding tone she'd acquired from her mother and grandmother. "This is me turning down a ridiculous business proposal that endangers my parental rights."

Cole tapped a finger on his chin. "What if we have a separate signed agreement where I acknowledge that you're already pregnant and I agree to give up any parental claims? I think it would be valid, as long as you don't ask for child support."

"That's good, because I don't want it." Her gut eased a bit when he didn't insist on behaving like the baby's father.

"That'll make Garner happy, too." He wiped his hand on his napkin and moved to the kitchen counter to grab his cell phone. "I'll jot off a note to him now, and see if he can whip up that contract."

"Wait a minute. Wouldn't it be simpler all around if you just married someone else? You wouldn't have all these extra complications if you were with my sister."

And I won't have to worry about getting my heart broken, again.

He looked up from his phone screen. "I'm sorry, but I'm not interested in marrying anyone else. If you won't do it, I'll just break the contract and pay the penalty."

"That doesn't make any sense." She pushed away from the table, her chair legs scraping on the floor, probably adding yet another chip to the ceramic tile. She carried their plates to the kitchen counter. "Why choose me? It's not like you're in love with me and want to spend the rest of our lives together."

"It's hard to explain."

"Do you think I'm so financially destitute that you need to make me your pet project?" She scraped a plate off in the trash and put it down in the sink with too much force, clattering it in the stainless-steel sink. She whirled to face him across the narrow galley kitchen. "Because I'll be fine. I've got family. If I need to, I can always move home."

Not that she was looking forward to having her parents interfering in her life again. They meant well, but she dreaded their daily criticism.

"That's not it." He abandoned his cell phone and jammed his hands into his pockets, only succeeding with his prosthesis on the second try. "It's the fact that you're pregnant and you don't want anything from me."

"I still don't get it."

"I told you why I never want to get married or have kids." His gaze dropped to his white-socked feet. With one toe he traced the grout in the tile. "When you dropped into my life, it was like a sign from God."

"Meeting a pregnant woman was a burning bush that made you change your mind about everything? Now you want to get married?"

"No. Well, not exactly…" He cleared his throat. "It's a chance for me to try it out, with no consequences. I get to see what it's like to live with a woman and watch a baby grow… see the miracle happen. There's a chance I really will change my mind. Decide it's worth the risk. Then, if I meet the right woman, maybe I'll go on a second date and a third. And one day, if I can learn to trust her as much as Bran and Finn and Jarrett, maybe I'll get married and have children."

"You don't need me for that. You could do it with anyone." Impatience crept into her tone. "There are tons of women who'd be happy to marry you, for any length of time. You probably have a hundred thousand followers on your Twitter account."

"A million. But those women all want something from me. They like me because I have money. They don't want a guy who has flaws and hang-ups. They're only willing to put up with this thing," he said, waving his green hand in the air, "because I'm a billionaire. That's true of most people… not just women."

She gentled her voice. "I believe the opposite about people. I think most of them are genuinely nice and selfless. A lot of folks would like you for who you are, instead of your money and fame, if you ever gave them a chance to know you."

"But you're the only woman I know, with absolute certainty, who would marry me for a few months and be glad when it's over. You would never try to trap me into staying married."

For some reason, his words stung. Why did it bother her? He'd only stated a plain fact, right? Rather than argue the point, she spoke her just-now-solidified-conclusion.

"Being married is tough. It takes a lot of effort. I'm sorry, but I don't want to work that hard just so you can have a practice marriage with a practice pregnant wife to see if you like it."

"Even for $250,000?"

She refused to think about all the problems that money would solve. "I can't be bought."

"Plus, I'll do all the shopping and cooking and cleaning."

"I eat frozen dinners, so that doesn't really save me any time."

"I'm not even going to dignify that with a response." He made a face like he'd swallowed cough medicine. "I could also throw in a shoulder rub or a foot massage every night. How's that for a deal?"

She glanced down at her aching feet, still ensconced in cheap flats with no padding or support.

Be strong. Say no.

His smirk was at the edge of his lips. He could sense her weakening.

"If I said yes, could we not tell anyone we're married?" she asked.

It was unfair that even the scowl he made was mouthwateringly attractive.

"Why the secrecy?"

"I don't know how I would explain you to my family.

Especially my *sister*. And if the truth got out, you'd be in trouble for breaking your contract."

His right hand came up to rub the scruff on his chin. "We can try to keep it on the down-low, but I don't know how long that will last. I won't lie to you. My private life isn't very private."

"How do the other guys stay out of the public eye? I've seen a few things about Finn Anderson, but I've never even heard of the other two men."

"Bran and Jarrett have always stayed in the background. Finn and I were more outgoing, so it made sense for us to be the faces of Phantom Enterprises. But I took it a step further and courted the attention." His ribs expanded with a huge sigh, stretching the confines of his black t-shirt in a way that made her want to sigh in response. "It's too late to go back now."

"I don't see how we could ever pull it off. What am I supposed to tell my family? What are you going to tell your guy friends at Phantom? Are you going to tell them what's going on?"

"We'll convince our families it was love at first sight—that we're crazy about each other. My buddies would never be fooled—they know I don't do love."

"I'm not a great actress," she said. "It'll never work."

"It will. We just need a little practice pretending we're in love."

As he padded over to stand in front of her, his half-lidded hazel eyes smoldering, her pulse pounded inside her ears. His presence seemed to fill the entire kitchen. She had the crazy thought that he might try to kiss her. She wouldn't let him, of course. Her divorce had only been final a few days.

And besides, she needed to guard her heart against this man with the one-and-done dating policy. In that moment, she realized it would never work. One kiss from this guy and she would be as gone for him as Harper had ever been.

"To even consider it, we'd have to have strict ground rules," she said, hating that her voice sounded breathy. "Number one, no kissing on the lips. That way, we can keep this platonic and it won't get complicated."

"I agree, one hundred percent," he said, with a rasp of his own. "What about this?"

In the quiet, she heard a soft motor sound as his prosthesis moved. Both hands lifted, moving in slow motion, until they came to rest on the top of her shoulders. *Dagnabbit*—she got chills on both sides, even the one with the robot hand. As he bent toward her, she knew she ought to protest, but her brain couldn't form complete sentences.

His lips descended toward hers, but diverted at the last second, landing at the corner of her mouth. Moving at sloth-speed, they traveled down along the edge of her jaw, leaving a trail of fire behind. Then he came close to her ear and his mouth slid down, settling in the soft spot on her neck where her blood was pulsing like a wide-open firehose.

Her vision went black, her knees buckling.

"Brooke?"

Before she hit the ground, strong arms scooped her up, nestling her against the hard-planed chest. It would've been dreamy, if the room hadn't been spinning in circles. Jostled by his hurried strides, she was deposited on the couch, shoes off and feet up, a throw pillow under her head.

As her eyes fluttered open, his concerned face was inches away. "Do we need to go to the emergency room?"

"I think I'm okay."

"Was it something you ate?" His fingers gently brushed the hair from her forehead, then wandered down to tuck a strand behind her ear, in shiver-evoking fashion. "I thought maybe you weren't supposed to have tomato sauce. Aren't there certain things you can't eat when you're pregnant?"

"I don't think it was dinner. But Cole..." She grabbed his hand, putting a stop to its tantalizing movements. "I think we'd better stick to holding hands."

CHAPTER 7

3:15 p.m. Where is she?

A bead of perspiration rolled down Cole's forehead, probably because it was ninety-three degrees on his shady bench, unseasonably hot for May. On the other hand, he might be sweating because he was nervous. Technically, Brooke hadn't agreed to his unconventional proposal, though she'd promised to show up at the county clerk's office to apply for a marriage license. He'd finagled her cooperation based on the idea that she wasn't making a commitment by simply applying for a license.

He checked his phone for the eleventh time but found no message at 3:20, twenty minutes past their appointment time.

Maybe she chickened out.

He wouldn't blame her if she did. After that kiss last night, he was having second thoughts about his self-control around her. Her skin had been so soft. And he'd been further enticed by her perfume or shampoo or whatever it was that smelled so delicious. Not to mention the quiet moan she'd made, probably without realizing it. Luckily, she'd almost passed out. Otherwise, he might've gotten carried away. It was a mistake he was determined not to repeat.

It's 3:25. She probably filed a restraining order against me. She had his cell number, yet she hadn't called. Whatever the reason, it couldn't be good. She was probably creeped out that he'd been inside her apartment when she got home yesterday. At the time, it had seemed like an awesome surprise. In retrospect, he could see where it might look stalkerish... maybe even controlling.

The tap-tap of heels on the pavement drew his attention, but the harried-looking, middle-aged woman hurried past without sparing him a glance. Wearing his natural prosthesis and sunglasses, and dressed without his signature cowboy hat and boots, no one had recognized him.

A few minutes later, a couple walked by, their voices raised in heated discussion. Busy answering a work email on his phone, he didn't look up until they were about to enter the building. The woman, obviously pregnant, spewed out a string of curse words as they disappeared inside. He hoped, for their sake, they weren't applying for a marriage license. It didn't seem they were off to a very good start.

Not that I have any room to talk—I'm planning the divorce before we get the license, and my potential fiancée is a no show.

Then a movement drew his eye to the right. Jogging down the sidewalk, her purse bouncing on its long shoulder strap, Brooke waved. He stood to meet her, tucking his phone away.

"Sorry I'm late," she panted, bending over at the waist. "The exit I was supposed to take was under construction, and my map routed me on some street with about a thousand traffic lights."

"Calm down. You don't want to overheat. It's probably bad for the baby. Let's get you into the air conditioning." He tried to sound nonchalant, like he hadn't been panicking up until the moment he saw her. With his hand on the small of her back, he urged her toward the entrance. "It's no big deal. We may've missed our appointment, but we can always stand in line. This small branch office is supposed to have the shortest waits."

"You left Shrek at home?" she asked, still a bit winded.

"You mean my dog? His name is Argus. It means *watchful* in Greek," Cole said proudly. "I call him Gus."

"Shrek is my name for your green arm. Or do you already have a name for him?"

"I can't say I've ever named my body parts—biological or mechanical." He chuckled, surprised at her lightheartedness. He'd expected her to be uptight, maybe even to cancel. "If he's going to have a name, Shrek seems fitting. He's a tough green guy."

"The one you're wearing right now is kind of boring. I think we should call him… Arnie."

He lifted his prosthetic hand to his ear. "What's that? Oh! Arnie says to tell you thank you for naming him."

"You're very welcome, Arnie. Sorry about that *boring* remark. I'm sure you're a very fine prosthetic hand."

"Thank you," said Cole, puppeting the words with Arnie. He loved that it made her laugh. As he opened the door, he gestured inside. "After you."

But her good mood vanished as she entered the building. She took one step and froze in the doorway, her face the color of ash. With a one-eighty, she was striding away like an Olympic race walker. Cole trotted to catch up with her, grabbing her elbow.

"Hey, it's okay to be nervous. But don't run away. Remember, it's just a form—you won't be committed in any way. And I'm not going to get mad if you change your mind."

She wrenched her arm free and kept going, rounding the corner of the building, where she leaned against the brick wall. Her hands came up to cover her face, but not before he spied tears.

What am I doing, forcing this woman to marry me? She's totally traumatized.

He pulled her against his chest, hoping she wouldn't mind his slightly clammy state. This seemed to make matters worse, judging by the way she trembled in his arms. After a minute, she relaxed against him, but her tears had wet his shirt.

I am the scum of the earth.

"Shhhh," he whispered, stroking her silky, dark hair and attempting not to breathe in the same sweet scent that intoxicated him the night before. It must've been something in her shampoo. "Just forget about it. Okay? You don't have to do the marriage thing. I can afford to pay off the contract. I'll still help you with your bills."

"No," she croaked.

"At least let me move you into a safer apartment. I don't feel good about you living at that place, even with the deadbolt."

"No, that's not it." She looked up through wet lashes, swiping her arm across her face. "It's Nathan. He's inside, standing in line… with Wendy."

Every muscle in his body bunched up like a cat ready to pounce. He wasn't a violent man, but he was ready to punch this guy he'd never met for hurting Brooke so badly. She obviously still loved him, despite all he'd done. He forced his clenched fingers to relax, letting out a slow breath.

"Did he see you?"

"I don't think so." Her eyes squeezed shut, forcing out another tear. "The worst part is Wendy. She's big. She has to be third trimester. That means he started sleeping with her a long time ago."

"He must be a blind idiot to choose her over you."

Her sad-eyed, wobbly smile was a sure sign she didn't believe him. "You haven't seen Wendy. She's gorgeous."

He was about ready to declare her the most beautiful woman in the world, inside and out, just to banish her pain. But he realized a part of him was beginning to believe the superlative, and that scared him more than a little.

"What do you want to do?" he asked, forcing the confusing thoughts into the background. "You want to go home? Or go inside and make Nathan jealous? I'll be glad to play the part of doting boyfriend if you want me to."

"Look at me." She stretched out her fingers, which were shaking like it was below freezing. "I can't talk to him right now. He knows me too well. He'll know how upset I am."

Frustration boiled in his blood. More than anything, he hated feeling powerless. "Wait here. I'm going inside."

He whipped around, marching down the sidewalk toward the entrance. Something snagged Arnie and held him back.

"Don't make a scene." She clung to his arm. "It'll be even more humiliating."

"I won't, but I have to see this guy." He hadn't felt this angry since he'd been picked on in middle school.

"What are you going to do?"

"I don't know." Blood pulsed inside his head, so loud he could barely think straight. "I'll think of something."

BROOKE'S STOMACH turned over as Cole stomped to the doorway and disappeared inside. It wasn't the normal pregnancy stomach upset. This was cold fear. What if Cole picked a fight with Nathan, trying to defend her honor? Cole seemed to be in great physical condition, but he was no match for Nathan, who worked out with weights almost every day and bragged about how much he could bench press.

She only knew one thing... if Cole got hurt, it would be her fault. She wiped her face with her fingers and squared her shoulders. Nathan had taken so much from her, but there was one thing he couldn't take—her baby. No one was going to take her baby.

Before she could lose her courage, she jogged to the entrance and tugged the door open. She stepped inside the waiting room, facing the back of several lines. Under a hanging sign labeled *Marriage License Applications,* Cole's broad-shouldered form blocked her view of Nathan and Wendy.

She crept up behind Cole, listening to his conversation.

"Thanks for the pen," said Cole.

"No problem. It's awesome to meet you, Mr. Miller,"

Nathan gushed. "The guys aren't going to believe this. Could I maybe take a selfie with you?"

"Have you forgotten about me?" Wendy grouched. "I'd like to be in the picture."

"I don't do selfies." Cole's voice was stiff.

"I'm a big fan, Cole." Wendy's voice went velvety. "I've done some modeling, you know. I'd love to be on the Millionaire Matchup with you. I'll have this baby in June and be back to my pre-pregnancy weight by the time the next season starts."

Brooke couldn't believe Wendy was flirting right in front of Nathan. She almost felt sorry for him. *Almost.*

"You'll already be married," Nathan muttered.

"Not if you keep taking away my credit cards," she whined. "How am I supposed to pay for my hair appointment tomorrow?"

"Seems like the two of you fight a lot," said Cole. "Are you sure you want to get married?"

Brooke could sense Cole getting riled up. She needed to get him out before he made Nathan angry.

"Cole, let's go," she whispered. But Cole didn't respond. Had he even heard her?

"I gotta make an honest woman out of her," said Nathan. Brooke could picture her ex hooking his thumbs behind his suspenders and puffing out his chest. "That's my son she's carrying."

"Are you sure it's *your* son?" asked Cole.

"Hey!" Wendy protested.

"What's that supposed to mean?" Nathan's tone was accusing.

"Only that a woman who comes on to another man that

easily might be accustomed to it. I'd recommend a blood test when the baby comes."

Without seeing it, Brooke knew Nathan's face was deep red, by now. He would explode any second. Swallowing a gulp of air, she grasped the back of Cole's belt and tugged once... twice... with no response, not even a flinch of surprise.

"Come on, Cole. Let's go." She mumbled the words just loud enough for him to hear. Even after a third tug, he didn't budge.

"Next," called the lady at the desk, tapping a small bell.

"Forget him," Wendy said. "It's our turn."

"I think you just insulted my fiancée," Nathan snarled. "Do you want to take this outside?"

"No, he doesn't." Brooke shoved her way through to stand in front of Cole.

Nathan's mouth fell open, his eyes blinking. "Brooke? What are *you* doing here?"

"She's my fiancée," said Cole through gritted teeth.

His arm snaked around her waist and cinched her against him, like a caveman claiming his woman.

Ding, ding, ding! The woman at the desk slammed the palm of her hand on the bell three times "Sir, are you coming?"

But Nathan was still glaring at Cole, who relaxed his hold on Brooke's side, only to twist her around, his hands rising to cup her face. Her heart thrummed against her ribs like a wild animal trying to escape its cage. She braced herself for a repeat of last night, which had left her senses reeling. His lips moved toward hers, once again landing at the corner of her mouth.

That was all she could take. He'd better not move to her neck.

He didn't.

Those devastating lips edged their way over until he was kissing her full on the mouth.

CHAPTER 8

Cole had the marriage license in his hand, but a fat lot of good that did. If the cold fury on Brooke's face was any indication, he'd never get a chance to use it.

"Brooke..." He hustled to keep pace with her manic strides, though his legs had to be twice as long as hers. "Don't you think we should talk?"

"We have nothing to talk about."

Her icy tone chilled him to his marrow. He'd much rather she would rant and rave at him. That he knew how to handle.

"You seem upset," he ventured.

No response. The muscles flexed along her delicate jaw, her eyes fixed ahead on the sidewalk. Impossibly, her pace seemed to quicken.

"If you tell me what I did wrong, I'll apologize," he said.

"If you don't know, I'm not going to tell you." She reached the street corner and scowled at the poor, innocent drivers impeding her progress.

"That's not fair."

"Not fair, huh? Not fair?" The light turned and she exploded into the crosswalk, heedless of the cars speeding toward the intersection. "Was it fair that you stormed inside, looking like such a madman that I had to go in there? You knew I didn't want to face Nathan and Wendy."

"You didn't have to go inside."

"Yes, I *did*. I figured you might provoke Nathan, which is exactly what happened. I had to do something, because I thought Nathan might hurt you. He's a weightlifter."

"You thought I needed your protection?" Cole's pride stung. No doubt, she judged him weak because he was missing half his arm. "I lift weights, too. And I'm a black belt in taekwondo. I'm also trained in self-defense."

"How was I supposed to know that?" In an instant, her tone shifted from arctic to heated. "It's not like you ever mentioned it. And I've seen Nathan's muscles—I've never seen yours."

"We could remedy that any time you like." His hands went to his buttons, as if he might take his shirt off as they walked.

"I have no interest," she snapped.

Oops! Guess she wasn't quite ready to joke around.

"Everything turned out great, didn't it? I defended your honor."

"I didn't ask you to do that."

"It needed to happen. Nathan's a jerk."

"You bullied him."

"That's impossible. You said it yourself… Nathan lifts weights."

"You deliberately provoked him into taking a swing at you so you could do that little take-down move."

"He deserved it." It had been quite satisfying to put the man on the floor with his arm twisted behind his back. "After all, he's the one who tried to hit a guy with one arm."

"You're a black belt. That was like picking on a little kid."

"A little humiliation was good for him."

"It was *me* who got humiliated." Her voice went up an octave. "What part of *only holding hands* don't you understand?"

"I had to make it believable, didn't I?"

The grating noise she made was brimming with frustration or disgust or some other negative emotion. Whatever it was, it wasn't the warmth and gratitude he'd been expecting.

"I thought you'd like knowing your future husband is willing to stand up for you."

She reached her car, impressively wedged into a small, parallel parking space. "You're *not* my future husband."

"Look, I know you're angry right now, but give yourself some time to cool off. There's no need to make a hasty decision about the marriage. I think, with the proper perspective, you'll see—"

"What I see is a man who thinks he knows what's best for me. I have a brain and an opinion, and I make my own decisions." As she opened the car door, the interior heat hit him in the face. She climbed inside and slammed the door shut, starting the car and rolling the windows down.

"I won't push you around." He tried to lean on the car, but his hand jerked away from the hot metal. He switched, resting Arnie on the windowsill.

"That's right… you won't. Because we're not getting married."

She sounded like she meant it. How had things gotten so out-of-hand?

"Okay, I admit I might've been a little aggressive. But I'm not usually like that."

Truly, he couldn't ever remember picking a fight before. He wasn't sure what had made him lose control.

"I fell in love with Nathan and married him before I realized how dominating he was. I'm not making that mistake again."

Her window went up, and he had to jerk Arnie out of the way. With a few forward and back moves, she deftly maneuvered out of the tight space.

And she was gone.

I screwed up.

COLE HAD to apologize for being terse with his cheerful doorman. Edward had simply made a polite inquiry about Cole's day. How could he have known the benign question was hitting on a sore subject? Ever kind and fatherly, Edward had given him a sympathetic grimace.

"That bad, huh? Having woman problems?"

"Women are nothing *but* problems, Edward. I probably dodged a great big bullet. I should be grateful I found out in time."

Edward had lifted a skeptical eyebrow, but wisely kept his mouth shut. Cole knew just what he needed to forget his troubles... a weekend at his ranch. Now, with Gus in the passenger seat of the truck, Cole did his best to put Brooke out of his mind as they started the hour-long trip. Ten minutes out, with no improvement in his mood, he switched off the radio and called Finn through the truck's system.

Out of breath, Finn answered on the fourth ring. "Hey! Sorry! I was on the treadmill."

"At six thirty at night? I thought you did all your exercise in the mornings."

To combat the effects of cystic fibrosis, Finn was diligent about daily cardiovascular exercise, rising hours early to complete his health and fitness routine.

"It's seven thirty here. I switched my routine. Now I do an evening workout with Laurie instead."

"You changed your workout time?"

Cole must've done a poor job hiding his shock, because Finn laughed at him. "I know. Impossible to believe I would ever change how I do something, right? Especially to please a woman. But I don't mind—she's worth it."

"You've changed. A lot." Cole didn't mean it as a compliment.

"Marriage is all about change and compromise. It's hard work."

"Yeah, that's what someone else told me."

"You were talking about *marriage*? That's an interesting development," said Finn. "Was it in preparation for the Millionaire Matchup show?"

"No way. I'm going to pay the penalty and back off the show. Sorry we won't get that free exposure."

"I'm glad you're not doing it," Finn said. "I hope you know whatever I might've said on that conference call, I was only teasing. I want you to get married *if, and only if* you find the right woman and the two of you love each other, unconditionally."

"You're the voice of reason I need right now. I want you to tell me how lucky I am that I'm not marrying Brooke next week."

"Brooke? Is that the coffee girl?"

"Yes. The one from Hayward Home…"

Cole filled Finn in on the events of the previous two days. When the tale was done, Finn gave a long, low whistle.

"Cole, you know I don't usually do this, but I'm going to be serious with you. I think…"

He paused for so long that Cole grew impatient. "Tell me!"

"I'm trying to choose the right words. I think Bran may be right. For whatever reason, you seem to care more about this woman than you have any other. And maybe…"

"Maybe what? You think we should get married?"

"No. I think the marriage plan was a terrible idea. But maybe you should at least go on a second date, if you can talk her into it. See where it goes from there."

"Technically, we haven't even gone on one date. I haven't changed my rule about that."

"That's a sad fact," said Finn. "The poor girl deserves a lot more respect, especially after that stunt you pulled today. The least you could do is take her on a proper date."

"No chance of that happening. You didn't see how mad she was. She'll never forgive me."

"I've learned that when you mess up, a sincere apology accompanied by chocolate goes a long way."

"Is that so?"

"Yes. The worse the crime, the more chocolate I buy."

Could a box of chocolates really buy forgiveness? Maybe he could get out of paying that million-dollar penalty after all. He didn't tell Finn he totally disagreed with his assessment of the marriage plan. Cole knew the short-term, platonic union would be his best chance to experience marriage. Especially after hearing how Finn had adapted to please Laurie. There was no way Cole would ever change his whole life to suit a woman, even one as sweet and attractive as Brooke.

Cole spotted the highway exit at the last minute and swerved off, stomping on his brakes to make the curve. Only his grip on Gus' harness prevented the dog from tumbling to the floorboard.

"Any particular kind of chocolate?"

Brooke was trapped.

Thanks to her tantrum that afternoon, she'd driven straight to her apartment, too frazzled by the incident at the county clerk's office and the bumper-to-bumper traffic to stop at the store on the way home. Hunger didn't strike for another hour. But when it did, she didn't get up and look inside her empty refrigerator for food.

Resigned to making a grocery run, she opened her front door with an armful of reusable sacks, only to be greeted with camera flashes and shouts of, "Ms. Ponzio! Ms. Ponzio, is this a picture of you and Cole Miller at the district clerk's office today? Ms. Ponzio, how long have you been dating Cole Miller? Ms. Ponzio, when is the wedding?" The entire third floor landing was lined with reporters.

She stepped back inside and slammed the door, her heart racing. She knew without a doubt her ex was responsible for the reporters at her door. Even if some other stranger had spotted her with Cole, no one but Nathan would've known her name and address.

Someone knocked on her door. A muffled voice called out, "Ms. Ponzio, we just want to ask you a few questions."

What was she going to do? She'd seen Cole's temper. How would he act when he learned what Nathan had done? She imagined her ex lying on the ground, beaten to a pulp, with the police leading Cole away in handcuffs. She had to find a way to get rid of the reporters before Cole found out. What could she say that would protect his reputation?

Steeling herself, she opened the door and held up her hand to silence the crowd. More flashes exploded in her face, but she kept her composure.

"I won't answer questions, but I'll make a statement." She raised her voice and spoke in what she hoped was a commanding tone. "But then I want all of you to go away."

A man with wavy red hair and a matching beard stuck a microphone in her face. "Go ahead."

"Cole Miller and I are *not* getting married. It was all an act. He pretended he was going to marry me so I could make my ex-husband jealous."

So much for keeping the divorce a secret from my job.

"Your ex-husband, Nathan Riggs?"

"That's right. Cole and I have no relationship. We're not even friends. In fact, I never expect to see him again."

"Do you have a relationship with one of the other owners of Phantom Enterprises?"

"I've never met any of them. Now, if you'll excuse me, I—"

"Why were the two of you at the county clerk's office this afternoon?"

"I told you, I was trying to make Nathan jealous."

Lying made her stomach even more upset. She hoped she didn't have to go running for the bathroom. The reporters might guess she was pregnant.

Imagine that in the news!

"This doesn't make any sense, Ms. Ponzio. Why would Cole Miller go to such elaborate measures to help a complete stranger?"

"Because he's a nice guy. No more questions, please."

She tried to shut her door, but someone stuck a foot in the way. "Your ex-husband reports that Cole Miller assaulted him. Is that true?"

"Nathan tried to punch Cole, and Cole twisted Nathan's arm behind his back. That's all. Now move your foot, or I'm calling the police."

The foot moved and she shoved the door closed, leaning against it and breathing heavily while she tried to calm her racing heart. She'd made it worse instead of better.

A quick look through the peephole revealed the group appeared to be making themselves comfortable on her porch.

Now what?

Her phone rang. Part of her wanted to cry with relief when she saw Cole's name on the screen. She wanted so badly to let him handle the whole situation. But deep down, she knew he had to stay as far from her as possible.

"Listen," said Cole. "I called to let you know I'm coming over."

"No, no, no! Don't come!"

"Please. I need to talk to you... to apologize."

Apologize? She didn't have the luxury to show her amazement.

"An apology would be nice, but whatever you do, don't come now."

"Actually, I'm already here. I'm in the parking lot," Cole said, sounding insecure. "I have Gus with me, too. I hope that's okay."

"No! Get out of here, now, before they see you!"

"Before *who* sees me?" His voice morphed to the stern tone she was beginning to recognize as his I'm-about-to-flex-my-muscles-and-beat-my-chest voice. "Who's here?"

"Please don't get upset, okay? It's just some reporters who heard about us getting a marriage license. I told them it was all an act to make Nathan jealous."

"Why did you talk to them? People at your work will see it." A deep growl erupted from the cell phone. "Be quiet, Gus. He gets upset when I do."

"I took care of everything," she told Cole. "All you have to do is go home and pretend you don't know me. But promise me you won't hurt Nathan."

This time, the growling sound seemed to come from Cole. He was getting wound up, just like she'd thought he would. How could she calm him down?

"Nathan's a bag o' you-know-what," said Cole, "but this isn't his fault."

"It's not?" A puff of air would've knocked her to the ground. What had happened to the enraged Cole who'd picked a fight with Nathan that afternoon?

"It's my fault." Cole sounded beyond exhausted, exactly the way Brooke felt. "I didn't think about him going to the media, but I should have. That's what happens every time I encounter someone, even if I'm only saying hello in the grocery store. I should've realized he'd talk to the reporters when he saw us getting a marriage license. He probably got paid well for breaking that story."

"Maybe they'll ask for their money back, since we're not getting married."

"Whatever happens, I'm not letting you take the flak for this. I'll explain it, somehow."

"I already took care of it." Her hands were shaking, more from frustration with Cole than the reporters who were just doing their jobs. "I told them we aren't even friends."

"But that's a lie, and I bet you're already kicking yourself for it."

"Not really." She swallowed bile in her throat.

"And there's another one. Look what I've driven you to."

"I'll be fine. All you need to do is go home."

"I'm sorry, Brooke, but I can't do that. This is my responsibility, and I need to take care of it. I got you in this mess, so I'm going to get you out." She heard his car door open and slam shut. "I have to go talk to them, even if you never speak to me again."

"You're going to make things worse! Stay in your car!"

"Too late."

She stomped her foot. This man had some sort of overdeveloped protection complex. The last thing she needed was him spouting off to the press. He might contradict everything she'd said. "But what are you going to tell them?"

"I'll tell them the truth."

"Which is?"

"If you want to know, listen at your door."

CHAPTER 9

"We'll take care of them, boss."

"Thanks, Mack. I'm hoping they'll be gone by the time you get here." Cole talked on his cell as he walked across the parking lot, his arms draped with shopping bags and Gus on a leash.

"Could be. But it sounds like she'll need a security detail, anyway."

"If I can get her to agree to it," said Cole. "She's a bit on the stubborn side."

"All the good ones are." Mack guffawed. "We'll be there in fifteen, tops."

"Don't speed to get here. I don't think these guys are dangerous. Just a pain in the rear."

Cole juggled his bags to tuck his phone away and started up the metal stairway. Tugging on the leash, Gus growled, most likely feeding off of Cole's tension.

"It's okay, Gus. Settle down."

He answered with a low woof and went silent.

At the third floor, they walked down the breezeway then turned the corner to walk down the back of the building toward Brooke's apartment. Cole was glad the sun wouldn't set until after eight o'clock, since all but one of the overhead lights appeared to be burned out.

He spied the first of the paparazzi thirty yards ahead, a lanky man lounging against the balcony railing, a smoking cigarette dangling from his fingers. As they approached, Gus let out a low snarl, his hackles raised.

The noise emanating from his 130-pound body snapped the reporter to attention, and he scurried over against the railing. Though Gus had never bitten any living being, Cole felt no need to reassure the nervous reporter or any of his twenty or so companions. With Gus attracting most of the attention, Cole passed halfway down the line of reporters before someone noticed the growling dog's owner.

"It's him!" A woman's voice shouted over the murmurings. "Mr. Miller, is it true you and Brooke Ponzio were at the county clerk's office today, getting a marriage license?"

"Mr. Miller, did you assault Nathan Riggs?" asked a deep voice behind him.

"What's in the bags?"

"How long have you known Brooke Ponzio?"

"Mr. Miller..."

"Mr. Miller!"

The group swarmed closer, the clamor growing, until Gus let out a deep growl that startled everyone.

The crowd split and Cole made his way through to Brooke's door and backed against it. "If you want me to answer questions, you'll need to keep your distance. You're upsetting my dog."

The group edged a few more steps away, and Cole bent to whisper some soothing words to Gus. He faced the reporters with as friendly an expression as he could muster, considering they'd harassed an innocent woman. Though the paparazzi didn't rattle him with their cameras and videocams, he knew their aggressive tactics had sent Brooke into a panic.

"Mr. Miller, Brooke Ponzio stated that the two of you aren't even friends, and yet you're here at her apartment on a Friday night. Can you explain that?"

Cole recognized the red-haired man from H-Magazine. "Hi, Rick. What are you doing here? Don't you have bigger fish to fry?"

"Cole, there aren't any bigger fish than you." Rick sported a huge, smug smile, glancing over his shoulder, probably making certain everyone had noticed they were on a first-name basis.

"We both know better than that." Cole shifted one of the bags from the throbbing fingers of his right hand to Shrek's untiring grasp.

"I go where my editor sends me." Rick shook a finger at him. "Now quit dodging my question."

"I believe Brooke already told you the answer to that question. We definitely aren't *friends*."

"Then why are—"

"We're much *more* than friends." Cole raised his voice, wondering if Brooke was listening inside the apartment door. "I'd say we're crazy about each other. But Brooke would say we *drive* each other crazy."

Titters of laughter rippled through the crowd.

"Are the two of you getting married?" asked a woman from the back.

Cole scrunched his shoulders up and let them drop. "She turned me down, but I haven't given up."

"She turned down your proposal?" Rick asked, one eyebrow arched in doubt.

"It's hard to believe, right?" Cole gave a conspiratorial wink. "What girl wouldn't want to spend the rest of her life with a hot-tempered, sarcastic guy like me? I was hoping to change her mind, but I'm afraid you guys aren't helping my cause. So I'm going to have to ask you to leave. My security team will be here any minute."

"You can't force us to go anywhere," said a male voice, and several others shouted their agreement.

"I'm afraid I can," said Cole. "I'm sure none of you would really be surprised to learn that, as of noon today, I own this entire apartment complex. So you can leave now, or my security team can escort you off the grounds when they arrive, which should be about five minutes from now."

A chorus of grumbles arose, but Cole only chuckled at them. "Seriously? You have nothing to complain about. You got your scoop and now you have an excuse to go home and enjoy your weekends. Your editors can't ask you to break the law, can they, Rick?"

Cole could barely see the red glow on Rick's cheeks in the fading sunlight. "Let me cover the wedding and all is forgiven."

"Sorry, Rick." Cole increased his volume, hoping Brooke would hear him. "But if I try to make any decisions about this wedding by myself, there won't be one."

"Sounds like you're hen-pecked already, Cole."

Cole kept his grin steady, even though Rick's remark confirmed what he'd already been thinking.

It's a good thing we only need to be married for five months. There's no way I could act like this the rest of my life.

"The coast is clear. Will you open the door please?" Cole's muffled voice filtered inside the apartment.

Brooke stood on her bare tiptoes to look through the peephole as he thudded against the door with his shoulder. Miraculously, the landing appeared to be empty, except for him.

"Why should I let you in?" she asked, still peering out. "You keep trying to make decisions about my life without asking me."

"But, I have something for you." He lifted the reusable grocery sacks toward the peephole.

"What's in those?"

"Open the door and I'll show you," he said in a teasing, sing-song tone.

Her eyes crossed, trying to discern the contents of the bags through the distorting lens. "If I let you inside, do you promise you won't try to talk me into getting married?"

"Ow! I think my arm is about to fall off... *literally*."

"Gracious!" She flipped the deadbolt and swung the door open, reaching to relieve his prosthetic arm of its burdens. "Here. Hand those bags to me! I didn't know you were straining your arm."

"Not Shrek. He's perfectly fine." Cole strolled inside like

he owned the place and dumped all the sacks on the table, arranging them in a perfect line. "It's my real hand whose fingers are about to fall off."

Though he'd tricked her into letting him in without making a promise, she was already having a hard time holding onto her anger. After all, he had gotten rid of all those reporters.

Leash trailing behind him, Cole's huge dog came to sniff her hand. From his intense stare, she had the distinct feeling the dog was assessing her worth, yet his tail was wagging. He pushed his head under her hand, and she obediently rubbed his ears.

"You've made a friend for life." Cole returned to take the leash off.

"What did you say his name was?"

"I call him Gus, but his real name is Argus."

The huge dog edged closer and pushed against her leg, almost knocking her off balance.

Cole chuckled. "Watch out—he's a leaner. And he's stubborn. Plus, he slobbers a lot. But other than that, he's a great dog."

Cole directed Gus to lie down close to the door, and he obeyed... eventually... after nosing around a bit.

"I see what you meant by *stubborn*. I like dogs, but I doubt one would be happy staying in the apartment all day." The thought reminded her of his earlier announcement. "By the way, why did you buy these apartments?"

Cole's dimples winked at her. "I don't own the apartments."

She refused to be swayed by his adorable, lopsided smile. "So you lied? And earlier you were fussing at me about lying."

"I didn't actually say anything untruthful. All I said was that none of them would be *surprised* to learn I had bought the apartment complex." His eyebrows bobbed. "That was completely true."

"Technically, I suppose…" Her gaze flicked to the orderly display of shopping bags. "Are all those for me?"

"Yep!" He stepped to the side and swept his hand toward the table. "It's chocolate! Finn told me he always apologized to Laurie with chocolate, so I thought I should do the same."

"Chocolate?" Her mouth watered. "All of that is chocolate? Why did you get so much?"

"For one thing, I didn't know what kind you like, so I got some of everything. Dark chocolate, milk chocolate, nuts, no nuts, caramel, cherry, chewy centers, soft centers…"

His anxious eyes followed her as she explored the bags. He must've bought out an entire chocolate store. Some were assorted boxed chocolates. Others were individually wrapped in tissue inside white paper bags. She selected a piece of dark chocolate almond bark. One bite, and taste-bud heaven exploded in her mouth.

"Oh my gosh! That's amazing!"

"You like it? Am I forgiven then?"

Her happy tongue wanted her to say, "Yes! Of course!" But she had to stay strong. While she'd been with Nathan, she'd constantly pushed her own wants and needs aside, trying to please him. Her mom and her sister had warned her, but she'd refused to believe it. If she allowed Cole to manipulate her now, wasn't she doing the same thing?

"I love the chocolate, but I'm still waiting for the apology you promised."

He folded his hands together and held them to his chin in

a pose of prayer. "Please forgive me for this afternoon. I don't know why I acted without thinking things through. And I didn't mean to make you uncomfortable. All I can say is, I lost my temper."

"You seem to have a bad one."

"I'll admit that's true." His hands fell to his sides. "But I'm not usually like that. Years of martial arts have taught me self-control. There's no excuse for my behavior, except that I was so angry with your ex that I couldn't think straight. I wanted him to feel sorry for what he did to you. I wanted him to regret it."

"And that's why you kissed me on the lips?"

"That was an accident." The toe of his boot scuffed the floor.

"It didn't *feel* accidental."

He moved close and reached for her hand, his thumb caressing her skin. "If you'll forgive me, it'll never happen again."

"Okay, you're forgiven." She jerked away from his tempting heat. "Now, it's time for you to go."

"Wait. We need to start making some plans. My security team will be here any minute."

"Security team? I thought that was another exaggerated truth you told to get rid of the press."

"We'll work out the details after Mack gets here, but something has to happen. Either we move you tonight or set you up with a bodyguard. You can't stay here without protection."

"This sounds like you telling me what to do again."

"I don't want to control you, Brooklyn. I just want you to be safe."

"No one but Dad calls me that. And he only does it when he's angry."

"I have no desire to be your father, but you need to listen to me. This apartment is too dangerous."

"It's plenty safe. You put a new lock on, remember?"

"Someone could still break in. Or you could be ambushed. Once this story hits the airwaves, you could be a target for crazies."

After her encounter with the paparazzi, she was inclined to agree. But she didn't dare concede. "I'm no more a target than you are, and I don't see you walking around with a bodyguard."

"If you were a black belt, I wouldn't be worried about you, either."

"It's. Not. Happening." She crossed her arms.

A strangled grunt came out of his throat.

"If you don't want a security detail, at least let me move you to a safer place."

She hated her apartment, but it was all she could afford, since Nathan had left her. If not for her pride, she would've caved in an instant. "I don't want to owe you anything, Cole. We need a clean break."

His eyes went wide. "A break? I thought you said you forgave me?"

"I did. But we still need to end this one-sided friendship or whatever it is. You've done enough for me."

"Not by my accounting." He pulled a chair out from the table, turned it sideways and sank into it, rubbing his fingers on his temples. "All I've done is to make dinner, put in a deadbolt, and buy you some chocolate. In exchange, I've probably cost you your job."

"I would've lost it anyway, you know." She rotated an adjacent chair to face him and found another piece of chocolate-covered almond bark before sitting down. "They'd have found out about the divorce, eventually."

"But not this soon." He shook his head. "I've really made a mess out of things, but I can fix it. I'll offer Hayward Home a large donation if they'll agree to let you stay on. It's the least I can do."

"No way! I'm not letting you spend any more money on me." She flexed her feet, which had started to ache. In fact, every muscle in her body felt sore. What she needed was a soak in a hot tub. Was it even okay to do that when you were pregnant? She had so many questions. Maybe she could get a doctor's appointment early next week, before the board at Hayward Home had time to meet and vote to fire her.

"Put your feet up here and I'll rub them for you." Cole patted his knees. When she hesitated, a hurt look crossed his face. "I can just use my real hand if you're afraid of Shrek."

"I'm not afraid of him. I was thinking my feet aren't all that clean."

"They're clean enough." He bent down and lifted a foot into his lap. The prosthetic motor whirred softly as both thumbs massaged the muscles on the bottom of her foot. Soon she was dissolving into a relaxed puddle.

She groaned her appreciation. "My right foot is getting jealous."

"We can't have that." He gently placed her left foot on the floor and replaced it with the right one. From his pleased-as-punch expression, she realized he was simply the kind of guy who enjoyed doing nice things for people. Her dad was like that. As a teenager, she'd often woken up to a tap on her door as he brought a cup of hot tea to her bedside.

"We should move to the couch before you slide onto the floor."

"Too late—my bones have turned into Jell-O. Walking is out of the question."

"Then I'll carry you."

Before she could blink, Cole had scooped her into his arms, ignoring her protests.

"I was kidding. Put me down!"

Pressed into his chest, she got a whiff of something wonderful—probably some fancy men's cologne that cost a thousand dollars an ounce. Whatever it was, it made her want to bury her face against him.

She didn't tell him how surprised she was that Shrek could support her weight. He seemed awfully sensitive about it. And if he'd been repeatedly teased by his classmates, she could understand why.

With no sign of strain on his face, he carried her to the couch and eased her onto it. Gus lifted his head to observe them, but never moved from his place by the door. Soon Cole was working his magic on her feet. "You could have a foot rub like this one every night, you know. All you have to do is agree to marry me for a few months."

She sighed with pleasure. Maybe he wouldn't be so awful to live with, after all. And she'd be saving him a million dollars, so she wouldn't have to feel guilty if he made a donation to Hayward Home.

Three short raps on the front door had Cole bounding to answer it. Gus sprang to his feet, his tail wagging.

"Hey, Mack. Come on in."

The man who steamed in must've gotten his name from a Mack Truck. About six inches taller than Cole, with a thick neck, his shoulders were so broad he was bursting the seams out of his black t-shirt. His entire head was shaved, but he sported a dark, close-cropped beard.

Brooke sat up straight, with her feet on the floor. She didn't want it to look like they'd been lounging on the couch together.

"You already got 'em cleared out." He bent to give Gus' head a rub. "I was looking forward to chasing them off."

"They ran when they heard you were coming." Cole clapped him on his brick-wall back.

Mack gave a sharp nod. "What's the plan? Are we moving her out or making this a safe zone?"

Cole opened his mouth to answer, then glanced at Brooke and snapped it closed. He tilted his head in her direction. "Talk to Brooke. It's her decision."

Mack moved toward her and stuck out his hand. "I'm Mack Shaeffer, head of security."

"Brooklyn Ponzio." Her hand disappeared in his huge one. Thankfully, he tempered his grip.

"But don't call her Brooklyn," said Cole, with a wink. "She prefers Brooke."

"Mack can call me anything he likes," she said, in a challenge.

"Oh, I see what's going on here. You prefer Mack over me, huh?"

To her surprise, Mack turned about fifty shades of red and backed away from her like she had the plague. "I'm just here to work, boss."

Cole laughed. "You know I'm teasing you. Don't worry. Brooke's not that kind of woman."

"I'm certainly not."

She'd hoped her broad smile would put him at ease, but it seemed to do the opposite, judging by his shifting stance and the way his hands searched for a place to rest.

"Tell Brooke what her options are," said Cole.

"For the weekend, you could stay in Cole's complex. Our security team has an apartment on the floor below Cole. That would work if you guys want to stay in town. My personal preference would be for both of you to spend the weekend at the ranch, because no one can even get close to you. As for a permanent place, we could locate a new apartment and have all your things moved over by the time you come back Sunday night." Back in his comfort zone, Mack's posture relaxed. "Andrea's prepared to spend the night with you if you insist on staying here."

"I don't need anyone with me. Besides, there's no comfortable place for her to sleep."

His bushy brows drew downward, obscuring his eyes. "If Andrea's here, she'll be on the job. She certainly won't be sleeping."

"Why don't you come out to the ranch?" Cole's eyes danced like an excited kid. "I'd love to drive you around and show you everything. If it rains tomorrow, like they're predicting, I can take you mudding. Plus we have a lot of newborn calves right now."

Mudding! For some crazy reason, she'd always wanted to go. And who could resist seeing baby calves?

"It sounds fun," she admitted, "but leave all my things here. I haven't agreed to move."

"That's fine." Cole offered his hand. "Pack a bag with your clothes and bathroom stuff. That's all you need for now."

"But boss, I thought you wanted her moved to a safer place."

"It's what Brooke wants that matters," said Cole. "Can you make this place secure so that nothing will happen to her things?"

Mack's chin tilted up. "Of course we can."

Cole's hand hefted her off the couch.

"Don't go to any trouble. I don't have anything important here. Nathan got all the good furniture in the divorce because we still owed on it." She scanned the dreary room, furnished with pieces from the secondhand store. "Everything that means anything to me is either at my parents' house or in one of the boxes in my bedroom. I never had the heart to unpack them."

"Whatever you want," said Mack.

A meaningful look passed between the two men, and Brooke suspected Mack would use all his resources to protect her measly possessions. She was too tired to fight it. And *hungry*. Her stomach made rude noises that didn't subside when she pressed her hands against it.

"Grab your suitcase. We'll get something to eat on the way."

Cole's smile was so big that she could see all of his perfect white teeth. Knowing she'd put that smile on his face made her feel strangely warm inside.

"Okay."

I can't believe I'm doing this.

CHAPTER 10

"Hang on a minute, Garner." Winded, Cole answered the cell phone on his watch as he pressed the button to gradually bring the treadmill to a stop. He wiped his face with a towel before collapsing on the weight bench. "What's up? Why are you calling before seven a.m. on a Saturday?"

"Because the attorneys at Millionaire Matchup started trying to reach me at midnight. They were surprised to hear you're getting married." He cleared his throat. "As was I."

"What do you mean? I told you that was the plan." Cole took a long drink from his water bottle.

"At six p.m. yesterday, you told me the wedding was off."

"I thought it was. But last night I gave her chocolate and brought her out to the ranch. In fact, she's asleep in the guest suite right now."

"So you're getting married after all? Have you both signed the prenup and the parental rights form?"

"You're kind of jumping the gun," said Cole. "I haven't quite talked her into marrying me, yet."

Garner groaned, "*Unbelievable!*"

"I was going to call you as soon as I had a definite answer," Cole defended.

"Cole, if all you need is someone to marry for a couple of months to get out of the Matchup contract, I'm positive I can line up at least three women in my office who'd be *glad* to do it. One of them is my law partner. And you wouldn't have to go to extreme measures to *persuade* them."

"If I wanted to marry someone who *wanted* to marry me, I'd go ahead and do the show. That's what I'm trying to avoid."

"Let me get this straight… Your goal is to marry a woman who has no desire to marry you?"

"That's right. A strictly platonic relationship with no strings attached. Marrying Brooke gets me out of the contract, and it's guaranteed to be drama-free when it's over."

"Can I point out the absurdity of mentioning a pregnant woman and 'drama-free' in the same sentence?"

"Not if you want to remain my attorney."

"That's currently up in the air."

"Well, if you're done," said Cole, ignoring Garner's sarcasm as easily as his attorney had ignored his. "I need to get back to my run."

"There's one more thing." Garner used the gentler tone he reserved for bad news, and Cole's gut tightened. "That news report mentioned Hayward Home, so now you're on their radar. I've got no hope of making anonymous inquiries into your birth mother's records. If they pull her file and see her baby was born thirty-five years ago with a deficient arm, they're bound to put two and two together."

For a moment, Cole couldn't swallow. He hadn't considered that particular complication, but it made sense.

"I guess I'll never find out the truth, then... at least not from Hayward Home."

"To be honest, there was never much chance of that," said Garner. "The privacy rules have always been strict, especially at religious institutions."

"You told me that. But I was hoping for a miracle." Cole didn't feel like finishing his workout. He tossed the towel over his shoulder and headed to take a shower. "I'm sure you'll think of some way to get me the information about my birth mom. I'm counting on you."

"And I'm counting on *you* to give me a big fat ulcer." Garner's sarcasm returned with a vengeance. "Oh! What do you know? Already happened."

SATURDAY MORNING, still in her sleepshirt, Brooke sat cross-legged on the comfy cushion that covered the bay-window seat in her bedroom. Her first daylight view of the ranch revealed a grassy expanse littered with oak trees that were probably older than the state of Texas. Beyond a barbed wire fence, a herd of cattle milled about, heads to the lush green grass beneath their feet.

She nibbled on a saltine cracker, one of several from a Ziploc bag Cole had insisted she have at her bedside. The trick had worked to settle her morning queasiness, but now she was craving something to drink. Her mouth was bone dry, but not simply because of the saltines. Before she went out to face the day with Cole, she had to make a decision. One that could change the rest of her life. Thus the reason for the cell phone in her hand. With a quick selection from her recent calls, she had her sister on the phone.

"Hi," said Harper in a soft, muffled tone, as if her hand might be scooped around her mouth. "I got called in to work in the clinic today, so I hope you're not on the way here."

"No, but I need your advice."

"Just a sec. Let me move into the hallway, so I can talk." A few seconds later her voice was back, her concern evident. "What's going on?"

"I'm guessing you didn't see me on the news last night."

"No! What happened? Are you in some kind of trouble?"

"Yes and no. I need to tell you something, but you have to swear not to tell a living soul. Not even Mom and Dad."

"Elbow promise!" It was their own sister-to-sister, linked elbows, stronger-than-linked-pinkies, 'til-death-do-you-die promise.

"And you can't be mad at me."

"I promise, but you've got me really worried, now. What is it?"

"There's a guy who's offered to marry me." She hurried on before Harper could interject a question. "It would only be for about five months. He thinks he can help me keep my job until I finish my counseling hours, and there's a prenup that gives me $250,000 when we divorce. I've done some figuring, and that would be enough to pay off my school loans, buy a decent car, start a college fund for the baby, and put a down payment on a house."

Harper responded with silence.

"What are you thinking?" Brooke asked.

"You may not want to hear it."

"Go ahead. That's why I called." Brooke's pulse raced.

"I'm sorry, but I think this sounds a lot like being a prostitute. Some rich dude is basically paying you for temporary sex. There's no commitment. That's not a real marriage and you know it. And how do you know he'll even come through with the money?"

"But—"

"Brooke, you don't have to do this. When I finish school, I'll make enough money to pay back both our school loans."

"But we aren't going to sleep together."

"What did you say?"

"We aren't going to sleep together. We'll be married, but we'll have separate bedrooms. No sex whatsoever."

"If you're not having sex, then what does he get out of the deal?"

"He'll save a million dollars, minus the quarter million I get when we divorce. So he nets three-quarters of a million."

"And how does marrying you save this dude a million dollars?" Harper asked in an I-can't-believe-you-fell-for-that voice.

"It gets him out of his contract to be on Millionaire Matchup."

Harper's tell-tale gasp signaled the moment the puzzle pieces clicked together. "Cole Miller? Cole Miller wants to marry you?"

"Yes." Brooke cringed. "Don't be mad at me. I suggested he'd be happier marrying you, but he's never met you, so…"

Harper let out a squeal that must've surprised anyone in hearing distance. "This is fantastic!"

"It is?"

"You guys are only friends, right? I mean, obviously you haven't fallen madly in love, or you wouldn't be planning a temporary, sexless marriage."

"No, it's completely platonic. We don't have any feelings for each other." Why did the words stick in her throat?

"It's the perfect chance for me to meet him. He won't be on the show, so he won't fall in love with some rich girl and be lost forever. Instead, he'll marry you. I'll come to the wedding and then visit you guys a few times. You'll divorce and get your money. Cole and I will start dating. Etcetera, etcetera. And we'll live happily ever after!"

"Wait. Let's go back a few steps. You want to come to the wedding? I was thinking we'd make it small and quiet, since it's not real."

"Whatever you do, you have to invite me," Harper gushed. "I have to meet him."

"I'm not even sure I want to marry him."

Harper came back in a panicky voice. "Oh my goodness! Is he abusive? I wasn't even thinking! I'm so sorry. If he is, don't marry him. I don't want to marry a guy like that, either. It's not worth it, even for the money. He just seemed like such a nice guy on TV, but—"

"No, he's not abusive," Brooke cut in. "He has a little temper, but he's super sweet to me."

"Then what's wrong with him? You can tell me. I already elbow-promised to keep it a secret."

What could she say? That Cole Miller was too nice and she might fall for him? That she couldn't handle getting her heart broken again? The seed of an idea sprouted in her head. If she went into the marriage with the attitude that she was setting Cole up to fall for her sister, she wouldn't get so attached. In a weird way, it would be like being a surrogate mother. Only in this case, she would be a surrogate wife.

"I'm mostly worried I'll let him push me around too much," Brooke said. "After being with Nathan, I never want that to happen again."

"I don't think you will," said Harper. "These last few months it feels like I finally have my sister back. Nathan really wore you down, but I can't imagine you'll ever bend to someone else's will again. You were already pushing back before he cheated on you. Didn't he try to make you give up on your counseling license?"

"You're right." Brooke thought back to the last few months of the painful relationship. "The closer I got to finishing, the more he complained about it. I think he felt threatened."

She was surprised to find the memory wasn't as raw as before. Maybe the pregnancy was giving her some endorphins.

"What about Mom and Dad?"

"Your best bet with them is to pretend you're both in love. I don't think they'd go for this temporary marriage thing."

"I can't lie to them."

"You don't have to. You know Mom is almost as in love with Cole Miller as I am. She'll be so excited you're marrying him, she won't question the timing."

"I haven't even told them about the baby yet."

"Weren't you going to wait until you were in your second trimester?"

"Yes, but I'm almost there, already." She chewed her lower lip. "Mom'll be so upset when I get divorced again."

"After all the divorces Aunt Patty's had, she's still Mom's favorite sister."

"True." Her stomach churning, she took another bite of her cracker.

"When is the wedding supposed to happen?" asked Harper.

"Early this week, I guess. We have to be married before the show starts filming on Friday."

"I have to work every day next week. Can't you get married tomorrow?"

"We got a marriage license, but it has a seventy-two-hour waiting period. Monday night is the earliest we can do it."

"Not if you fly to Vegas. You can be married and back home tomorrow night."

Brooke's stomach heaved. "I gotta go!" She barely made it to the bathroom before she lost her saltines.

COLE WAS on his third cup of coffee by the time Brooke appeared in the dining room, her beauty making him catch his breath. Each time they were apart he almost convinced himself he wasn't physically attracted to her. But this time, the heat in his chest as he gazed at her left no doubt of the truth. She was the most beautiful woman he'd ever seen. Oh, he'd been around plenty of women who were more polished and perfect after applying layers of makeup and styling their hair just so. But Brooke had walked in with a fresh-scrubbed face, her deep brown eyes so sultry he was dying to kiss her again. Having her around the whole weekend was going to be dangerous. Time to muster his self-control.

"Good morning!" He put on a casual air, yawning and stretching. "I thought you might've gotten lost in the guest wing."

"Sorry you had to wait."

Her eyes darted around the room. What was she looking for?

"Gus isn't allowed in the dining room," he offered.

"That's fine." She walked to the kitchen door and peeked inside.

"Can I help you find something? There's decaf coffee in that insulated carafe."

"That sounds heavenly." She poured a cup and carried it to the table. "Is there anyone else around? I kind of need to talk to you in private."

"I've got permanent staff, but they all have their own living quarters on the grounds. No one's here but us."

If she needed privacy, he had a feeling he wouldn't like whatever it was she had to say.

She lifted the coffee to her lips, took a sip, and set it down with trembling hands. "I've decided I'm willing to do the temporary marriage thing."

He held her gaze, unwilling to take her at her word when she seemed so distraught. "Why do you look like you just volunteered to walk the plank?"

"Mostly because I'm worried what everyone will think."

Cole chuckled. "That's one thing I'm *not* worried about. I enjoy keeping people off guard. If you don't believe me, ask my attorney."

"Then what are *you* worried about?"

He was afraid her vulnerability made her even more irresistible. If they got married, he'd have to limit the time they spent alone together, or he'd be tempted to let his guard down.

"I don't want you to feel pressured into something you're not comfortable with."

"I don't feel pressured. I just want everyone to be happy." Her fingers drummed on the table.

"Ha! Now there's an impossible task."

"That's one of my faults—trying to please people." She'd chosen a seat on his left, so he tentatively covered her hand with his prosthetic one, watching for her reaction. Her tiny shudder was almost unnoticeable. *Almost.* He withdrew his hand, as color rose in her cheeks. In a way, he welcomed her aversion to his prosthesis. It might keep his attraction from growing.

"I'm also afraid you'll fight me about spending money on you."

Her sharp glare darted his way. "There's no need to spend any more than what's spelled out in the prenuptial agreement."

He lifted his chin, enjoying the fight. "How will I ever make this look real if I do that? Do you think the public will buy it if the wife of a billionaire drives around in a wreck of a car?"

"Fine. You can buy me stuff, but I'm not going to keep it. Or we can subtract it from the $250,000."

When she tugged her lower lip into her mouth and chewed on it, he had an insane desire to do the same. Just one more little kiss. Maybe she'd make an exception to her no-kissing rule at the wedding.

Unaccustomed to feeling off-balance, he threw out a

distraction. "You're as stubborn as my sister. In fact, you remind me of her."

Except I have no desire to kiss my sister.

"Are you going to tell your sister the truth?" she asked.

"I'll have to. She can see right through me." He shrugged. "But Garner says, as long as we're legally married with a normal prenuptial agreement, Matchup would have a hard time proving fraud. After all, plenty of marriages end in less than a year."

"I told Harper this morning."

"What did..." His train of thought vanished as she did it again—chewing on her lip in that tempting way. Why did his mouth feel so dry? He gulped down some coffee, grimacing at the now-tepid temperature. "What did your sister say?"

"That she wants to come to the wedding and her only day off is tomorrow." Her voice grew softer and softer with each word, until he was straining to hear the last one.

"Tomorrow? We can't get married that soon unless we go to Las Vegas."

"It's really important to me for Harper to be there."

"Then, tomorrow it is." Cole stood, his mind racing. He was back in his element—making plans and taking action. Best of all, he'd have his family and friends in an uproar. He hadn't had this much fun in years. "We've got a lot to do in the next twenty-four hours."

Why was Brooke's face so ashen? Of course...she needed food!

"You must be hungry," he said. "Can I cook you some breakfast? Scrambled eggs? Bacon? Pancakes?"

Her hand clapped over her mouth as she bolted from the room.

CHAPTER 11

"Try this one on, too." Laurie, Finn Anderson's wife, brought yet another dress to Brooke's fitting room. "There's one more I want you to try, but I'll have to get the manager to get it down. It's hanging in the display."

Branson Knight's wife, Steph, gave Brooke a rueful smile. "If she brings any more dresses back here, we may have to start a second fitting room."

"All of these dresses are too expensive, anyway," Brooke complained. "I told Cole I wanted a simple, quiet ceremony, but he's turning it into a three-ring circus. The dress I brought with me would've been fine if he hadn't decided to wear a tuxedo."

"Don't worry," said Steph. "Cole can afford any dress you like."

"But I don't want to waste his money on a fancy dress for a wedding that…" She dropped her voice to a whisper. "For a wedding that isn't even real."

Cole had explained their plan to his sister and all his

buddies, who'd shared the story with their wives. Only her parents and his were in the dark about the true nature of the impending marriage.

"This will quite likely be Cole's only wedding." Steph hung the latest rejected dress on the overflowing hook. "Don't you want it to be memorable for him?"

"I hadn't thought of it that way. I guess it needs to be special." Brooke peeked through the slats in the dressing room door to be sure no one was listening. "Even though the whole thing is fake."

"I'm not so sure about that." Steph tapped a fingernail on her front tooth as she studied Brooke's current dress, a fluffy white ballgown.

"You're not sure about this dress?"

"No, I'm positive that's not the dress for you. You're not the fairy princess type." She perused the untried choices, hanging from every available hook in the room. "What I'm *not* sure about is this whole fake marriage thing. You're both swearing this is a temporary, platonic relationship, but I'm not convinced."

"What else could it be?" Beads of sweat broke out on Brooke's forehead, even though the room was chilly. "We can't be in love. We only met five days ago."

"I think I'm going to like this one on you." Steph held up a dress with drapes of soft satin. "Look, I've known Cole for a couple of years now, and Bran talks about him all the time. He tends to buck the system, so-to-speak. He's a billionaire who drives a pickup with 100,000 miles on it and wears boots that've been re-soled, twice."

"You see, I didn't even know that." But secretly, she thought it was awesome.

"My point is he's acting like this is just another one of his rebellious stunts, but I don't buy it. And neither does Bran."

Brooke slid the silky dress over her head and struggled with the side zipper. "It's more than a stunt... I'll give you that. Cole put a lot of thought into this decision, and so did I."

"Yes, but as far as women are concerned, this goes against everything that's always defined him." Steph helped her close the zipper. "The back is beautiful, the way it dips down. Let me see the front."

Brooke turned to face the mirror. The creamy-white satin fell from her shoulders in a low cowl-neck and clung to her form like a forties-style Hollywood glam dress, the folds miraculously camouflaging the slight rounding of her tummy.

"That's the one!" Steph declared. "It looks gorgeous on you!"

"But how much is it?" Brooke tried to read the price tag, but Steph jerked it out of her hand.

"Cole will love it, and he can afford it. He doesn't spend money on himself, but he loves to spend it on other people. This will make him happy."

"Do you really think so?" She realized how woefully unprepared she was for this marriage. She barely knew this man she was going to be living with for the next five months. Since she obviously wasn't going to make him happy in the bedroom, she needed to meet as many of his other needs as possible.

"I know so."

"Let me in." Laurie tapped on the door. "I've got one more dress."

Steph opened the door. "What do you think of this one, Laurie?"

Her mouth dropped open. "Wow! That's gorgeous!"

Brooke smoothed her hand over her belly. "I know, right?"

"You're going to want some pearls, and I know just the right shoes." Laurie dashed off again, a dress still in her arms, calling, "Be right back!"

"I appreciate both of you for helping me shop," said Brooke. "My sister isn't flying in until seven o'clock, just in time for the ceremony, so it's a good thing you were able to come early."

"I wouldn't miss it for the world. Fortunately, the nanny was happy to watch our toddler for the day."

"How old is he?"

"Twenty months. And we've got a daughter who's ten. They grow up so fast." Steph gave a happy sigh. "As you're about to find out for yourself. When are you due?"

So Cole had told them about the pregnancy. Brooke was glad. At least she could get some advice. "I haven't been to the doctor yet, so it doesn't seem real. By my best calculations and a little internet research, I'd say I'm about thirteen and a half weeks, due the first week of December."

Steph's brows pinched together. "You're pretty small."

"I lost a lot of weight during the divorce, and I haven't been very hungry." Dread swirled in her chest as she dropped her hands protectively across her belly. "Do you think the baby's okay? I'm hoping I get my appetite back soon."

"I'm sure the baby's fine." Steph patted her arm. "I'm just surprised you're that far along."

"I'm back." Breathless, Laurie knocked on the door, and

Steph let her inside the fitting room, which was beginning to feel a bit cramped with three women and twenty wedding dresses. "I've got some pearls and some satin pumps. They're a size eight instead of seven-and-a-half, but the lady told me they run small."

"How much are they?" Brooke jutted her chin forward. "I know you think Cole can afford it, but I plan to pay him back every dime he spends on me."

Laurie folded her arms. "When you get divorced?"

"Right!" Brooke punctuated with a sharp nod.

"Or *if* you get divorced." Laurie's eyebrows danced, and she exchanged a glance with Steph. "Because Finn and I have a bet going. A thousand dollars says the divorce will never happen."

"I hate to tell you, but you're going to lose that bet. Neither one of us wants a long-term relationship." *Not to mention, I'm setting him up with my sister.*

"Either way, you can't pay Cole back for any of this," said Steph. "He said he wanted it to be your wedding gift from him."

"He did?" Sudden tears stung her eyes. "I don't have a present for him."

Drat that man! Why does he have to be so nice?

"All Cole needs as a wedding present is you in some little lacy lingerie."

Laurie threw her head back and laughed, while the blood rushed to Brooke's face.

Steph grimaced. "Uhmm… Laurie. There won't be any lingerie. They plan to have a platonic relationship."

"*Platonic?*" Laurie stomped her foot. "Finn didn't tell me that! No wonder he made the bet!"

Steph gave Brooke's arm a squeeze. "Don't worry. Cole won't be expecting a present."

"This is all so stressful. I was so uptight I barely remember riding in the private jet this morning."

"Sure beats flying commercial, doesn't it?" asked Steph.

"I wouldn't know," said Laurie. "I've got aerophobia. I take two sleeping pills and they carry me onto the plane."

"Which is why the four of us flew over last night." Steph gave Laurie a hug. "But I still love you, phobias and all."

"Let's have all these things sent to your room and go grab some lunch," said Laurie. "I've been married to Finn for over a year now, so I'll teach you my ways."

"I've been married to Bran for over *two* years," said Steph. "You might learn more from me."

"Nah!" Laurie gave Steph a playful shove. "It doesn't take any skill to live with Bran—he's way too nice. Cole's a lot more like my husband. Finn hasn't stopped teasing me since the day we met."

"Cole does tease me a lot," said Brooke, as she searched for her clothes under the yards of white lace and satin littering the settee. "But sometimes he's also super sweet and thoughtful, like the last two nights when he gave me a foot-rub."

"You got your man to massage your feet? Two nights in a row?" Laurie looked at her sideways. "Girl, I think you could teach Steph and me a thing or two."

"Brooke seems like a nice girl," Jarrett said, as he buttoned his tuxedo shirt.

"I agree." Already dressed, Finn lounged on the couch in Bran and Steph's expansive hotel suite, the designated dressing room for the men. All the women were getting ready in Finn and Laurie's suite. Finn added, "Way too nice for the likes of Cole."

"You're right." Cole laughed, enjoying the easy banter with his friends. He'd have enjoyed this day so much more if his cohorts were going to be the only people at the wedding. Who'd have dreamed his entire family would insist on flying to Vegas for the impromptu ceremony? His plan to throw his family into an uproar had backfired. He was counting on his sister, Mariah, to keep his parents from causing a scene, though she'd made it clear she didn't approve of his "phony marriage." As for Brooke, she'd turned chalky white when her parents announced they were also coming.

"Is everything ready for the ceremony?" asked Bran, as he navigated smoothly to the kitchenette area, having already memorized the layout so he could move around without his cane. His buddies were careful to keep the floor clear of obstructions, a habit instilled since their early days together at camp. "I know you haven't had time to shop for rings."

"The wedding concierge made all the arrangements, including buying the rings for us."

"Did you buy a band to fit your prosthetic hand?" Bran dispensed a glass of water from the refrigerator door.

"I thought I'd just wear it on my right hand."

"Guess it doesn't matter," said Finn, "since it's not a real marriage."

"It *is* real!" he argued, though Finn's sentiments expressed his exact reasoning when he ordered the ring. "And I say our practical motives for marriage with mutual benefits is just as legit—maybe even more—than people who get married because of a physical attraction."

"I'm on your side." Finn lifted his palms. "I wasn't trying to criticize."

"Sorry. Didn't mean to bite your head off." Cole forced out a slow breath, hoping his steam would go with it. "I'm a little uptight, with Mom coming. She can be a bit overbearing."

"I understand completely." Finn chuckled. "You've met my mum, right?"

"Mine makes yours seem like a pushover." Cole collapsed onto a white leather chair opposite Finn. "She has an opinion on everything. Take the wedding rings, for instance. It's a good thing Brooke wanted something simple, because Mom would've had a fit if she'd heard I threw away my money on a huge diamond."

"She does realize you're filthy rich, right?" asked Jarrett.

"She knows, but it doesn't matter. She reuses *everything*. This is the woman who's been known to wash paper towels and lay them out to dry. To say she doesn't believe in wasting money is a huge understatement. Almost every gift I've given her is still in the box, stored in a closet, because she's *saving* it until she really needs it."

His mother was also known for speaking her mind, and he worried what she might say to his friends if she saw any sign of extravagance. It was one of the main reasons he'd never invited his buddies to meet his parents.

"Ah-ha!" Finn exclaimed. "So it was your mom who made you so stingy you've had your cowboy boots re-soled multiple times."

"Stingy is a harsh word. I call myself *prudent*."

"What I don't get," Jarrett said, "is why you won't buy yourself a new truck, but you'll shell out $5,000 for a new Stetson."

"You don't get rid of a truck just because she's getting a little older," Cole said. "A good one will run 150-200,000 miles. As for hats, I have cheap ones I wear when I'm working, but a high-quality Stetson will last a lifetime... *if* you take care of it."

A knock on the door interrupted them, and Cole leapt to his feet, praying it wasn't his mother.

"I'll get it," said Bran, who was closest.

The door burst open and in came Cole's sister, wearing a stunning sapphire dress that complimented her athletic build. She gave Bran a hug.

"Hi, Bran. Haven't you talked my brother out of this harebrained idea, yet? I figured you have the most common sense out of this group."

"That would be me." Jarrett crossed to exchange embraces. "I'm the only one in here who hasn't done anything insane because of a woman."

"Be careful, it might be contagious." Mariah chuckled, tossing her auburn curls behind her shoulder.

"I'm trying to keep my distance, just in case." Jarrett threw his head back, laughing. "You look amazing, Mariah."

"Thanks." Her face turned red to match her hair.

"My turn." Finn tapped on Jarrett's shoulder.

She started to hug Finn but pulled back. "I've just been on an airplane with a hundred other people. I changed clothes and washed my hands, but I haven't taken a shower."

"It'll be fine," said Finn, though he kept his face turned to the side while he hugged her. "But thank you for being considerate."

Cole was proud his sister had remembered how susceptible Finn was to infections. She came to Cole last, folding him in a bear hug. "Where is this poor unfortunate woman you've roped into your crazy scheme?"

"All the women are in Finn's room, Suite B. But I—"

"Great! See you later." She turned on her heel, heading for the door. "Good luck with Mom, by the way. She'll be up here any minute."

"Wait!" Cole caught her by the elbow before she could escape. "You can't leave me alone when Mom comes. I need you to run interference."

"No way! I'm done trying to cover for you. Three long hours, all the way from Kansas City to Vegas, and all she wanted to talk about was you and Brooke. She's in Heaven right now. She'll be crushed if she finds out the marriage is fake. And if she doesn't, she'll be devastated when you get a divorce."

"We'll hardly see her enough for her to get attached to Brooke."

"Mom's already attached." Mariah finally succeeded in jerking her elbow from his grasp. "In fact, she's planning for grandbabies. So, once she finds out Brooke is pregnant, she's going to go ape."

Cole's stomach churned. "Do you think I should tell her the truth?"

"I gave you my advice," said Mariah, backing out the door. "To call this whole thing off. But you didn't listen. You've dug your grave. Let's see if you can dig yourself out."

"Where are you going now?"

"To meet my future sister-in-law and warn her about Mom." She glanced to her right, down the hotel hallway, and whispered, "Speak of the devil… here she comes."

Cole tried to shut the door. "Stall for me. I'm not ready."

Mariah raised her voice. "Hi, Mom! Cole's right here! He's dying to see you."

Her grin was pure evil.

"Someday, you'll pay for this," Cole mumbled.

"By the way, she brought a few surprises for you." Mariah's laughter trailed behind her as she flounced down the hall toward Finn's suite.

STEPH AND LAURIE chatted with Cole's sister while the makeup artist put the finishing touches on Brooke's face.

"Now, don't touch your face!" the woman warned. "And don't cry or talk or laugh too much. Absolutely no eating until after the ceremony."

"That's not true, Brooke." Laurie must've overheard, because she corrected the woman. "You're allowed to eat those saltines if you need them. Better to mess up your makeup than throw up on your dress."

Brooke stood as the tailor slid the silky white dress over her shoulders and zipped her into it, pronouncing the fit "perfect."

If perfect means it's so tight you can't breathe.

"So you're the woman who finally got my brother to the altar."

Mariah approached as the other women gathered their supplies and slipped away. The tall redhead was intimidating

—her sleeveless blue dress exposing the sinuous muscles in her arms and shoulders. She could probably bench-press a hundred pounds with Brooke sitting on the bar.

"This whole marriage thing was Cole's idea." Brooke shifted, trying to relieve the pressure on her aching feet. She didn't dare sit down for fear she would rip her gown. "I promise, I'm not trying to take advantage of your brother."

"I'm sure you're not."

Mariah's tone was hard to read. Was she against the marriage? Did she think Brooke would go after her brother's money?

"I didn't want to spend a lot on the wedding, either."

"That's the truth," said Laurie, who was relaxing on the couch beside Steph, the delicious-looking glass of water in her hand emphasizing the desert in Brooke's mouth. "Steph and I had to twist her arm to get her to buy a wedding dress."

"Don't worry. I believe you." Mariah arched an eyebrow.

"I just don't want you to be angry with me."

Her expression softened. "I'm not angry with you, Brooke. But I can't say the same for my irresponsible brother. In fact, I want to warn you what you're up against."

"Like what?"

"Like the fact that he's nerdy. Plus, he's lived alone so long he doesn't know how to think about anyone else."

"Well, I'm pretty self-sufficient, so I'm not worried."

"I can attest he's self-centered and hard to live with."

"Maybe you don't know him as well as you think you do. He may be a little arrogant, but he's not selfish."

"You don't say." Mariah's arms folded and Brooke knew her words were falling on deaf ears. It broke her heart that Cole's sibling wasn't supportive. Harper had her faults, but she was always ready to back up Brooke's decisions, whether or not she approved. She'd been an absolute rock during the breakup with Nathan. Cole needed that kind of loyalty.

"As a matter of fact, Cole's extremely considerate." Brooke jutted her jaw forward. "He's gone grocery shopping for me and cooked dinner. He picked flowers for me. He even ran me a bubble-bath."

"I'll bet he did," Mariah chuckled. "No offense, but a man will show you his best side to get what he wants. I'm glad you made him work for it."

Brooke sputtered as heat raced from her collarbone to the roots of her hair.

Steph came to the rescue. "I'm guessing your brother didn't mention he and Brooke aren't sleeping together—before or after the wedding."

"Not even *after* the wedding?" Mariah's mouth dropped open. "Why not?"

"Because it's not that kind of relationship." Brooke grappled for her composure, blood throbbing in her face almost as intensely as in her swollen feet. "And Cole's not that kind of guy."

Mariah's lip twitched then curved into a mischievous grin. "What kind of guy is he, then?"

"He's the kind of guy who gives a ton of money to help kids with disabilities. And he's willing to ruin his own reputation to protect someone else's. He's tough enough to stand up to a bully, but sweet enough to massage a pregnant girl's feet."

"Well, well, well..." Mariah stroked an invisible beard on her chin. "That's very interesting. Seems I have a lot to learn about my brother."

"I'm glad you're finally seeing it." Brooke reached for a cracker and nibbled on the corner. "I hope this means you'll be there for him when he needs it."

"I have a feeling that job isn't likely to fall to me."

Mariah looked over her shoulder toward the couch. Steph grinned back at her and Laurie thrust a thumbs-up. Obviously, Mariah was counting on Bran, Finn and Jarrett to give Cole any encouragement he needed, rather than accept her responsibility. How would he ever learn to trust women if his own sister wouldn't stand by his side?

Steph stood up, glancing at her watch. "It's time to head downstairs."

Brooke's tongue grew thick and heavy. "Now?" she rasped.

"Didn't you say your family was going to meet us at the chapel?"

"Yes, but..." A glance at her cell phone revealed the time as seven o'clock, on the dot. Her sister and parents were due to arrive any minute. "Hopefully, I'll feel more courageous once Harper gets here."

"That's your sister?" asked Mariah.

"Yes. She's the one who gave me the courage to do this." A frightening thought occurred. "I hope no one says anything about me being pregnant—I haven't told my folks about it yet."

"No worries." Steph checked her face in the mirror. "Cole threatened us with certain death if we spilled the beans to your parents."

"Ready to go?" asked Mariah.

"I can't believe this is really happening," Brooke said, her mouth getting dryer by the second.

Laurie frowned, coming to put an arm around her waist. "It's only happening if that's what you want. You can change your mind right now. Call the whole thing off, if that's what you want. You're way more important than any old bet."

With her eyes trained on the hem of her dress, Brooke felt three sets of eyes boring into her forehead. She looked up, with as much courage as she could muster. "No, nothing's changed. I want to do this. I feel good about it."

"Are you sure?" Laurie asked. "You look kind of green."

"Nothing a saltine won't fix." She ripped open another packet and stuffed one of the two crackers into her mouth in its entirety.

"I can't wait to meet your sister." A smile bloomed on Mariah's face as she flanked Brooke's other side, herding her toward the door. "On the way down, I'll give you the heads-up about your future mother-in-law."

"Why? Is she against the marriage?"

Mariah laughed, shaking her head. "Not by a long shot."

CHAPTER 12

"Don't lock your knees," Finn murmured. "You look like you're about to pass out."

Cole shifted his feet to get the blood flowing. His antiperspirant seemed to be failing, despite the frigid air conditioning. Standing at the front of the hotel chapel with his three friends, he tried to avoid direct eye contact with anyone in the miniscule audience consisting of Steph, Laurie, his anxious parents, and Brooke's beaming mother. The gentle strains of the string quartet playing through the ceiling speakers did little to calm his nerves.

"I'm worried about Brooke. I have no idea what my sister told her."

"Whatever it was, it didn't change Brooke's mind. You'd know if she backed out."

"You're probably right, but I wanted to talk to her before we started. Your wife insisted it was bad luck to see the bride before the wedding, so Brooke doesn't even know about my uncle."

"She's not going to care if your uncle does the ceremony instead of the guy the hotel hired."

"But my uncle is a pastor—that's going to make it feel more real." Cole tried, without success, to talk without moving his lips

"It *is* real." Finn gave him a you're-losing-it look.

"I know, but she wanted it to be a casual, civil ceremony. That way she wouldn't feel as guilty when we got divorced. Then the families decided to come, and I pushed her into buying a dress and having the ceremony here." He scanned the opulent chapel, complete with an intricate, painted ceiling gilded with gold. "I didn't realize it would be so fancy. She'll hate it, and she'll probably go ballistic when she realizes Uncle Jack is an ordained minister."

"You didn't know your uncle was coming. Brooke won't be upset with you."

"But I don't want her to be blindsided."

"You could've told your mom no," Finn mumbled.

Cole glanced at his mother, whose disapproving gaze was trained on him. She sent him a scolding frown and mouthed, "Stop talking!"

He gave a fake cough behind his hand and muttered, "One doesn't simply say no to my mother."

Finn chuckled. "Yeah, I get that. Mum's the same way. It's easier to agree with her in person and do whatever I want when she's gone."

"Exactly!"

"Maybe you can smooth things over when you get home," said Finn.

Home... we haven't even discussed our living arrangements.

The double doors in the rear of the chapel swung open,

and Cole's pulse kicked up a notch. Mariah stepped into view, sporting the same wicked grin she'd worn when she sauntered off a few hours earlier. With a single long-stemmed red rose in her hands, she moved down the aisle and took her place on their uncle's right, her narrowed gaze never leaving his. What was she up to?

He was still staring at her when Brooke's sister arrived at the front of the chapel, wearing a strapless green cocktail dress. In contrast to his own sister, Harper gazed at him with bright, adoring eyes, like every other female fan. He wasn't worried about her, though. She wouldn't be so doting once she got to know him, and his mystical public aura wore off. She wouldn't like him any more than Brooke did.

An elbow jabbed in his ribs.

"There she is," Finn whispered.

His eyes went to her, a vision in white in the rear doorway. For a moment, he forgot to breathe. He'd known Brooke was beautiful, but now, with yards of silky white fabric draping in graceful folds, a stark contrast to her olive skin and the shiny dark locks, she was nothing short of exquisite.

His chest swelled with some weird feeling. *It must be pride.* Fans would go wild for her when they saw the pictures. No doubt, the publicity would increase stock values, as well. For a temporary bride, he'd chosen well.

"It's funny," Finn murmured. "From the way you're gaping at Brooke, one might think you had feelings for her."

Cole snapped his jaw closed. "I don't."

Paused at the back with her hand gripping her father's arm, Brooke radiated tension. Her dad took a step, but she didn't move, her face blanching. Her eyes squeezed shut, and she shook her head at whatever question her father asked.

She's backing out.

It would be the ultimate humiliation, especially when word got out to the media. He ought to be upset with her, but instead, he felt sympathy.

Shaking off Finn's restraining arm, Cole trotted down the short chapel aisle. He put his arm around Brooke's shoulder and wedged her away from her dad.

She jumped when she opened her eyes and saw him, her tears welling. "I'm sorry."

"Don't be." He lifted the bouquet from her limp grasp and handed it to the confused wedding coordinator. Then, ignoring everyone else, he retreated with her into the empty vestibule, away from listening ears. "I don't blame you for getting cold feet. I pushed you into this."

"That's not it," she said in a wobbly voice. "It was my decision."

"Then what's wrong?" He held her petite fingers with his hands, careful not to exert too much pressure with his mechanical hand. Her earnest expression tore at his heart.

"Would you mind being the one who files for divorce, instead of me, like we planned?"

"Why? I thought you said it would be embarrassing if I dumped you."

"But if I'm responsible for ending the marriage, everyone will hate me. Your mother, who wants a grandbaby. My parents, who are excited to have a celebrity as their son-in-law. All your fans who'll think I'm a jerk for leaving you." She studied their joined hands. "I won't be able to handle it."

He checked over his shoulder to be certain no one was

eavesdropping. At the hallway entrance to the vestibule, he could see Mack's broad form standing guard, too far away to hear their conversation. "There's no reason I can't file for divorce, if that's what you want."

Her shoulders remained stiff. "There's one more thing."

"What?"

"Tell me you don't want to be a father."

"I don't." As soon as he made the declaration, he realized it wasn't quite accurate. He dropped her hands, stuffing his in his pants pockets. "I mean… I might change my mind someday, if I can ever come to terms with what happened with my birth mom. But definitely not now. Anyway, what difference does it make?"

"It's me and my stupid, people-pleasing personality. I want sole custody of this baby."

"That's guaranteed in the contract we signed."

"I know. But if you were all sad about it, I don't know what I would do. I'd probably let you stay in contact, and then I'd regret it."

He could see her doing that. He wondered how many times she'd sacrificed her own happiness for someone else's.

"You want me to divorce you and stay completely out of your life, from that point on?" Could he do that?

Her lip was doing that thing where it folded between her teeth, mesmerizing him so he almost didn't hear her question. "Am I asking too much?"

He gave his head a little shake, refocusing on her pleading eyes. How could he disappoint her?

"I promise, after the divorce, it'll be like we never even met. Except you'll have a quarter million dollars, of course."

Her brows bent. "Minus whatever money you spend on me while we're married."

"Don't start that again." He folded his arms. "We both agreed it would be too hard to keep track."

"You said it, but I didn't really agree." Her lower jaw protruded. "Besides... do you know how much this dress cost?"

"Whatever I paid, it was worth it. You look amazing." He let his gaze wander down her bare shoulders to the satin fabric that graced her curves.

Her cheeks flushed. "You really think so?"

He tilted her chin up, sorely tempted to press his lips to hers. "I'd be as blind as Bran if I didn't notice."

She turned her face away. "Okay. I'll let you buy the dress. But that's all."

"We can talk about it on the way home tonight." He twisted to look back inside the chapel. Though their family and friends had kept their distance, every head was craned their direction.

She swallowed, her throat bobbing, and started for the door. "I'm ready. Let's do this before I chicken out again."

He grabbed her hand and pulled her back to him. "Before we do this, there's something you need to know."

BROOKE'S SKIN tingled where Cole's thumb caressed her hand, distracting her so that his words barely registered. She pulled free of his grasp, trying to recall what he'd just said.

"What do I need to know?" she asked.

Cole wrinkled his forehead. "My mother brought her

brother along to do the ceremony."

"Is that a bad thing?" She blinked, picking up on his anxiety.

"No, but he's an ordained minister."

"Oh." The blood drained out of her face. She wasn't sure how God would feel about her getting married with the intention of getting a divorce, so she would've preferred to leave Him out of it.

"I'm really sorry. She's just so excited that I'm finally getting married." To his credit, he looked as miserable as she felt.

"I'll be fine. God probably won't count it as a real marriage anyway, since we're not... you know..." Her cheeks heated.

"Consummating the marriage?" A crease appeared on his cheek.

"Yes. That."

"You aren't mad at me?"

"I can't be upset when you're only trying to keep your mother happy."

He gave a rueful laugh. "I'm glad you feel that way, because she also wants me to give you this ring."

His hand slid into his pocket, and he held it out for her inspection. Small diamonds sparkled in an antique setting, encircling a central round diamond that appeared to be about a carat in size, maybe more.

"That ring is way too valuable. She should save it for your sister." Brooke refused to even look at it.

"I tried that argument, but Mom says she has another ring for Mariah, because this one isn't her style."

She used both hands to rub her temples, pressing hard to

dispel the headache forming between them. "She's going to hate me when we get divorced, isn't she?"

His arms encircled her, strong and protecting. Her face pressed against the hard planes of his chest, and she breathed in his clean scent mingled with a pleasant aftershave. He said, "No one's going to hate you. I promise I'll take the flak, and I can handle it."

For a moment she stood still, relishing the comfort of his sweet embrace.

Of course I'm physically attracted to him. So is almost every other woman in the country. Whatever I do, I can't let myself get attached. This isn't a real relationship.

She pushed away from him, wrapping her arms around herself. "We should say it's a mutual decision. It wouldn't be fair to make you the bad guy."

His brows knitted together in a baffled expression. "But a minute ago, you said—"

"It's a woman's prerogative to change her mind."

He laughed so hard he choked. "I've always heard that, but I didn't realize it happened so fast."

With pursed lips, she tried to keep a straight face. "Well, now you know."

His smile gradually faded, his expression growing serious. "Please, can I hold your hand?"

With his green prosthetic fingers stretched toward her, she couldn't bring herself to say no, lest she hurt him. She put her hand in his and told herself it didn't affect her in the least. Was it a sin to lie to yourself?

"I'll be happy to take the blame for the divorce. You don't realize how much I…" He stopped in mid-sentence, averting his eyes.

What had he been about to say? Was it possible? She waited, holding her breath, as her pulse quickened.

He cleared his throat and continued. "How much I *owe* you. Thanks to you, I'm saving three-quarters of a million."

Her heart dropped into her stomach. There it was, in a nutshell. He was marrying her to avoid being on the show and to save himself a lot of money. She was a fool if she read anything into his sweet mannerisms. He was simply protecting his investment. Now, more than ever, she had to guard her heart, or it would be broken again. And this time, she had a baby to protect.

Not trusting her voice, she gave him a nod. So severe was the ache in her chest she was tempted to call the whole thing off. She might've done it if their families and friends hadn't flown across the country for the ceremony.

But she'd come out of her disastrous marriage with Nathan a stronger person, hadn't she? Now was the time to prove it. She could handle anything for a few months. Cole was a decent and caring man, and a platonic relationship with him would be far better than her stifling life with Nathan. In exchange for a few months of her time, she would have financial freedom for her child.

His hand tightened on hers. "Are you ready?"

"Ready as I'll ever be." With a bright smile plastered on her face, she forced her wooden legs to move.

Reunited with her father, she watched as Cole trotted down to take his place, his perfectly tailored tux accentuating his athletic form.

"Are you okay, Brookster?" Her father tucked her hand in the crook of his elbow and gave it a fond pat. "Do I need to take that boy out back and give him a talkin'-to?"

The crinkles at the corners of his eyes didn't fool her. His half-hearted smile told her he was worried.

"I'm fine, Dad. Just some wedding-day jitters."

Everyone was staring, waiting for them to walk down the aisle, but her father held back, ignoring the orchestra music that announced the bride's entrance. "I don't understand why you need to be in such an all-fired hurry to get married again. Your Mom and sister are excited because this guy is rich and famous, but you've never cared about stuff like that. You've always been sensible, like me."

"I've thought it through, and this is what I need to do."

"That doesn't sound like a woman in love." The furrow between his brows deepened. "I should've spoken up when you married that jerk, Nathan. I kept my trap shut, and I've always regretted it. I don't want to make that mistake again."

"It's okay, Dad. Cole's nothing like Nathan. He's going to help me get my counseling license." She swallowed hard. "I want to marry him."

He caught her gaze with his penetrating stare and held it so long she was afraid he saw through her façade. "Are you sure?"

Rising on her tiptoes, she kissed his cheek. "I'm sure."

She put all the confidence she could muster in those two words, praying she'd made the right decision.

COLE SLIPPED the antique ring onto Brooke's trembling finger.

"With this ring, I thee wed, in the name of the Father, the Son, and the Holy Spirit." His tongue felt like sandpaper as he repeated the words his uncle spoke. Why did saying the vows make him feel so guilty? Even though they both knew the marriage would be temporary, his objectives were noble. And he intended to keep every promise he made, except for the part about *as long as we both shall live*. He hadn't had the guts to suggest his uncle leave that section out of the vows.

Brooke's voice was so quiet he barely heard her as she mumbled the identical phrase and pushed the white gold ring onto his finger. It felt thick and heavy, and would probably be harder to get used to on his right hand, since he used it so much.

"I now pronounce you husband and wife. Cole, you may kiss your bride."

The face she lifted toward him was full of fear, and when he held her arms to pull her closer, he realized she was shaking from head to toe. He forgot his own distress, knowing hers was even worse.

"I won't leave your side," he whispered in her ear before he moved his lips to hers. He could only hope she understood his words of encouragement, since the group erupted with whoops and hollers. Though stiff at first, her sweet mouth responded to his tender kiss, stirring something deep in his gut… something he needed to ignore.

The next two hours passed quickly, but he kept his promise. The wedding coordinator had arranged dinner in a private meeting room. Toasts were made, with plenty of laughter. True to their word, his buddies made no mention of the pregnancy, but he suspected Brooke was dying from having kept the secret from her parents.

In a rare, private moment he bent close and asked, "Do you want to tell them about the baby now?"

"Not today." Her eyes were wide, and he saw her gulp. "Next week."

Before he thought about what he was doing, he leaned in and kissed her forehead. "Okay. Good plan."

Rosy spots bloomed on her cheeks. Clearing her throat, she stood up. "I'm going to the ladies' room. Be right back."

He felt a tap on his arm and turned to find Mariah sitting beside him, with one eyebrow arched high. "Platonic relationship, huh?"

"Shhhh!" His face burned as he scanned the area, relieved to see that his mother, seated at the adjacent table, didn't appear to be listening. "Keep your voice down."

"Don't worry. Mom's thoroughly convinced the two of you are madly in love." She leaned back in her chair and crossed her arms, one corner of her mouth kicking up. "In fact, so am I."

"What are you talking about?" he hissed.

"I'm talking about you, acting all sweet and protective, and Brooke, who looks at you like you hung the moon. I want to know what's really going on here."

"Nothing is going on."

"Even Mack thinks it's more than *nothing*."

"Mack? When did you talk to him?"

"We ran into each other out in the hallway. By the way, don't you think Mack ought to be invited to eat dinner? He's more than just an employee, after all these years, isn't he?"

Her cheeks flushed bright red. Why was she so angry about Mack being on duty during the wedding?

"Mack's not offended," said Cole, "and there's no one else I trust with security. This isn't an easy job."

Her lips blanched as she squeezed them together. "Back

to the subject at hand... I think you feel more for Brook than you're admitting. Isn't it possible you're falling in love with her? Would that be so bad?"

"Listen," he said, grinding his molars. "Brooke is doing me a huge favor. She's really stressed out right now, so yes, I'm being protective. That's *all* that's going on."

He would never let himself fall in love. He'd be a fool to be that vulnerable. If there was one thing he'd learned in life, it was how to make sure no one could ever hurt him again. Except for his family and a few select friends, he kept everyone at a distance. He might've shared more of his personal feelings with Brooke, but only in her role as a counselor.

"Keep telling yourself that." Mariah chuckled, rising to her feet.

"Mariah..." He used his best big-brother-warning-tone to no effect as she sidled away, still laughing.

Another feminine chuckle sounded behind him. He jerked his head around as Harper slid into Brooke's chair. With a conspiratorial look, she propped her chin on her hand, resting her elbow on the table.

"Sisters can be such a pain, right?"

"They can be." Remembering Brooke's insistence that Harper was *in love* with him, he scooted his chair back to put a comfortable distance between them. She was an attractive woman, though somewhat lacking when compared to Brooke. Harper projected an air of availability, while Brooke did the opposite. And while he regularly got lost in the depths of Brooke's deep brown eyes, Harper's pretty green ones did nothing for him.

"I didn't hear what she was saying, but it sounded like she knows how to get you riled up." Harper said.

"She does, and she did," he admitted. "I love my sister, but she makes me crazy. I guess you and Brooke aren't like that. She's never complained about you... at least, not to me."

"You mean, she hasn't complained once, in all the time since you met?" Harper gave an exaggerated wink. "How long has it been now? Maybe a week?"

Relaxing, he chuckled. "We talked a lot in a week."

She lowered her voice. "I'm not trying to give you a hard time. I appreciate what you're doing for Brooke. She deserves a break after everything she's been through, and that money will be life-changing for her."

Her assessment annoyed him. She made it sound like Brooke was a gold-digger.

"She's saving me even more."

"Oh, I know. She told me." Her hand reached out and brushed his arm for the briefest of seconds. "No explanation needed. What I want to talk to you about is your dog."

"My dog?"

"Yes. I read that article in *Prominence Magazine*, and I want to hear about your Blumastiff. I've always wanted one because they're so cool. I wondered how one would do in an apartment."

"Gus doesn't bark or shed much. He does fine in my apartment, but I pay someone to walk him every day." Cole spent the next five minutes entertaining Harper with stories of the dog's antics, his eye on the door where Brooke had disappeared.

"I'm getting worried about Brooke," he said, scanning the room for a sign of his bride. "She ought to be back by now."

"Brooke's up in her room." Harper looked confused. "She told me she was pooped."

He stood so fast he knocked his chair over. "Why didn't you tell me?"

"I thought you knew." She shrank away from him. "She said to tell you not to hurry, but she was ready to go when you were."

Why hadn't Brooke mentioned being tired? Was she afraid to be honest with him?

He was stomping across the room when Harper caught his arm. He shook free and muttered, "What do you want?"

Harper moved to stand between him and the exit, her hands on her hips. When she spoke, it was barely above a whisper, but there was no mistaking the fury in her tone. "You obviously have a problem with your temper. And I'm warning you right now, you'd better not hurt my sister. *Ever!* Or you'll answer to *me!*"

"I'm not that kind of man," he grumbled, offended at the accusation. "I've never been anything but kind to Brooke."

"Then why are you racing upstairs with your fists clenched?"

He forced his fingers straight, glancing around at his friends and family, who'd stopped talking to watch the exchange.

"Come talk to me in the hallway," he hissed. "People are watching."

She marched outside the banquet room and whirled to face him, her lips pressed together in a flat line.

"I'm not angry with Brooke," he mumbled.

"It sure looks like you are."

"Well, I'm *not*. I'm just frustrated she wasn't honest with me. How am I supposed to take care of her if she won't even tell me when she's tired? What am I doing wrong?"

He didn't flinch under her accusing stare. A long ten seconds passed, and then her furrowed brows lifted, her stance relaxing.

"It's not your fault," Harper said. "She always hides things like that."

"Always? I thought maybe it was a pregnancy thing."

"I don't think so." A ghost of a smile flitted across her face. "She doesn't want to bother anyone. It's like she listens to other people's problems all day, but she can't admit she has any. Or at least, she won't admit she needs any help."

"But she talks to *you*?"

"I'm her sister, but she doesn't tell me everything." Harper sighed. "Nathan did a lot of damage."

"I'm not Nathan." Surely, she wouldn't compare him to her ex. They were nothing alike. "She'll learn to trust me."

"Don't push her to change or make her feel guilty about it." Harper's eyes narrowed again. "It's not like you'll be together that long, anyway."

His mind was protesting her insight, even though she was probably right. Why did it exasperate him so much to admit he wouldn't have time to gain her trust within the next five months? It must be his competitiveness coming out.

"Harper, would you do me a favor?"

"Maybe…"

"Go back inside and tell everyone I'm leaving here in fifteen minutes." He looked up at the ceiling, like he could see through the thirty floors between him and Brooke. "I'm taking my wife home."

CHAPTER 13

"Good morning!"

Brooke blinked her scratchy eyes open, as Cole's bright smile came into focus. She tugged the sheet up to her neck, even though she'd purposefully worn a modest t-shirt and yoga pants to bed.

"I've got decaf coffee for you and an English muffin with some of my homemade cactus jelly." He nodded toward the tray in his hands as he set it on the bedside table. "What else can I do for you?"

"Stop being so perky." She closed her eyes. "That cheery face is giving me a headache."

"I guess you're not a morning person, huh?"

"No," she mumbled, resenting that he was forcing her to speak before six in the morning.

"I've already done a workout and taken a shower," he said. "Been up since a quarter 'til five."

She grunted, unable to think of a pleasant response, though quite a few scathing replies came to mind.

"Did you sleep well?" he asked.

"Like a rock."

It was true, but only after lying wide awake, tossing and turning, until three a.m. The flight home had been anything but romantic, as they'd sorted through all the logistics of living together for the next five months or so and the exact phrasing to utilize when discussing the marriage in public. By the time she'd arrived at his country home, she'd taken two Tylenol and climbed into bed, knowing she had to get up early to make it to work on time.

"I have some meetings today," he said, picking up one of the two coffee mugs on the tray and settling into a nearby wingback chair. "So I'll drive you in to work and pick you up at the end of the day."

"That's not necessary," she said, hoping he would leave, since her bladder was complaining. "I can drive myself."

"We already agreed about this." He sounded almost as impatient as she felt.

"No, you told me how it was going to be, but I never agreed."

"Brooke, it's not safe. When word gets out, reporters might show up at Hayward Home."

"So what? I'll show them my fancy ring and say the stuff we agreed to say. It'll be done and over with. If I avoid them, it'll make them think there's some great hidden story, and they'll be even more intense."

"I'm not worried about the reporters. I'm worried about the crazies who might see you as an easy target."

Unable to ignore her screaming bladder, she threw the covers back and hurried toward the bathroom, tossing her reply over her shoulder. "If they think I'm easy, they'll learn a hard lesson."

She barely heard his mumbled response. "No kidding."

Fifty minutes later, despite her protests, she was pouting in the passenger seat of his Ford pickup.

"You didn't tell me you'd put my car in the shop," she complained, idly twisting the foreign ring around her finger. It was a beautiful, but constant, reminder of how completely out of her element she was, married to a billionaire.

"If you call that hunk of junk a car."

"This old truck has more miles than my car." She eyed the odometer, displaying some number over 180,000.

He patted his dashboard. "You can't compare Betsy here to that thing that you drive around. She's still young in truck years."

Her lips twitched with a threatening smile. "Don't let Andretti hear you criticize him like that."

"Andretti? You named that car after a race car driver?" He choked out a laugh. "It probably tops out at seventy miles an hour." As if to make a point, he picked up speed as he merged onto the highway.

"I gave him a strong name, so he'd have something to aspire to."

"Is that why you named this guy Shrek?"

He waved a green hand at her, the motor purring, and she laughed.

"Let me buy you a new car. I can't have my wife driving around in something that looks like it belongs in a junkyard."

"If my car embarrasses you that much, I'll drive something else while we're married. But when we divorce, I'm taking Andretti with me."

"Fine."

From his pleased-with-myself expression, she figured he would try to change her mind when the time came.

Stubborn man.

Coming from outside town into the heavy Houston traffic, it took a full ninety minutes to reach Hayward Home. She was surprised when he parked the car and got out.

"I can walk inside by myself, Cole. There's no one waiting around to attack me."

"I'm aware of that. But I have an appointment this morning. I'm going to arrange a monthly donation... with the implied understanding that it will continue as long as my wife is employed here."

"Isn't that unethical, somehow?"

"It happens all the time. Some people donate millions to get their kids into the top schools. In this case, you're not getting anything you don't deserve. I'm just making sure you don't get fired for something that isn't your fault."

"Part of me feels guilty, like I'm taking a handout. But Hayward Home helps a lot of women, so at least you're donating to a good cause." As she fell in step beside him, she realized she felt lighter inside. Marrying Cole really had taken the weight of the world off her shoulders. "Can you also make sure I can keep my health insurance for a couple of months after I quit working? I'll finish my counseling hours four weeks before the baby comes."

"As of yesterday, you're on my insurance." His hazel eyes clouded. "And you'll be on it until after the baby is born."

"But I don't need—"

"It's in the contract you signed, so it's too late to argue."

She wondered what else she'd missed reading in the multi-page prenuptial agreement. He'd hired an attorney to represent her interests. But everything had happened so fast she hadn't had time to fully grasp all the details. Her main concern was keeping sole parental rights, which her attorney had assured her was the case.

"Fine." She would find a way to pay him back out of her divorce settlement, which would dwindle to nothing if he continued to lavish his wealth on her.

He opened the lobby door and caught her hand before she could escape, pulling her into his embrace. Though brief, the fiery kiss he placed on her lips felt like he'd branded her.

"Why did you do that?" she whispered, so breathless, she couldn't have spoken in a normal voice, anyway.

"We're newlyweds, remember?" His eyes darted toward the wide-eyed guard standing inside the door. "We need to make it believable."

Of course it had been for show. He hadn't tried to kiss her or even hug her in the privacy of his ranch home. Not that she wanted him to. In fact, she'd demanded they keep a respectful distance, knowing she couldn't handle the temptation of physical contact. But he'd conceded a little too easily for her fragile pride.

For a few dreamy seconds, he held her close and she melted against him. When he released her, she went rigid, mortified at her response.

"I'll see you after work." She spoke loud enough for the guard to hear. "Have a good day."

COLE'S WORK kept him busy, but Brooke had been in the back of his mind all day. Even his PA noticed.

"Did you hear anything I said?" Phillip asked, his mouth pursed in disapproval. He'd been a bit put off to learn about the marriage after the fact, though Cole assured him he was one of the first to know.

"I'm sorry. I wasn't listening."

"You've been completely distracted all day. And we're already behind after last week. Is this how it's going to be now that you're in love?"

He almost denied the emotional attachment but remembered Phillip didn't know the true story.

"It's a new thing for me," Cole said. "I imagine I'll get better, once I'm used to it."

"To be honest, I wouldn't mind if you slowed the pace a little bit." Phillip flopped into a chair in front of Cole's desk. "With the new baby, I'm hardly getting any sleep."

Cole realized he hadn't even bought the child a gift. He'd given Phillip a bonus, but now that seemed too impersonal. He resolved to send a present before the day was over.

"How's little Mallory doing?"

Phillip beamed. "She's beautiful! Amazing! Even though all she does is eat and sleep and poop. It's just the most incredible thing I've ever experienced."

"Congratulations." Why did Cole feel a little jealous?

"Now that you're married, maybe you'll find out for yourself what it's like to be a father." Phillip tilted his head, his gaze curious. "I hope you're not offended when I tell you this, but the way you went through women without ever being in a committed relationship, I thought you'd never settle down. That's why I was so shocked when you told me you got hitched."

Cole repeated his carefully planned response. "I'm surprised, too. We haven't known each other long, but everything just clicked. I knew I couldn't survive without her. But I was scheduled to be on Millionaire Matchup and the contract said I had to marry someone from their pool of contestants. The only solution we could find was to get married right away, before the filming started."

"To be honest, I get it." Phillip stood, his hands pressed to his lower back "I knew I wanted to marry Marcy by the end of our first date. But don't tell her that. She brags about how hard she worked to get me to fall for her."

Cole nodded, relieved his story had passed muster. And the way it was worded, every single word was true. His statement about not being able to survive without Brooke might've implied that they were in love, but he'd never made that claim.

"The phones have been ringing off the hook all day," said Phillip. "I know you have a press conference planned for tomorrow, but I think the word may already be out."

"I knew it would be. What have you been telling them?"

"I read your statement, word for word. 'Mr. Miller will make a public announcement concerning his relationship with Brooke Ponzio at nine a.m. tomorrow morning. Until then, we have no comment.'"

"Perfect. That ought to work them into a frenzy."

And with any luck, Millionaire Matchup would be ready to announce his replacement on the show. This morning, Garner had reported his lead was already in negotiations.

With a new millionaire getting all the publicity and Cole losing his bachelor status, his story would fade into obscurity. Everything was proceeding as smooth as clockwork.

Well... almost everything. He needed to follow Brooke's advice about keeping his distance. After his strong reaction this morning, he knew kissing was out of the question... even on the cheek. He'd already promised a nightly foot rub, but even that contact had filled his mind with thoughts that couldn't be classified as *platonic* by any stretch of the imagination.

Yet, he wasn't really worried about her magnetic attraction. After all, she was pregnant. Each month, as her belly grew larger, he ought to find her less and less desirable. It had to work. He was counting on it.

And he would still be safe, despite his strong physical attraction to Brooke, as long as he kept a tight hold on his emotions. It was okay to want her, as long as he didn't love her.

CHAPTER 14

When Cole pulled into the parking lot at Hayward Home thirty minutes early with hopes of finding Brooke in her office, she was waiting outside under an oak tree. He assumed the current ninety-six degree temperature was responsible for her grumpy countenance.

With country music still blaring on the radio, he hopped out of the truck and jogged around to open her door. "Why aren't you waiting inside the building? Isn't it dangerous for the baby if you get overheated?"

She climbed up, flounced her back against the seat, and yelled over the music. "I'm standing outside because my boss—who suddenly loves me after treating me like a piece of dirt for the past six months—said I should go home early, since I now have a secretary to schedule my appointments for me. I was so shocked I walked all the way out here before I remembered I didn't have a car. And then I was too embarrassed to go back inside. Especially since that guard from this morning was teasing me on the way out!"

He grinned as he shut her door and trotted back to the driver's side. Funny how she was amusing even when she was ticked off. What had he done to entertain himself before they met?

He turned the volume down as he pulled out of the parking lot. "Isn't it a good thing that your boss is being nice to you?"

"No, it's not! I've been working my tail off for the last six months without so much as a 'Nice work, Brooke.' Then *you* show up and throw some money at them, and they're all syrupy-nice to me. It's so fake! It's infuriating!"

He chuckled. "Welcome to my world."

"Oh my gosh!" Her eyes went as round as a wombat's. "Is that really how people treat you? All fake and pandering? I don't know how you stand it."

"I'm used to it, by now. But it makes it hard to have a real relationship with anyone, that's for sure. Just one more reason I've never dated seriously."

He turned toward his downtown apartment, where his security team had already relocated all of Brooke's clothes and toiletries. Eventually, he'd get her a double set, so she would have what she needed at either home.

Complaining about her boss evidently made her feel better, because she launched into a monologue about her day, including one client who shared every gruesome detail of her recent delivery, unaware that her counselor was newly pregnant.

"But she had the baby with her and he was adorable."

He heard a hiss and glanced over to see her hands

cupping her belly. His fingers tightened on the steering wheel.

"Is everything okay?"

"I'm fine." She grimaced, not meeting his eyes.

"Something hurts?"

She nodded, her lower lip trembling. "I've been having sharp stabs of pain down here all day. I'm afraid it means I'm losing the baby."

"That's it. We're going to the emergency room." He slammed his foot on the gas and sped up, whipping across three lanes of traffic to exit the highway.

"Cole!" she shouted. "Stop! You're being crazy!"

"I won't let you lose the baby."

"If that's what's happening, you can't stop it."

"Maybe not, but I'll die trying."

"That's not really helpful, if you kill us all in the process," she squeaked, one hand gripping the door handle while the other braced against the dashboard.

Though his heart still raced, he slowed the vehicle and tried to reason the fastest way to the medical center in Houston. "You're going to see a doctor, right now."

"I'll get an appointment tomorrow," she said. "I don't want to be one of *those* women."

"Who are *those* women?"

"The kind of women who demand special treatment."

"You certainly aren't that kind of woman," he said. "Fortunately for you, I *am* that kind of man." He punched the hands-free call button on his steering wheel to contact his friend, Dave Harrison, who answered on the second ring.

"Dave, I've got a medical emergency! Where are you right now?"

"Hey, Cole." He was out of breath. "I'm working out, but I'm in the gym above my office. What's wrong?"

"I've got a friend with a problem... actually, it's my wife."

"Your *wife*?" He used the same inflection one would expect if Cole had mentioned a pet rattlesnake.

"Yeah, I got hitched last night."

"Well, congratulations! What's going on with your wife?"

"She's pregnant, but having pains."

"Okay. How far along?" He didn't even question that Cole's wife of less than twenty-four hours was pregnant.

"Thirteen weeks, right?" He looked to Brooke for confirmation.

"Almost fourteen."

"What kind of pain?" the doctor asked. "Sharp, stabbing pain? Or achy cramping pain?"

"Sharp." Brooke answered the question herself.

"Any bleeding?"

"No."

"First thing—stay calm. I don't think it's anything serious, but I want to check things out. I'll meet you at my office in ten minutes."

"I CAN MAKE an appointment and come back during your regular hours, Dr. Harrison."

She'd been mortified that Cole had imposed on him, accusing Cole of being rude, simply because he had money and power. Enjoying her misdirected rant, Cole hadn't bothered to explain.

"Brooke," Dave said as she continued to balk, "this is what

I do, and I get paid well to do it. I'm a concierge doctor. People like Cole pay a lot of money so they can be seen in a private setting whenever the need arises. In addition, he's also one of my best friends."

"And one of our neighbors in the building," Cole added.

"You could have mentioned that before," she muttered, her narrowed eyes slicing Cole to shreds.

"But you're cute when you're riled up."

Her glare told him she hadn't taken the comment as a compliment.

Maybe I should give her an extra-long foot massage tonight.

At Dave's direction, she climbed onto the examination table. With no nurse present, he instructed Cole to stay in the room. Cole didn't mean to stare when Dave exposed Brooke's stomach for the ultrasound, but he was fascinated by the sight of her slightly rounded belly.

"This'll be a little cold," Dave said, as he squirted some clear jelly on her skin and moved the sensor across her stomach.

An image appeared on the screen, and Cole's heart leapt against his ribcage.

"That's him?" Without thinking, Cole grabbed Brooke's hand and squeezed it. "That's really the baby?"

The picture clearly showed the profile of a face. It was the most amazing thing Cole had ever seen. The image shifted to something strange and abstract, and then Cole could see something moving.

"That's the blood flowing through the heart," Dave said, shifting the sensor again.

"The heart's already working? At fourteen weeks?" Cole's

own heart was working overtime, pumping way faster than it needed to.

"The heart starts beating twenty-two days after conception." Dave moved the sensor again, and something that might've been an arm or a leg appeared. Then he stopped in a position that almost showed the entire baby in profile. "Everything looks good. I'll take some measurements and confirm the due date, but since you know the date of conception, it doesn't really matter."

"What about the pain I felt?" Brooke asked.

"It's common to have sharp pains from the round ligament about this stage of pregnancy." Dave put the sensor up and removed his gloves. "There's a great book I recommend to all my expecting parents—it explains a lot of this stuff. I'll text the name to Cole."

"Thanks, Dave," Cole said.

"Congratulations to both of you!" Dave clapped Cole on the back. "For getting married and for the baby. I'm so happy for you!"

A true friend, Dave had the grace not to question the circumstances of the hasty marriage or the pregnancy.

"Thanks." Cole choked the word out, a small part of him wishing Dave's assumptions were true.

"I'll order some blood work, and see you again in about a month." Dave handed Brooke some tissues to wipe her skin. "And in case you were worried, having sex won't harm the baby."

Fortunately, Dave seemed not to notice the pink color spreading on Brooke's face.

"That's a relief." Cole said what he assumed his friend expected him to say.

"Next time, when we do the ultrasound, we'll be able to determine whether it's a boy or a girl. You'll need to decide if you want me to tell you, or if you'd rather be surprised. Or, I can write the answer down and put it in a sealed envelope."

"I think I want to know the gender," said Brooke.

Dave shrugged. "Some couples like to be surprised at a gender reveal party."

Her mouth drooped. "We won't have one of those."

Cole wondered if she felt like she was missing out on some of the joy.

"We could have one if you want," he said.

Her surprised eyes whipped over to his. "We can't! No one even knows I'm pregnant."

"Everyone will know soon enough," said Cole.

"I hope you're not starving yourself, trying to hide this pregnancy." Dave's face was stern. "I expect you to gain about a pound a week."

"I don't know if I can. I'm just now getting my appetite back."

"She'll gain the weight," said Cole. "I'll make sure it happens."

A flash of anger told him he should've kept his mouth shut.

"You aren't going to make me do anything! I'll eat whatever I choose."

"Sorry." His apology met an impassive expression. "I meant to say I'd help as much as I can. Cook some great meals for you. Stuff like that."

Dave chuckled as he offered Brooke a hand to sit up. "You've got a tough job—trying to keep Cole in check. I think he's used to giving orders."

Her scowl softened. "I'm not easy, either."

"Brooke doesn't need to be controlled," Cole said, with a wink he hoped would brighten her mood. "It's too fun to watch her when she's *out* of control."

She stood up and gave him a playful shove.

"Here are your pictures to take home." Dave handed her a set of five or six images, which Brooke slid into her purse. He had a feeling she wouldn't take them back out until she was alone in her room.

"Can we have a second set of pictures?" Cole wished the words back when Brooke shot him an anxious look. "I... uhm... thought your sister might want to see them."

She beamed at him. "Good idea."

Whew! That was close. No wonder they say marriage is hard work.

COLE WAS SPOILING her and she didn't like it.

Well... she liked it, but it wasn't a good thing. If their relationship was going to be a mutually-beneficial, friend-roommate thing, she had to pull her own weight. So far, Cole was doing all the heavy lifting.

When they arrived home to the immaculate penthouse apartment, which had more square feet than her parents' home, Gus greeted both of them with equal helpings of enthusiasm and slobber. While Cole tended to Gus, she retreated to her room.

Cole had stocked her closet with an array of maternity clothes, tags still attached. She had no idea who'd chosen them, but whoever it was had great taste. She changed into an adorable green-striped tunic in a buttery soft fabric. And her maternity yoga pants were admittedly more comfortable without the tight elastic at her waist.

In the mirror, she scrutinized her growing belly. She couldn't imagine how she would look when she was nine months pregnant. Part of her wondered if Cole would be grossed out by her appearance. Not that it mattered, since they'd be divorced by the time the baby came.

She sighed, surveying the new clothes, which included a dresser full of maternity undergarments. He'd even bought her a huge assortment of new shoes, allowing that she could return the ones that didn't fit. He'd already informed her the ranch had been stocked with a full set of clothes and toiletries to match the ones she already owned. Whoever had done the shopping—undoubtedly a woman, from the thoroughness of their selections—was probably chuckling at her measly collection of cheap makeup. Well, no reason to get used to fancy toiletries. She'd be back on her own in a few months, and she needed to make her settlement money stretch a long way. *If there's anything left when I pay him back for all the money he's spending on me.*

"This is way too much!" she'd complained the night they arrived home from Vegas. "I don't need all this stuff."

"After I go public Tuesday morning, everyone in the country will be dissecting you from head to toe. If I don't spend money on you, people will wonder why."

"You don't wear fancy, expensive clothes." She'd nodded toward his boots. "I hear you've had those re-soled twice."

"Three times. Nothing could ever replace them. In fact, I plan to be buried in them." He'd admired his booted foot as he lifted it in the air. "But everyone knows I could buy new ones if I wanted to. I don't, because I don't need them, and I don't like to waste money."

"Then why waste money on me?"

His shoulders had gone up and down, as if her question didn't have any merit. "Because I wanted to."

She hadn't argued that he was, in fact, using *her* money, since he didn't know she intended to deduct his expenditures from her ever-dwindling settlement. She couldn't even imagine how much a concierge doctor cost, but she reasoned her insurance wouldn't cover Dr. Harrison's services.

Somehow, she had to get his spending under control. She propped herself up on the pillows on her king-sized bed, feeling like a character in a Hallmark movie... a commoner pretending to be a princess. Closing her eyes with the intent of resting for a second, she fell asleep, awakening to a mouth-watering aroma.

She made her way back to the main living area, vainly trying to shush her growling stomach. With an apron over his shorts and t-shirt, Cole was busy at the stove.

"What are you making?"

She peered around him at the sauce pan, amazed at his deft use of Shrek, along with his flesh-and-blood arm.

"Sautéed shrimp and scallions. It's almost ready."

It was then that she noticed, for the first time, he had on a short-sleeved shirt, exposing a metal spike where Shrek was attached, just above the elbow.

"I hope it doesn't bother you too much." The muscles along his jaw rippled. "I can cover it up, if it does."

Embarrassed to have been caught staring, she jerked her gaze away. "I'm sorry. I was just wondering how it attaches."

He turned the fire off under the sauce pan and twisted

toward her, holding his arm out for inspection. She felt like he was testing her reaction.

"I'm fortunate to have a rod and sensors implanted in my body, so I don't have to wear a harness. I can do pushups and lift weights without any pressure on my skin where the implant attaches. That's a luxury most amputees can't afford."

"So that rod never comes off?"

If her blatant curiosity bothered him, he didn't show it.

"No, that's a permanent part of me."

"But you can take Shrek off and trade it out for the other one?"

"If I want to, yes. But I hardly ever do. I have to take it off in the shower."

Images of Cole in the shower filled her mind, and her face caught on fire. She bent toward the floor, hoping he wouldn't notice.

"You can't stand to look at it, can you?"

Great… she'd hurt his feelings.

"No, it doesn't bother me at all. I was just noticing my feet are swelling again." She fanned her face. "And it's hot in this kitchen."

His smile returned.

Thank goodness! Her explanation had worked, and he had no idea where her thoughts had been.

"I'm glad you aren't grossed out by it," he said, carrying the sauce pan to the table and placing a serving on each of their plates, "because I usually exercise without a shirt."

"That won't matter, anyway, since I make it a point never to set foot inside a gym."

"All that changes tonight," he said, as he heaped a pile of

salad on each plate and pulled her chair out, motioning for her to sit.

"What are you talking about?"

"While you were in your room, Dave dropped by and left a ton of information about how to have a healthy pregnancy." He sat down at the end of the table, beside her. "Turns out it's really important to exercise while you're pregnant."

"That pamphlet was probably written by someone trying to sell gym memberships."

He stabbed a shrimp with his fork and pointed it at her. "You're just trying to get out of exercising."

"Because I hate it. I don't believe in sweating." She took a bite of shrimp. "Wow! This tastes like Heaven!"

"Thanks," he said. "But, you live in Texas. How can you not believe in sweating?"

"That's what air conditioning is for."

"Exercise can give you more energy, help you sleep, help you have an easier delivery and recovery, and help prevent pre-eclampsia—whatever that is—and gestational diabetes." With amazing agility, he ticked the points off, one mechanical finger at a time. "You don't want to get insulin shots multiple times a day, do you?"

The room swam at the idea of daily shots. Did he know she was secretly needle-phobic? Yet she had to find an excuse to avoid working out with Cole. She knew for an absolute fact she couldn't handle seeing him without a shirt. Not when his t-shirt-covered chest took her thoughts where they shouldn't go.

"I don't have time to exercise." She pushed her salad around on her plate.

"You can get up an hour early and exercise with me."

Aha! The perfect solution!

"I'm not a morning person," she said, triumphantly.

"How could I forget? You were a real grouch when you woke up this morning."

"Only because you were smiling and talking in a happy voice."

He threw his head back and laughed. "Okay. No morning exercise for you."

"I'm afraid not." She pulled her lips down as if she were disappointed.

"I guess you'll have to do your exercise in the evening."

"Fine, I'll do it." Without his supervision, she could probably get by with a few minutes walking on a treadmill. Then, she could stay in the gym a little longer, playing on her phone.

He took a bite of shrimp and chewed, lost in thought. Just as she sipped her water, he spoke again.

"I'll exercise with you."

She sucked in a surprised breath, choking on the liquid.

"Are you okay?"

Eyes watering, she continued to cough. "I'm fine," she wheezed.

"We'll start off easy," he said, forking a piece of lettuce. "Twenty minutes of cardio, and then some yoga."

"Great," she mumbled, picturing Cole, shirtless, his muscles flexing as he stretched into various yoga poses.

She was fairly certain waterboarding would be a preferable form of torture.

CHAPTER 15

Cole had ripped off the proverbial bandage, and it could've been worse. He reasoned if they were going to be living in the same house for months, Brooke might as well get used to seeing his arm implant. He had no intention of wearing long sleeves in his own home like he did whenever he was in public. She'd responded reasonably well at first, displaying only mild curiosity. But during the exercise session, it was obvious she was uncomfortable with his appearance. She'd mostly kept her eyes glued to her treadmill display. The few times he'd caught her glancing his direction, she'd quickly averted her eyes, deep red spreading all the way down her neck on to the part of her chest exposed by her tank top.

Not that he'd been staring at her chest or anything. Though he had noticed she looked really nice in her exercise outfit. He kept stealing peeks at her shapely legs. Did pregnancy make her extra curvy? It would be interesting to watch the gradual change as the baby grew. With any luck, she would continue to work out with him each evening, so he could observe the transformation and eventually get her accustomed to his arm's strange appearance.

So far, things were progressing better than he'd hoped. The Hayward Home director hadn't even blinked upon learning that Brooke got divorced and remarried without their knowledge. In light of Cole's proposed donation, Hayward Home had enthusiastically agreed that their policy excluding divorcees from professional positions was more of a *general guideline* that certainly wouldn't apply in Brooke's case. Especially since Brooke was now legally married, the director had reasoned, while drooling over the check in his hand.

Likewise, his press conference had gone smoothly, the reporters mollified when he described a whirlwind romance and shared select photos from the wedding ceremony. The host of Millionaire Matchup was present, as well, to congratulate Cole and Brooke and announce that the next season would begin filming that week, as planned, with a new bachelor. The identity of the new millionaire would remain a secret for now, though fans could visit the website for clues. The reporters were excited to get a double scoop, and none protested at his firm but gentle suggestion they not hassle his bride.

Cole's workday, on the other hand, had been anything but smooth. He cringed when Phillip walked in his office at four fifteen, wearing a guilt-ridden expression.

"What is it, this time?" Cole asked.

"You know that Economic Development Committee

meeting that was supposed to be today, but got rescheduled for next week?"

"Let me guess. It's back on for tonight?"

"Yes. And the Macy Road property is on the agenda."

Cole groaned. He'd been looking forward to picking Brooke up from work. But this property had been sitting idle for too long.

"Can O'Reilly or Hutto cover it?"

"O'Reilly's at that conference in Chicago. And Hutto's on vacation. He moved it forward a week so he'd be in town next Tuesday for the meeting." Phillip scrunched up his face. "Sorry, Cole. After the day you've had, I'm sure you don't feel like working late."

"Yes, I'm beat. I'd love to go home and fall into bed."

"I'll bet." Phillip chuckled. "You newlyweds…"

Cole's face warmed, and he bent his head, pretending to search for something in his bottom desk drawer. He should've expected this type of friendly ribbing, but he'd been caught unprepared. By tomorrow, he'd have some witty response, but nothing appropriate came to mind. "Thanks for letting me know about the meeting."

Phillip took the hint and left him alone. He called Mack on his cell phone.

"Hey, Mack. I need you to pick up Brooke for me."

"I know. I'm already on my way to Hayward Home."

"Why?" His heart hammered against his ribs. Something bad must've happened.

"I'm going to rescue Brooke from the reporters. Isn't that why you're calling?"

"No, I just got hung up at work." Why were they

bothering her at her job? Cole had thought he had a *gentlemen's agreement* with the press to leave her alone in exchange for the wedding images he'd shared. "I can't believe they double-crossed me," he muttered.

"Hayward Home invited them." Mack's voice conveyed his disapproval. "Brooke told me it's a publicity stunt. She doesn't want to participate, but she doesn't really have a way to escape, either. That's why she called me."

"Why didn't she call me, instead of you?"

He could picture Mack's huge shoulders lifting in a shrug. "Maybe because this is my job, and we told her to call me if she had any problems."

Mack was right, but it didn't take away the sting of knowing she'd turned to another man for protection. *Forget the economic development committee!* "I'll be there in fifteen minutes. Twenty, tops."

"We'll be gone by the time you get here," said Mack. "You stay and get your work done, and let me do my job. I'll make sure she gets home safe and gets something to eat."

It could be nine o'clock or later by the time Cole made it home. He didn't want her to be alone. But his gut twisted at the thought of her spending so much time with Mack.

"That's a bit outside your pay grade, to be a babysitter. Do you think Andrea could stay with her until I get home?"

"You want Andrea instead of me? Are you afraid I'm going to flirt with your wife?"

"I didn't say…" Cole sputtered. "I just thought Brooke would enjoy a woman's company. And Andrea is certainly competent for the job."

"Whatever you say." Mack gave a snort of laughter. "For

the record, not only would I never betray you, but Brooke doesn't strike me as the cheating type, either."

"Don't worry. I trust both of you."

He wasn't lying. He had complete faith in both Mack and Brooke. Cheating wasn't the issue. His greatest fear was she would compare him with another man and develop a sort of buyer's remorse. His ego wouldn't be able to handle that, even from a temporary wife.

"But how much overtime pay will you get?" Brooke tried to camouflage her question as curiosity, when, in fact, it was all part of her ongoing accounting efforts. Only her second day of marriage, and she'd already had to call Cole's security team to rescue her. She could've blamed it on Hayward Home. But admittedly, Hayward wouldn't have been pandering to the press if Cole hadn't promised them an exorbitant amount of money to secure her job. That made the whole fiasco her responsibility.

Now one of Cole's employees was wasting her time babysitting Brooke at the apartment. Nothing Brooke said had persuaded Andrea to leave before Cole arrived home. At least she'd agreed to sit down and share dinner.

"That's not how it works," said Andrea, as she pushed her empty plate away. "I'm paid to be on call. And this is about the easiest gig I could possibly draw… eating dinner with the boss' wife inside his penthouse. The pack is going to be *soooo* jealous."

"Are days like today pretty commonplace? Dealing with the press?"

"Not really. I've been on board for two years, and this is only the third time we've had problems with reporters."

"Was last week one of the other two times?" Brooke asked, dreading the answer.

"Yes, although there've been other crazies to deal with." Andrea closed her mouth tight, as if she were afraid she'd said too much. "Do you want some more chicken or veggies?"

Brooke looked down, surprised to find her plate empty. How had she been able to eat with all that was going on? She must've chewed and swallowed on autopilot.

"No, thanks," she responded, standing to carry the plates to the kitchen.

While loading the dishwasher, her mind swam, searching for an answer to her dilemma. As she'd suspected, her presence in Cole's life was causing more problems than he could've possibly predicted. And today, his sister, Mariah, had tracked down her work number to call and warn her that Cole's parents were planning a surprise visit that weekend.

"Why are you telling *me*?" Brooke had asked. "Why not warn Cole?"

"Because Cole would probably leave town to avoid them. Heck, he'd probably leave the country. But I think I can convince you it would be better to get it over with."

"Get *what* over with?"

"Letting Mom satisfy her curiosity about you."

"Cole doesn't like having his mother interfere."

"She's not interfering… not really. She just loves him and wants to be part of his life. But she wants to be more involved. Cole's always shutting her out. In fact, he shuts his whole family out—including me."

"What do you expect me to do?" Brooke had asked. "I don't have any say in his decisions. We aren't even going to be together that long."

"You have more power than you think. And I mean that in a good way. He never listens to me, but you have his ear. Wouldn't you feel better about this whole marriage if you knew you'd helped Cole get closer to his family?"

"I don't know," she'd replied, though it wasn't true. How could Mariah already have her pegged? There was nothing Brooke would like better than to feel their temporary marriage had accomplished something worthwhile.

"Besides," Mariah had added, "you might have fun!"

Brooke had found Cole's mother way too overbearing for comfort, even during the short time they were together in Las Vegas. A weekend with Cole's parents sounded about as fun as getting a root canal. But she was willing to do almost anything to help Cole. She owed him so much, and the tab was getting higher by the day. Perhaps the amount she reimbursed him could be adjusted for "pain and suffering." A weekend with the in-laws would certainly qualify.

"I'll see what I can do," she'd told Mariah, "but I'm not making any guarantees."

"I don't expect any. After all, this is my brother we're talking about."

The doorknob rattled, drawing her back to the present. She turned in time to see Cole trudge inside, the dark circles under his eyes attesting to his fatigue. Without thinking, she hurried to his side, and he pulled her into his arms like any newlywed husband who'd missed his wife. For a moment,

Brooke basked in his fervent embrace. All her worries melted into nothingness. Then she remembered he was simply performing for his audience.

"We'll send a full report tomorrow, Mr. Miller," said Andrea, as she slipped out the door and shut it behind her.

Brooke pushed herself free, as if she'd been pretending, as well. "What can I get you? Have you had dinner?"

"I'm okay. I ate a couple of protein bars." He collapsed on the leather couch, patting the seat beside him. "I'm afraid I'm too beat to work out with you, tonight."

She danced a little celebration jig on the inside—all the exercise she needed for the evening.

"Did your meeting go well?" She sat next to him, though not as close as he'd indicated.

"We got most of what we wanted. But I was gunning for a few extra tax breaks. That's not happening."

"Would a back rub help?"

Why did I say that?

His eyebrows arched in surprise. "You'd do that?"

She held her breath to keep from hyperventilating as she nodded her head.

"Let me go shower off, and I'll trade you a ten-minute back rub for a twenty-minute foot rub." He stood up and moved toward his bedroom with a bit more pep in his stride.

Frantic, she was on her feet, pacing, trying to think of a way out of her predicament. In what seemed like less than sixty seconds, he was back, shirtless, his hair damp from his shower, smelling so clean and yummy she was tempted to press her nose against him.

Blood rushed into her face, and she prayed he wouldn't notice. "I'm not great at giving massages."

"I promise I won't judge you."

As he moved closer, she began an intense study of her hands to avoid looking at his bare chest. Exercising with him last night had been bad enough. How on earth would she be able to keep her composure when her fingers were massaging the same delectable muscles that had invaded her dreams and ruined her sleep?

"My nails are probably too long to do a decent back rub." She cleared her throat, trying to get the squeak out of it. "I should go cut them."

She started toward her room, but his hand grasped her arm.

"Brooke." His voice broke. "Look at me."

Her eyes met his pain-filled ones, and her heart twisted inside her. In the moment, she forgot her discomfort. "What's wrong?"

"Look at my arm."

Confused, she blinked, her gaze falling to his left arm, where the bare implant extruded from its end. On the table beside him, Shrek lay like something from a science-fiction movie. Cole must've taken it off for his shower.

She locked eyes with him again, trying to find the cause of the hurt radiating from his tortured expression. "Did I do something wrong?"

"When my shirt is off, you manage to look everywhere in the room except at me. You did the same thing last night." His eyes glinted steel. "Is it that disgusting to look at me without my prosthesis on?"

It took a moment for the accusation to sink in. When she finally realized what he'd been thinking, a nervous giggle bubbled out, expanding to full-blown laughter. Her knees went weak, and she collapsed on the couch, still laughing.

"What's so funny?" His bitter note testified he found no humor in her reaction.

When she caught her breath, she knew she had to confess, no matter how embarrassing it was. "The truth is, I could care less what your arm looks like, with or without your prosthesis."

"Sorry, but I don't buy it."

"I can't believe I'm going to tell you this…" She covered her face with her hands, so her words came out muffled. "The problem isn't your arm. The problem is you look a little *too good* without a shirt on, and I'm doing my best to keep my mind out of the gutter."

After a moment of silence, she peeked between her fingers and spotted a goofy grin on his face.

"And I swear," she growled, "if I find out you tricked me into admitting that, I'm going to smack that smile right off your face."

That remark got an outright laugh.

"It wasn't a trick." His fingers attempted unsuccessfully to pry her hands away. "I promise I didn't know."

"Well, I hope you're happy now, because I'll never be able to face you again."

He wedged two of her fingers apart. "Would it make you feel any better if I told you I feel the same way about your legs?"

She wished she believed him. At least she wouldn't have to feel lecherous on her own. But she doubted a guy like Cole Miller would find any part of her that attractive. Most likely, he'd made up that story because he felt sorry for her.

"Yeah, right," she said, with enough sarcasm to make her point.

"It's true," he said. "Especially when you're wearing those shorts."

"These capris?" She lifted her hands away to glance down. "They cover most of my legs. All you can see are my calves."

"But they're tight, so…" His grin twitched on one side. "Trust me, they're totally sexy."

Her face was hot enough to fry an egg, so she redirected his attention. "Maybe you should put a shirt on."

"Okay, but I'm not letting you off the hook for a back rub."

He disappeared down the hallway and came back looking like a model in a t-shirt ad… one that would've had her groping for her credit card.

"Much better." She gulped, hoping she could forget what he looked like underneath the thin cotton.

His smug smile reminded her she'd revealed too much of her attraction for him. But instead of teasing her about it, he graciously offered to do the foot rub first.

With Shrek's assistance, he performed a bone-melting massage on her left foot. As he began her other foot, she remembered Mariah's phone call.

"Mariah called to let me know your parents want to come visit us."

He stopped rubbing and stared at her, slack-jawed. "Mariah called you?"

"Yes. And I want you to know I'm in favor of the visit."

"Well, I'm not." A glower descended as he returned to the massage. "Mom's way too nosy, and she's been getting worse about it."

She knew better than to tell him it would be *good* for him.

"She's just being a mother." She rubbed her belly. "I imagine this little one is going to complain about me being nosy someday. I'd be heartbroken if I thought he didn't want me in his life anymore."

His hazel eyes aimed toward the ceiling. "I've never said that."

"Does she know you've been looking for your birth mom?"

"Sure she does. But she also knows why." He jutted his jaw forward. "She isn't upset about it."

"Don't you think she could be a little insecure, even if she hasn't admitted it?"

His scowl softened. "I guess that's possible."

"You could invite your folks out to the ranch this weekend. Keep them really busy, and there won't be much time to talk."

"That's true. They love it out there, and I haven't invited them in a while." His fingers slid up to her calf and began kneading the muscle. "Does this feel good?"

It did. *Too* good! She lost her train of thought as warmth furled in her belly. Warning sirens went off in her head, and she jerked her leg away to sit up.

"It's your turn." She pointed to the floor. "Lie down, and I'll rub your back."

He grabbed a pillow for his head and stretched out on the thickly padded area rug. She knelt beside him and began to knead his knotted muscles through the thin t-shirt. Even with fabric between her fingers and his skin, she got a thrill from touching his well-formed back and shoulders. And when he let out a groan, she almost responded with one of her own.

Time for a distraction.

"Do you want to talk about your day?" she asked. "Sorry you had to work so late."

"Normally, I wouldn't mind staying past five." The pillow dampened his voice. "But today I wanted to be the one who picked you up from work."

"If you'll get my car out of the shop, I'll drive myself and save you the trouble."

"But it's not far out of the way." He turned his head toward her. "Plus, I enjoy driving you. Weirdly, I actually like talking to you."

"Weirdly?"

"I'd always heard stories about how wives talk too much, though I have to admit Bran and Finn never complain."

She smiled at his thoughtful expression. Then she found a knot in his right shoulder muscle and dug her thumbs in, producing another gratifying groan.

She'd also enjoyed their commute together, but for a different reason. Riding with him in his pickup truck while having long discussions felt like something any normal married couple might do. For that brief time, it had felt like a real marriage.

"If you really wouldn't mind having my parents visit, I'll let Mom know they're invited." He shifted his head, aiming his face down while she massaged his neck. "They probably would've shown up, anyway. That's what usually happens."

"Are you going to tell them the truth about us while we're all together at the ranch?"

His muscles stiffened. "I probably won't tell them at all.

No use spoiling it for Mom. At least she can be happy until the divorce."

She wanted to argue with him, except she felt the same way about her own mother. Yet, one thing was certain… soon, everyone would know she was pregnant.

CHAPTER 16

"They'll be here any minute!" said Brooke, as she dug in the back of the dining room hutch and pulled out another set of dishes.

From his place at the stove, Cole couldn't tell any difference between the plates. "What was wrong with the first dishes?"

Banned from the kitchen and dining room, Gus lounged on a ginormous elevated trampoline bed in the family room.

"They were china. Too fancy for what we're eating." She refolded each napkin for the umpteenth time.

"Why not use the regular plates in the kitchen cabinet?" The timer dinged, and he retrieved the cornbread from the oven, a perfect golden brown.

"It's my first time to have my mother-in-law at the house since we got married." Brooke stared at him like he'd lost his marbles. "I want the table to look special."

He could've told her his mother would be critical, no matter what she did, but he didn't want to burst her bubble.

Maybe he could try to be a buffer and keep her from being hurt. He took off his oven mitts and stole behind her as she reached across the table to rearrange the flower stems in the centerpiece.

As he slid his arms around her waist, she jumped.

"You scared me," she said, speaking over her shoulder from the circle of his grasp.

"Thank you for going to so much trouble to make Mom happy." He planted a chaste kiss on her cheek, noting her fresh scent, with a hint of strawberry. He resisted the urge to nuzzle her neck, an act which would violate the touching rules they had discussed at length. With satisfaction, he noted a row of chill bumps had formed on her arms. He shouldn't enjoy teasing her, but it felt good to know he had the ability.

She peeled his hands away. "I'm not sure that hug is allowable."

"The rule is, 'No full-body hugs facing each other.' If side hugs are okay, back hugs should be fine, too."

"But your hands—"

"They were on your stomach, one of very few safe zones you left me. Essentially, I can touch your stomach, your hands, your feet, and the top of your head, and that's it. Well, maybe the tip of your nose."

"No, the nose is definitely off limits." A grin snuck onto her face. "I can't help it. I'm sensitive everywhere."

"I'm well aware. With all the strict guidelines you set, I'll have to be creative around my folks, or they'll be suspicious. Most newlyweds do a little more touching than that."

She worried her lower lip between her teeth, which made him want to toss the no-mouth-to-mouth-kissing rule out the window. Maybe he should make lip chewing against the rules.

"I guess we can stretch the limits a little bit, while your parents are here," she said.

He conjured a pained expression. "Stretching the limits is outside my comfort zone, but I'll go along with it, if that's what you want..."

"Very funny." She shoved him so hard he stumbled, laughing, back into the kitchen.

"I put some of your special chocolates in that candy dish. You should have a piece." Though he'd been told his chocolate purchase had been a bit excessive, she'd already managed to make a significant dent in it.

She opened the lid and squealed with delight. "Dark chocolate! Just what I need!"

One went into her mouth and several into her pockets. Then the door-knocker clanged, and she froze, with a deer-in-the-headlights expression.

"We're here!" His mom burst in, only her blonde hair visible around the tall paper sack she carried. "We have peaches. Came from the roadside stands on the way here. Sweetest ones you ever tasted."

"Janet bought enough to share with you and the entire county." Bill, the only father Cole had ever known, followed behind her, toting two more sacks, brimming with peaches. His blue eyes sparkled with humor. "We would've been here an hour ago if your mother hadn't insisted on stopping at every roadside stand along the way instead of buying peaches at the first place we stopped."

"We had to wait until we knew we were getting the best

peaches at the best price," she said, setting her sack on the cabinet.

His dad added his sacks to the collection. "Which meant we stopped at seven places and then drove all the way back to the first one."

"But we saved eight dollars!"

"We probably wasted ten dollars in gas," his dad whispered, and Cole had to stifle a laugh.

He exchanged a bear hug with his mom, who then turned to Brooke and did the same, cinching her arms so tight Brooke's eyes bugged out.

"Sorry, Brooke," his mom said. "I'm a hugger. You might as well get used to it."

It probably made Brooke even happier the marriage was only temporary.

"Our family's big on hugs, too," said Brooke.

"Yes, but Janet's been known to break bones." His dad gave Brooke a gentle, one-armed side-squeeze. And both of them went to greet Gus, who was waiting impatiently at the tile border, his tail wagging a hundred miles an hour.

"Dinner's about ready," said Cole as he ditched his apron.

"Let me wash my hands." His mother headed to the kitchen sink. "By the way, I noticed you're finally using those dishes I bought you a few years ago. It's about time."

"Those came from you?" Cole rubbed his chin, hoping his mother wouldn't notice he hadn't shaved. "Well, you can thank Brooke for that. She chose the dishes and did all the decorating."

Brooke's cheeks pinked up, but she kept her composure. "Your plates are beautiful, Ms. Miller."

"Please, call me Janet. *Ms. Miller* sounds like a little old lady in a nursing home… the kind who tucks tissues in the sleeves of her sweater."

"A serious waste of a great hiding place," Brooke said, without blinking an eye. "I'll be storing *chocolate* in my sleeves."

His mother laughed so hard, she choked, and Cole couldn't help being proud of Brooke. She was holding her own, and that wasn't easy to do with his mom around. Though he had to admit, his mother hadn't complained about a single thing since she'd arrived. Come to think of it, most of her recent complaints involved Cole being too busy for his family. Maybe she wasn't as bad as she used to be.

He motioned his parents to the table and turned the burner off under the greens. As Brooke helped him put the serving dishes on the table, his mother cleared her throat, the way she always did when she was going to make an announcement.

"Now that you're married, I hope you won't wait too terribly long to start a family." She raised her eyebrows at Cole, peering over the pair of reading glasses perched on her nose. "None of us are getting any younger, you know."

Nope. She's as bad as ever.

"We haven't decided yet." Brooke jumped in before he could reprimand his mom. "But we might try to adopt. It's so awesome to give a kid the gift of a loving forever-home, like you did."

For the first time in his life, Cole witnessed his mother in a state of speechlessness. Tears welled in her eyes, and his dad leaned over and placed an affectionate arm around her shoulders.

"Thank you for saying that," his dad finally spoke in a

strangled voice. "It means a lot to your mom... to both of us... to hear it."

Cole ought to say something, but his tongue felt like a chunk of wood.

Again, Brooke came to the rescue. "I'd like to say thank you for the way you raised Cole. He knows what's really important in life, and I'm sure he learned it from you."

Cole's mom sniffed. "Now I wish I had one of those tissues up my sleeve." She gave a sheepish chuckle.

"I'd offer you one, but this is all I have." Brooke extended her hand, a piece of gourmet dark chocolate on her palm.

In the laughter that followed, Cole realized marriage had other advantages besides sex and procreation. A wife like Brooke could make dealing with his family much less stressful... even pleasant. Of course, he and Brooke weren't going to stay married long, so he would have to look for a woman with a similar personality. He refused to think about the fact that he'd never met a woman like Brooke before.

Meanwhile, he owed Brooke big time for making his mother so happy. In fact, his mom had been cheerful for the rest of dinner and hadn't uttered a negative word during the entire hour-long drive around the property. Too bad his parents were going to be around that evening, or he could've paid her back with a phenomenal foot massage. They'd both agreed that the nightly massages—innocent as they were—felt too intimate for company.

After a friendly game of spades, during which Brooke revealed an intense competitive streak, they all retired to the family room to read and watch television. When he saw Brooke battling to keep her eyes open, he suddenly remembered she was pregnant. She had to be exhausted! She'd been up since six a.m.

"I think Brooke and I need to hit the hay," he said, standing and stretching his arms over his head. "We've both had a long day."

Brooke shot him a look of gratitude and accepted the hand he offered. She said her goodnights and started toward her bedroom, while Cole went to turn out the kitchen lights.

"Where are you going?" Cole's mom asked, looking up from her e-book. "Aren't you sleeping in the master bedroom?"

Brooke stopped in mid-step, while Cole's mind raced for an explanation. How could they have forgotten his parents would expect them to sleep together? Should he break down and tell his parents the truth about the marriage?

Brooke turned to face his mother, her cheeks flushed. "I stayed here before we got married, and all my clothes are still in the front guest bedroom. We haven't had time to move them."

His mother beamed her approval. "Call me old fashioned, but I think that's admirable. I know most young people don't think anything about living together before they get married. I wouldn't have said anything, but I'm glad to know you waited until you tied the knot."

"Thank you, Mom," Cole said. "And if possible, I don't ever want to hear my mother talk about sex again."

She threw her head back and cackled in laughter, his dad joining in. Meanwhile, Brooke went down the hallway and reappeared, suitcase in hand. With her face so white he feared she might pass out, she made her way toward the master bedroom, and Cole followed her inside.

"Are you okay?" he asked.

"I'm fine," she said, standing at the foot of the massive custom-made bed, clutching her overnight bag against her like a lifejacket. "But I hate lying."

"You didn't lie... not really. Everything you told Mom was true."

"You know what I mean." Her posture was fence-post rigid.

"I do." He sat on the edge of the bed and dropped his face into his hands. "But I've never seen Mom this happy before. I hate to tell her the truth before we absolutely have to."

"I get it."

He looked up in time to see her entire body wilt. She dropped her bag and moved to sit beside him.

"I dread telling my mom, too," she said. "But I won't be able to hide this much longer."

Her hands moved to rest on her tummy, and she let out a weary sigh.

"Listen, I won't make this awkward," he said. "I'll sleep on the floor."

She looked over her shoulder at the bed. "This thing is the size of the US. Why don't you sleep on the west coast, and I'll sleep on the east?"

"Okay. But fair warning... I move around a lot, so I'll probably end up in Kansas."

"You may be taking your life in your hands. Nathan refused to cuddle with me because he said I kick in my sleep. Five years of marriage and it never got any better."

Cole chuckled. "Maybe I should wear protection to bed."

"Not a bad idea." She stood and walked toward the

bathroom, picking up her bag on the way. "But remember the rules. You have to keep that chest covered up."

Cole went into his closet to change into a t-shirt and athletic shorts. He intended to ditch his shirt once the lights were out and don it again before she woke in the morning. She'd never be the wiser.

When he returned, she emerged from the bathroom, face freshly scrubbed, her form draped in an extra large t-shirt that read, *RUNNING LATE IS MY CARDIO*.

"If you want, I could still give you a foot massage," he suggested. "It might help you fall asleep."

"That sounds great," she said as she flopped onto the bed. "I'm tired but keyed up at the same time. Plus, my feet are really sore."

"I'll be right back," said Cole. "Let me brush my teeth."

Only minutes later, he returned to find she'd already nodded off, her dark hair splayed out on her pillow, framing her sweet face. One smooth leg was on top of the sheets, the other buried under the covers. Her plump lips were parted in sleep, begging to be kissed.

As warmth furled in his gut, he forced his gaze away.

A cold shower sounds like a good idea.

BROOKE AWOKE WITH A START. Her eyes tried to focus in the dim light, but nothing looked familiar. Then she remembered... she was in Cole's room. In his bed! As she groped for the mattress edge, she realized she must've migrated to the middle.

The air conditioner must've been set to sub-zero, because

her nose was cold, as was the mattress when she felt for the edge. She hated to move from her cozy, warmed-up spot, but she needed to get back on her side before she delivered a damaging kick to her sleeping husband.

She tried to scoot over, but she couldn't move. A pressure at her waist held her in place.

It was then that she noticed the uniform warmth against her back. She reached down, to find an arm draped over her side, the hand on her belly. Carefully sliding her hand under the arm, she attempted to push free, but the arm tightened, tucking her snugly against the warm chest behind her. She'd never felt so secure in all her life.

Part of her wanted to give in and simply enjoy the warm embrace, given in sleep, and thus completely platonic. But what if she kicked him? He was so vulnerable while sleeping, she didn't dare risk it.

She struggled again, but his arm cinched even tighter, and his warmth lulled her toward sleep.

Maybe it would be okay if she rested her eyes for few seconds. Then she would find a way to escape his embrace without waking him.

Her heavy lids drooped, a slow blink…

CHAPTER 17

Cole's internal alarm never failed to wake him at five a.m.... until today. When his scratchy eyes worked their way open, he saw daylight flooding through a crack in the curtains.

Can't believe I slept in.

Something next to him shifted, and he jolted awake.

Brooke!

She was in his bed! *And* he was pressed against her. *And* he had his arm around her. *And* he didn't have a shirt on. That had to break about a million rules! He didn't move a muscle. How could he extract himself without waking her?

His hand was draped over her side, with her arm resting on top of his arm. The sweet scent of her hair filled his nostrils. Her soft form fit perfectly against him, as if she belonged there.

A knot formed inside his chest. She didn't belong. He couldn't let himself think that way. That's why they made the rules.

Moving slowly, he worked his arm out from under hers and rolled himself away from her, a millimeter at a time. Careful not to tug the covers or jar the mattress, he swung his legs off the bed and retrieved his t-shirt from the nightstand, deftly maneuvering it over his head and down his torso with one arm. Relieved, he let out the breath he'd been holding and lay back against the padded headboard.

"You know you didn't get away with it, right?"

Brooke's voice made him jump about six inches off the mattress. A glance to his left showed her sitting up on one elbow, her grumpy morning expression even more pronounced than usual.

"What are you talking about?" He opened his eyes wide, giving his best impression of innocence. He wasn't sure when she'd wakened, and he wasn't about to give anything away.

"You didn't wear a shirt to bed. That's a clear rule violation."

"Since I only had my shirt off while it was dark and your eyes were closed, no harm was done."

"Nice try." She sat up and propped herself against her pillow. "But a rule is a rule. You broke it, and now you have to pay the price."

"Ughh!! Fine. Which chick-flick do I have to watch with you?"

"Hmm…" She tapped a fingernail on her tooth. "I think the Hallmark Channel is having their Summer Christmas Movie Marathon."

"Noooooooo! Not a sappy Hallmark Christmas movie!" he wailed, as he fell back, jerking and writhing as if he'd been poisoned. With strangulated noises coming from his throat, he flopped onto the floor and gave a final twitch of death.

She peered over the edge of the mattress. "Seems that will be sufficient punishment for going shirtless."

He opened one eye. "Yes. I've learned my lesson."

At least she doesn't know we were spooning. That was close!

BROOKE'S PULSE WAS RACING. When she'd awakened to Cole pulling his shirt on, she realized he'd been without it during the night when he'd had his arm around her. The last thing she needed was that image in her head, but it was there. Embedded a mile deep. Maybe two.

"You have to promise you won't do anything else to tempt me," she told him, using the firmest tone she could muster.

Though both of them had admitted to a physical attraction, Cole hadn't been concerned about it. She'd had to convince him they needed to squelch those urges. For her, it was crucial, because her emotional attraction seemed to grow along with the physical one. Obviously, Cole didn't have that problem.

"Okay. I'll be good."

That was a little too easy.

"Promise me."

He raised his hand as if he was swearing an oath. "I promise."

A buzzing sound at her elbow drew her attention. On the bedside table, the mechanical hand moved, all on its own. She yelped, scrambling away.

"What's wrong?" Cole asked.

"Oh my gosh! I swear I just saw Shrek's fingers moving! Is that normal?"

"Are you sure it wasn't your imagination?"

She heard the noise again. This time she was watching closely.

"There! It happened again!" She pointed, still not getting too close. "Look… his fingers are crossed."

She heard peals of laughter. Cole was rolling on the floor.

"Were you making the arm move?" she accused.

"Your face… That was priceless!" He spoke between chuckles. "I crossed Shrek's fingers when I made the promise. But then, you squealed like it was going to crawl off the table and attack you."

In a flash, she grabbed her pillow and flung it at him, hitting him on the shoulder. He only laughed harder. She threw another one, this time connecting with his face. By the time she lifted the next pillow, he was scrambling to his feet.

"This isn't fair. I can't defend myself with one hand."

"Ha! I'm not falling for that, Mr. Blackbelt." She launched her pillow. His arm shot up and batted it away, as he loomed closer, a threatening look under the smirk on his face.

"Be careful what you start…"

She sat up and grappled behind her for another pillow, but he snatched it away from her. Giggling, she raised her hands to protect herself, but the force of the pillow's blow sent her toppling to the mattress. Before she could pick it up, another pillow came flying at her, connecting with her face. She was laughing so hard, all she could do was hug the pillow to protect herself. Over and over, she was pummeled with a soft weapon.

"Uncle! Uncle!" she yelled.

The barrage ceased, and she lay still beneath her fluffy protection until she caught her breath. When she pulled the pillow away, a triumphantly-grinning Cole was attaching the prosthetic arm to his implant.

"How did you make Shrek move like that?" she asked.

"It has a wireless receiver that responds to surgically implanted sensors."

"I had no idea."

"Yeah, I noticed." He smirked.

She climbed out of bed and put her hands on her hips. "You may have won the pillow fight, but I'm holding you to your promise. No more tempting me. And crossing your fingers doesn't count, no matter where your hand is."

"I was only kidding. I plan to keep my shirt on."

He stretched both arms to the side and moved them around in slow circles, his chest muscles straining against the thin cotton.

She swallowed a gulp.

Shirt or no shirt... he's still tempting.

THE VISIT with Cole's parents went by without another hitch, aided by the fact that Cole made a pallet on the floor the second night. Brooke felt so guilty about it, she told him he could take off his shirt when the lights were out.

On their way back to Houston, Cole told her she must've worked some kind of magic on his folks, because they'd been so easy-going. She wondered how upset his mother would be when they divorced but kept the thought to herself.

Two weeks passed, and they fell into a comfortable

routine. The news reporters appeared to have lost interest in their relationship, though the same couldn't be said for her coworkers or clients. It seemed she spent much of each counseling session turning the conversation away from questions about Cole, and she was beginning to doubt her effectiveness.

That Friday, on their way home from work, she was brooding about the problem, when Cole broke into her thoughts.

"You haven't heard a word I said, have you?"

"I'm sorry. I've got a lot on my mind."

"Your hands are on your belly, so it must be about the baby, right?"

"You guessed it." Seemed like all she thought about, these days.

"Still haven't decided how to tell your mom?"

She'd been ignoring her mother's phone calls.

"I don't know what to say."

"Tell them the truth… you're pregnant. Maybe they won't ask any questions."

"When I tell them the due date, they'll figure out the baby isn't yours. They'll want to know why we got married."

"Let them believe it was a whirlwind romance, like I announced at the press conference. It's no secret we got married fast because the show was about to start filming. You don't have to lie to them at all. There's no reason to mention the divorce until it happens."

"I guess you're right. Is that what you're going to tell your folks?"

He scrunched up his face. "I think that would be best. In the long run, my mom will be a lot more upset. At least, when you tell your mother about the divorce, she won't be losing a grandbaby."

It was on the edge of her lips to say Janet could see the baby if she wanted. But that would mean continued contact with Cole, something Brooke knew she couldn't handle. It had to be a clean break.

"Maybe she won't care, since the baby isn't yours, anyway."

"You're talking about the woman who adopted me. She doesn't think that way."

"You have a point." She picked a piece of lint from her pants. "Do you regret getting married?"

He kept his gaze on the road—a good thing, considering the traffic. "Not at all. As far as I'm concerned, breaking the news to my folks is the only drawback. It'll be hard when that happens, but we'll be okay."

"Especially if this means you'll be willing to get married again and have kids of your own."

The enthusiastic tone in her voice hid the fact that her stomach was churning. What was wrong with her? The scenario she'd described was the best possible outcome for both of them. If he had a wife and children, she wouldn't have to worry that he would change his mind and decide to fight for custody. In spite of the contract, her anxiety lingered.

"I don't think this is enough for me to change my mind about marriage," said Cole. "I thought it might be, but I still need... no, I *want* to talk to my birth mother. I can't make myself forget about it, even though the chance of it happening is zilch."

"What's going to change if you talk to her?"

"If I knew exactly what happened and why she made the choices she made, I think I could learn to trust women."

He was so agonized about his mother. Maybe she could secretly find out some information and see if there was anything she could ethically pass on to him. Probably not, but it was worth a try. She made a mental note to check into it the next week when she was at work.

"It's hard to believe all this distrust is based on what she did or didn't do," she said. "Especially when you have a great relationship with your adopted mother and your sister."

"What are you saying?"

"I'm not saying anything. I'm asking if it's possible there's more to it." She watched his fingers tighten on the steering wheel, his knuckles blanching. "Because most trust issues have to do with giving up control."

After a moment, he answered, his muscles flexing along his jaw. "You're right. I like to be in control, and that's not going to change."

"But if you love someone, it's not like that. You gain so much more than you give up."

His eyes narrowed and she knew she'd hit a nerve.

"It's not something I need," he muttered.

"That's the saddest thing I—" She gasped and grabbed her belly, feeling a sudden flutter.

"What's wrong? Should I call Dave?"

It was cute how easily he panicked. She'd better watch out, though, or she'd end up in the emergency room.

"No, I'm fine. But I think I felt the baby move."

"Really? Can I feel it?"

"I don't think so. It's only a little flutter on the inside." She hated to douse the little-boy excitement on his face. "But in a few weeks, I think you'll be able to."

This seemed to placate him, and he smiled, humming along with the songs on the radio. They each sat, lost in their own thoughts.

"I'm not saying it's impossible," he said after a while, as if she'd been listening to the conversation in his head.

"What's not impossible?"

"That someday... a long time from now... I might consider a real, long-term marriage."

Brooke smiled.

It's time to invite my sister for a visit.

CHAPTER 18

"Brooke!" Cole called, as he walked down the hallway toward her room, where she'd supposedly run in to take a 'quick shower' an hour ago. He should've known she would need more time. "We're going to be late, if you don't hurry."

Gus was at his heels, excited to go toward Brooke's room, where he usually wasn't allowed. Cole felt sorry for him, since they were headed out to dinner and leaving him behind.

It was their one-month anniversary, and Cole had decided to take Brooke out to a nice restaurant to lift their spirits. They'd both been a little dejected when Dave couldn't determine the baby's gender, even though he'd told them not to get their hopes up. He'd already scheduled another ultrasound two weeks later, when she would be almost twenty weeks along.

Breaking the news about the pregnancy had gone as smooth as one could hope with both sets of parents. Both mothers were more excited about the fact that a baby was coming than concerned about his parentage. That would probably change once they heard about the pending divorce.

When Brooke didn't answer his shouts, Cole wondered if she'd changed her mind about going out. Perhaps the idea of celebrating an anniversary was making the marriage feel too real for her. He understood her objections. She wanted to keep their relationship in the friend zone so she wouldn't be hurt when it came to an end. In fact, she'd even suggested that they were almost like a brother and sister, and Cole had spoken his agreement. But the truth was he'd never had a sisterly thought about Brooke.

He knocked on her door. "Brooke? Are you almost ready?"

Her croaky voice answered, "I don't feel up to going."

At his side, Gus whined, his nose against the door.

As Cole suspected, she was backing out. He hid his disappointment. Her feelings were more important than a steak dinner. He was becoming accustomed to the rise and fall of her emotions, changing every few minutes. From everything he'd read, this was a normal occurrence during pregnancy.

"That's okay. I'll cook something for you. Or order in. What are you hungry for?"

"Nothing." The noise that followed her choked word sounded like a sob.

His chest felt like someone was sitting on it. "Brooke? Are you okay?"

When she didn't answer, he tried the door. Finding it unlocked, he pushed it open, and Gus dashed inside. "I'm coming in. Are you decent?"

The only answer was another sob. The sight of her tore at his heart.

Gus paced around her where she sat on the floor, wrapped in a white robe, her back against the wall, hugging her knees against her. Her face was turned away, but he knew she was crying. On the floor beside her was her cell phone.

He moved on silent feet and sat against the wall beside her, praying he wouldn't say something idiotic and make things worse. Gus settled on her other side, nuzzling her arm until she relented, and moved her hand to rub his ears, her head still resting on her knees.

"What's wrong?" Cole asked.

After a moment, her muffled voice responded, "Nothing."

"This doesn't look like nothing."

She leaned her head back against the wall, exposing her tear-streaked face as she stared forward. "I'm overreacting. I shouldn't care. It shouldn't matter."

"What shouldn't matter? What happened?"

Her trembling hand reached for her phone. "Harper called. She can't come next weekend."

"I'm sorry. I know you miss her." It seemed like an extreme reaction, but at least he could fix the situation. "I can fly you down to Baton Rouge, any time."

"That's not the problem," she said, drawing a wobbly breath as her fingers punched at the phone screen. She handed it to him. "This is."

He recognized the couple on the screen—Nathan and Wendy. They'd had one of those trendy pregnancy photos made. Both dressed in all-white, he was standing behind her with his hands around her swollen abdomen. He appeared to be whispering something in her ear, while she wore a radiant expression.

Cole had a sudden urge to throw the man onto the floor again. He'd never felt so much hatred for someone he barely knew. While it stung his ego that Brooke still seemed attached to Nathan after being married to Cole for a month, he should've realized their temporary marriage didn't substitute for what she'd lost with her ex.

"I thought you blocked him," Cole said. "Where did this come from?"

"Harper sent it to me." She sniffed.

"Why did she do that? She had to know it would hurt you."

"She still follows him, but only because I asked her to be my spy." Brooke's head dropped forward. "I know it's petty, but I was kind of hoping Wendy would get some sort of pregnancy acne or her hair would fall out or something. So I asked Harper to send me a picture."

"She doesn't look as bad as you hoped?" Cole strained to keep a straight face.

"Look at her! She's beautiful!" Brooke flung her hands in the air. "Both of them are. And they look so happy together. They're practically glowing."

What could he say? He felt so helpless.

"She might have acne," he said. "This picture is photoshopped."

With hopeful eyes, she turned to gaze up at him through wet lashes. "You really think so?"

He looked at the image again. "Absolutely! In fact, there's one big zit they missed, right on the end of her nose. It's huge."

The corners of her mouth curved up. "You're lying."

"No, it's not a zit." He held the phone close to his face. "It's actually a wart! And it has a long black hair sticking out of it."

Her elbow jabbed weakly into his side. "Stop it."

She was almost smiling now. This was no time to stop.

"What do you think he's whispering in her ear?" Cole asked. "I bet he's saying, 'I can't believe you're making me do this stupid photo session. When we get home, I'm going to drink a six-pack and pass out on the couch.'"

"That sounds like something he'd say."

"I guarantee, whatever he's whispering, it's not sweet-nothings. Nathan was a sleaze before, and he hasn't changed." Surely she wasn't still in love with him after all he'd done.

"I know. I ought to be happy I'm away from him."

His eyes were drawn to her quivering lower lip and stuck to it, like super glue. She was upset, and all he could think about was how he'd like to kiss her. What was wrong with him? He blinked to break the magnetic connection and asked the question he was afraid to hear the answer to.

"Do you wish you and Nathan were still together?"

She hesitated for so long that he stopped breathing.

"I don't want to be with him." Her voice broke. "But seeing them together, looking so happy... I don't understand why it hurts so much."

He was done with having her so close and not touching her. "Want a side hug?" he asked, lifting his arm.

With a loud sniff, she nodded and leaned against him. His hand clasped her shoulder and snugged her close. Some weird emotion made his throat tight.

"Maybe," he said, "it makes you sad for what you lost. For the dreams that died."

It must've been the wrong thing to say, because she cried again, in earnest, until the side of his shirt was soaked. He couldn't conjure any comforting words to fix his blunder.

"I'm sorry," he mumbled, as her sobs ripped at his heart, washing away all thoughts of following their agreement. He slipped Shrek under her legs and lifted her onto his lap, holding her against his chest until, at long last, her sniffling subsided into regular breathing. Not to be left out, Gus did his best to join her, settling his head on top of Cole's right leg.

He steeled himself for the scolding to come. He'd gone past their boundaries, and they both knew it. But she was strangely silent about his lapse in judgement, as if she'd totally forgotten the rules, most of which she'd composed herself. She didn't even mention it later, when they were eating their Chinese food delivery or watching some mindless television show, each lost in their own thoughts.

With his self-control hanging by a thread, he didn't offer to rub her feet. Nor did he suggest they try to squeeze in their nightly thirty minutes of exercise. But when she got up to retire for the night, she stood before him with doleful eyes.

"Thank you for being there for me tonight. I'm sorry I ruined your plans."

Plans! He'd forgotten all about their reservation!

"We can go out to dinner another night," he said. "Maybe in two weeks, when we find out the gender."

A gamut of emotions flashed across her face, but the one

that stayed at the end looked like defeat. "Sure. That would be fine. And Cole, I…"

"Yes?" He encouraged her, when it seemed she wasn't going to complete her sentence.

"I want you to know I appreciate what you've done for me. You're a good friend… as good as I've ever had."

Why did her assessment make something boil inside him? He wanted to shout at her, "I'm way more than a friend!" Instead, he answered in a soft voice, "You're welcome. Anytime."

That night, as he lay in bed awake, he wondered if she was awake in hers. At one point, he even thought he might've heard her crying again. But he couldn't get to her. The sheetrock walls between them were as deep as the Grand Canyon, and twice as wide.

"We're supposed to find out the gender today." Brooke had her phone propped up as she Face-timed with her sister, simultaneously eating lunch in her office at work.

"Cole's going with you to the appointment?" Her innocent tone didn't fool Brooke. The last few times they'd talked, Harper had been questioning whether she and Cole were becoming emotionally involved.

"Yes, he's coming. The doctor is a friend of his. And Cole says it's the least he can do for me, for saving him a million dollars."

"Minus the quarter million when you get divorced, right?" Harper asked. "*If* you get divorced, that is."

"The divorce is going to happen, Harper. Trust me."

"It seems to me Cole's being way more attentive than he needs to be."

"He's gone above and beyond, but that's the kind of guy he is." Brooke trapped her lower lip between her teeth. "I want to get something nice for him, to thank him, but I can't think of anything he doesn't already own."

"I know something he'd really like," said Harper, who was munching on a sandwich of her own.

"Is it something I can afford?" Brooke asked. "He gave me a credit card, but I haven't used it for anything but groceries. I can't buy him a present with his own money."

"This won't cost you anything," Harper said. "And I guarantee he'll like it."

The lights went on when she saw the smirk on her sister's face. "Shut up, Harper. I'm not doing that."

"Why not?" Harper's eyebrows danced. "You're married. Why can't you sleep with him?"

"We're getting divorced, remember? This is only temporary."

Harper gave a slow eye-roll, showing the whites of her eyes. "It doesn't have to be temporary, Brooke. When are you going to admit you like him?"

"Sure, I like him. As a *friend*. But that's all it is and all it's ever going to be," she huffed. "Have you forgotten I'm doing this for you? You're supposed to marry him after we get divorced."

"Open your eyes, Brooke. Cole Miller isn't going to fall for me. And I don't even want him to. Not anymore."

"It won't happen if you don't try," Brooke said. "I've invited you to come visit, and every weekend you make an excuse."

"If I really thought you guys were nothing but roommates, I'd give it a shot."

"That's all we are. We barely even touch each other."

Harper shook her head as she swallowed the last of her sandwich. "Sometimes you're so naïve, it's hard to believe you were married for five years."

"What's that supposed to mean?" With her stomach turning flips, Brooke lost her appetite, and tossed the rest of her lunch in the trash.

"It means you're in love with Cole Miller, and I don't know why you refuse to admit it."

"But I'm *not* in love with him. Don't you realize I would never go after a guy you were in love with? What kind of sister do you think I am?"

"Brooke, don't be ridiculous. I had a *crush* on Cole when we'd never even met. But you… you're really in love with him. And I think he feels the same way about you."

"You're wrong." *She has to be wrong.* The room spun in a slow circle, and Brooke grabbed her desktop for balance.

"Not only that, but I think he's falling for your baby, too. Everything you want is right in front of you, Brooke. You just need to open your eyes."

The baby! He's falling for the baby. Her pulse rocketed into the sky. She couldn't lose the baby. It was all she had that belonged to her.

"I have to go," she mumbled, disconnecting before Harper could add any more fuel to the fire that was melting her insides.

COLE CHATTED HAPPILY on the way to Dave's office, but Brooke wasn't listening. She was too busy trying to decide how to break the news. At last, she decided there wasn't an easy way to do it. She had to be honest, and pray he wouldn't get his feelings hurt. It was better for it to happen now than when he was even more attached.

She cleared her throat, waiting until she had his attention. "I think it might be best if you weren't in the room when I get the ultrasound."

Confusion clouded his hazel eyes. "I could stand in a different place, where I can't see your stomach. All I need to see is the video screen."

"No, it's not like you stare at me, or anything. But…"

"What? What did I do wrong?" Pain replaced the confusion. She could always tell when she said something that hurt him. She could only hope she wasn't damaging his trust of women.

"I think you're getting too attached to the baby."

"That's not true," he spat back, aggravation in his tone.

"Are you sure about that?" she asked. "Are you sure you want to go through all these visits and ultrasounds and be okay when the baby is born and then never get to see him or her?"

He fell silent. "If you want to know the truth, the answer is no, I don't want that. But I've thought about it a lot. As long as I respect your boundaries, I don't see why I can't be a part of this child's life. You said it yourself… I'm like a brother. So why can't I be the baby's uncle?"

She imagined how hard it would be, especially if Cole remarried and had kids of his own. Yet the alternative, a life completely devoid of Cole, seemed even worse.

"I guess you could be an uncle, if you're sure you'd be satisfied with that."

"Yes." His relief was palpable. "I promise I won't interfere. I'll just do the uncle thing and buy him lots of noisy toy trucks to drive you crazy."

She laughed. "What if it's a girl?"

"Any niece of mine is going to like toy trucks as much as a boy. I'll buy her boots and turn her into a cowgirl."

"Cole, I'm not making any promises. If it gets—"

"I'll back off, any time you ask me to. Haven't I kept my promises so far?"

"Mostly."

"Mostly?" He said the word like she'd accused him of murder. "When haven't I kept a promise?"

"Well, two weeks ago, when you put me in your lap, that was clearly a broken promise."

"Says the woman who let me do it without objecting."

"I was in a vulnerable state." She pursed her lips and lifted her chin high in the air.

"Hmph!" He reached to turn the radio on, mumbling under his breath. It almost sounded like he said, "So was I," but that didn't make any sense.

ON THE ULTRASOUND SCREEN, the image squirmed. Mostly, it looked like a blob, though occasionally Cole thought he could make out an arm or leg.

"There's the spinal cord," Dave said, pointing to a long row of white dots. "And there's a kneecap," he pointed to a blob.

"That's not the parts we're interested in," Cole complained. "Is it a boy or a girl?"

"Hold on a second. You always were impatient," said Dave as he froze an image on the screen. "See this little part that looks kind of like a hamburger?"

Cole nodded, even though the blob looked nothing like a hamburger.

"That means... Are you sure you want me to tell you?"

"Yes!" they shouted in unison, chuckling afterward. Cole grasped Brooke's hand and squeezed tight.

"It's a girl!"

CHAPTER 19

"I sure hope Brooke is okay about this surprise baby shower," said Steph, as she arranged the plates and forks on the table. "She didn't really strike me as the surprise-loving type."

Cole glanced around the ranch dining room, with floating pink ribbons hanging from dozens of pink helium balloons. His sister had made short work of transforming the place to suit her vision.

"It was Mariah's idea, and you know how that goes."

"Right," Steph said. "Like trying to stop a freight train."

"Exactly."

"I'm glad Brooke's having a girl," Steph said. "I think it's easier to raise a girl as a single mom. My years alone with my daughter were really special. Not that it wasn't way better after Bran came into our lives."

"Right." Cole tasted bile in his throat, which seemed to happen every time he thought about Brooke leaving to raise the baby on her own.

"Have you felt the baby kick?" Steph asked.

"I have. It's crazy!"

He remembered the first time it happened. They'd been sitting on the couch together, with a sappy romance movie on the television. Brooke was holding his hand on her exposed belly, in hopes that the baby would move. Though he'd pretended he wasn't interested in the movie, in reality, he'd been caught up in the corny story. So when something kicked his hand, he'd sucked in an audible gasp of surprise. From that moment on, the movie was forgotten as he felt and watched for more ripples and bumps on her abdomen.

In that intimate encounter, something changed inside him. He realized he would readily lay down his life to protect that unborn child. And though he intended to keep his promise and distance himself from their lives, it was going to be more painful than he'd ever imagined. At last, he understood why Brooke had been so fearful. His money gave him immense power and, for the first time, he'd felt the temptation to use it.

"How far along is she, now?" Laurie's question brought him back to the present, as she carried a pitcher of punch to the table and poured it into the large, crystal bowl.

"Just over thirty weeks. The baby is the size of a zucchini."

"And how do you know this?" asked Finn, who appeared at his elbow and snatched a piece of cheese from the elaborate array of snacks.

"I'm listening to an audiobook, *Forty Weeks to a Brand New Life*."

Finn popped the cheese in his mouth and spoke around it. "Oh man! You've got it bad!"

"What are you implying?"

Finn merely chuckled as he walked away to rejoin the other men watching a football game on the television.

"Okay!" Mariah burst through the front door, her arms full of brightly wrapped packages. "Mom and Dad will be here in ten minutes. Brooke doesn't get back from shopping with her mom and sister for at least another thirty, so the timing should be perfect."

"Anything left in the car?" asked Jarrett, who'd come from the family room to refill his water.

"There's one heavy package in the back of my car—but Mack is bringing it inside for me."

"Mack? I told him to take the day off," said Cole. "His people have everything under control. And we're perfectly safe out here."

"Maybe he has a strong work ethic," Mariah said, as roses bloomed on her cheeks. "Anyway, we need to hide the rental cars before she gets back."

Cole's buddies and their wives had flown into the small private airstrip nearby. Normally Cole would've driven over to pick them up, but today they'd simply rented cars.

"That sounds like a job for the men," said Laurie, who promptly went into the family room to make a request that sounded more like an order.

Everyone had gone to so much trouble to make this happen, but it suddenly occurred to Cole that Brook might be upset. What if she hated the attention and the added pressure of pretending they were going to parent the baby together?

"What's wrong with you?" Mariah murmured as she pulled Cole into the utility room. "You look like you ate something sour."

"We shouldn't have done this." He crossed his arms, feeling like something might explode from his chest if he didn't. "This whole shower thing is dumb."

"What's got your panties in a wad?"

"She doesn't want this. Brooke isn't going to want a bunch of gifts from people who won't even be a permanent part of her life."

Mariah's mouth flattened, as if she were contemplating a kick to the shin. "Just because you and she are getting a divorce doesn't mean I can't still be the baby's aunt."

"I don't think that's a good idea." It hardly seemed fair for Mariah to have equal status with him, when he'd been so much more a part of the pregnancy. "She said she wanted a clean break."

"You told me she changed her mind." Her hands planted on her hips. "You told me you were going to be the baby's uncle after you split up. And you said how great it would be for Mom, because she could still see the baby."

"Yes, but she told me last week it's probably best if I don't come around more often than once a month or so."

"Too bad for you, bro." Mariah flashed an evil-villain smile. "She told me I could come see the baby as often as I like."

How is that fair?

Mariah flounced off, most likely to reorganize the serving table until it suited her. No... knowing Mariah, she'd probably rearrange the entire house.

Meanwhile, Cole stayed in the utility closet, fuming. How had everything gotten so twisted? Why should he do all the work and let his family reap all the benefits? He knew Brooke wanted him to file soon so that the sixty-day waiting period would be over and the divorce finalized before the baby came. The closer the time came, the less he was inclined to cooperate. Too bad his attorney had written such an iron-clad document.

"Cole?" Mariah stuck her head back in the utility room. "I'm moving your family room furniture around. Hope you don't mind."

She walked away without waiting for an answer.

"What if I mind?" he called after her.

She flipped her hand in the air. "I'm moving it anyway."

His cell phone rang. He was tempted to ignore the call until he saw who it was from. Dread fell to the pit of his stomach. His attorney never bothered him unless there was bad news.

"Garner. What's up?"

"Word has it Nathan Riggs has lawyered up."

"You mean he's filing assault charges? After all this time?"

"No. That would be easy to handle. We've got video that proves he took a swing at you before you took him to the ground. I'm afraid this is a little trickier. He's making noise about the possibility that Brooke's baby might be his."

"We haven't even announced that she's pregnant."

"People know. The press has pictures. And she's too pregnant to claim it's a honeymoon baby."

"But he can't prove it, right? You told us he didn't have the right to demand a DNA test."

"That's true, but only if you and Brooke are married when the baby's born. That's when the state of Texas presumes you are the father. If you're divorced… I can't say for sure what would happen. It's also possible the courts won't grant your divorce until the baby is born, especially if Nathan's trying to assert paternity."

"So now you're saying we should wait until after the baby comes before we divorce?"

"My advice, which you ignored, was not to get married in the first place. What you have here is a mess I can't fix."

"Then why did you bother to call me?" An edge of irritation crept into his voice.

"Because you don't seem to care about my advice anyway. Your only concern seems to be what's in Brooke's best interest."

"Which is what?"

"If you'd prefer to protect Brooke's reputation at the expense of your own and risk being saddled with millions in child support to make sure her ex doesn't claim parental rights..." Garner's tone left no doubt that he didn't approve of this line of thought. "If that's the case, you shouldn't file for divorce until after the baby comes. Alternatively, you might be able to buy Nathan off."

"I'm not giving him a dime," Cole growled.

"Okay, that's all, then," Garner said, cheerily. "Let me know what you decide."

The phone clicked, and he was gone.

"Dang it!"

Cole kicked the wall, with his boot, fully intending to dent the sheetrock. Unfortunately, he also rattled a shelf holding a precariously-balanced jar of screws, which tumbled to the tile floor and shattered, spreading a mixture of screws and glass shards over the utility-room floor.

Not my best day.

Brooke was glad she hadn't worn any makeup. At least she wouldn't have runny-mascara, raccoon eyes from all her crying. The baby shower was a sweet surprise, and she'd gotten way more stuff than any tiny baby could possibly need. But mostly, she was overwhelmed with the love and generosity Cole's friends and family poured out on her, especially the ones who knew the marriage was temporary.

"You guys shouldn't have done so much," she told Laurie when they were alone in the kitchen. She lowered her voice. "After the divorce, we may never see each other again."

"I don't see why we can't be friends after the divorce. *If* there is one," Laurie said, "which, in case you've forgotten, I'm rooting against."

"It's going to happen. It *has* to."

"Oh?" Laurie rinsed off a plate and loaded it into the dishwasher. "Remind me why that is, because it seems like the two of you are getting along just fine."

"Well, for one thing, I can't risk losing control of my daughter."

"You're afraid Cole would divorce you and take the baby?" Laurie asked, as she rinsed another plate.

Brooke studied her feet to avoid looking Laurie in the eye. "I don't really think he would, but I'm not a great judge of character. I was married to Nathan for five years before I realized how awful he was."

Laurie dried her hands on a dish towel and turned around to face Brooke. "Honey, when I met Finn, I didn't trust him as far as I could throw him. I almost lost him before I let myself believe the truth."

"I'm the opposite of that. I tend to trust everyone, and people take advantage of me. Ask my sister—she'll tell you I'm way too naïve." She covered her tummy with her hands. "But I'm a mom, now. It's time for me to grow up. I can't be naïve anymore."

"Just promise me one thing," said Laurie. "Talk to Cole. If Finn and I had communicated better at the beginning, we'd have saved ourselves a lot of heartache."

"We already talk a lot. Every day, on the way to and from work."

"I mean *really* talk to him. Ask him how he feels about you."

"We've talked about it. We like each other a lot, but that's as far as it goes."

At least, that was as far as it went on his part. For her part, she'd started making a list of all the bad things about living with Cole. Each day, she would add one reason she was going to be better off after they got a divorce. Sure, some of them were a bit of a stretch, like the one about having to shave her legs every day as preparation for her foot rub. As if that was really a hardship. But some days, reading over her sad little list was the only thing that kept her from stark depression.

"Are you sure about that?"

"I'm positive. We both want the divorce to be final before the baby comes."

Even as she spoke the words, she felt guilty.

"That's strange." Laurie's nose scrunched and she chewed on a fingernail. "I heard him talking to the guys, and he was hinting that the two of you would definitely stay married for a while longer, at least until after the baby came. That's what I heard. But maybe I misunderstood."

A chill ran down her spine, and it wasn't the good kind. Why was he suddenly changing his tune? And without consulting her?

∼

THOUGH COLE INSISTED there was plenty of room for everyone to stay the weekend, Bran and Steph were in a hurry to get back to the kids. Of course, Finn and Laurie flew back with them, and Jarrett seemed unusually anxious to return to Denver. But with both sets of parents and both sisters spending the night at the ranch, it was late before Cole and Brooke retired to his bedroom.

He'd been waiting all day to talk to her about Garner's news, but given her present mood, he wasn't sure he should. He'd hoped she would relax when she saw him setting up the air mattress so they wouldn't have to share the bed. But the way she closed her dresser drawer with more force than was needed and stomped her way into the bathroom to change clothes, he knew there was something else bothering her.

How would she react when he told her Nathan might be attempting to claim parental rights? She would likely freak out, and Cole wouldn't blame her.

Maybe it would be better if he kept the information to himself. If so, he faced an uphill battle to persuade her to stay married until after the baby came. While he was still wondering how to broach the subject, she marched out of the bathroom and stood in front of him, with her fists on her hips.

"You told the guys the divorce isn't happening before the birth!"

Heat radiating from his face, he tried to stay calm. "I was going to talk to you about it tonight."

"Are you sure this wasn't your plan all along? Let me believe you'd filed for divorce when you hadn't? To wait until after she'd been born to tell me the truth?"

His jaw clenched so tight he could hear his teeth grinding. "Is that what you think of me? After all this time and everything I've done? You think I'm trying to trick you? And then what? Steal your baby?"

"I didn't say that…"

"But you meant it, didn't you?"

"It's hard to trust you when it seems like you're lying to me." Her trembling lower lip snuck between her teeth in the way that usually made him crazy to kiss her. But this time, he ignored it.

"You want a divorce that bad? File it yourself! Do it Monday, for all I care."

"That's not what I said." A tear rolled down her cheek, and she swiped at it with the back of her hand. "But you scared me when you said one thing to me and something else to your friends."

Why did it tear at his heart so? He'd let his guard down, and she was getting under his skin. *How could I be such a fool?*

"You don't need to stay with me anymore if you're scared of me. Take your money and go."

"You're putting words in my mouth."

He grabbed his keys from the nightstand. "Better yet, *I'll* leave. I'm outta here!"

Her face contorted in pain, and his stomach twisted. He

ought to take his hasty words back, but his righteous anger wouldn't let him. He turned away and headed toward the door.

"Wait!" she cried. "I'm sorry!"

His chest cramped at her shaky voice, but he stormed out before he said something worse. The news about Nathan could wait until morning. For now, he needed to get away where he could think. On the way out, he grabbed a leash and took Gus along, knowing the dog would help him calm down. He was all the way to his truck before he realized he'd left his cell phone in the bedroom.

"I'll be fine without it," he told Gus, who was ecstatic about going for a ride. "Who am I going to call at midnight, anyway?"

He drove down the unpaved road toward the south end of his property, country music blaring on his radio. Twenty minutes later, he left the road and cut across the field on a seldom-used trail that led to an abandoned well site. In the secluded clearing, he turned the motor off but left the radio on as he got out and moved to the truck bed. Sitting on the tailgate, he leaned back and rested his head on a sack of corn, as he stared up at the stars. Beside him, Gus curled into a comfortable spot.

"What is it about her, Gus? She makes me absolutely crazy, half the time."

Gus lifted his head, the whites of his eyes glowing in the moonlight.

"Yes, I know she's pretty, but there are plenty of gorgeous women out there. Why am I letting this one get to me? You see, this is why I always had the one-and-done dating rule."

Gus brushed his muzzle against Cole's hand, leaving a pool of slobber behind.

"Ughh! Thanks for that." Cole wiped his hand on his blue jeans. "How could she accuse me of something like that? I've never done anything to make her distrust me."

Evidently bored with the conversation, Gus dropped his head to his feet.

"You're not much help." Cole groaned and shifted positions to get comfortable. "You know, all I ever wanted to do was protect her. Is that such a terrible thing?"

He closed his eyes, trying to clear his mind. If he got past his anger and hurt over her lack of trust, the facts remained. According to Garner, the courts probably wouldn't grant them a divorce, anyway. If that was the case, there was no reason to file the papers, since that would only open the door for Nathan to assert himself into Brooke's life. That man might've provided the DNA that brought the child into existence, but in Cole's opinion, it had been an act of rape. Brooke would never have slept with him if she'd known he'd already impregnated another woman and filed for divorce. That innocent child didn't deserve to have Nathan as a father.

Brooke had said she was sorry, but he'd been too hurt to listen. Tomorrow, he would have to eat humble pie and apologize for leaving, even though going for a drive had been the best option. He knew when he was on the brink of losing it, and tonight he'd been close.

Cole could go back in an hour or two and sneak into his bedroom without waking Brooke. In the morning, when both their tempers had cooled, he could lay out all the facts. Hopefully, he could explain it in such a way that she didn't start panicking about Nathan. There was no need for her to worry, because Cole would do everything in his power to be sure Nathan didn't get his hands on this baby.

Though he tried his best to block it out, the sound of her anguished voice kept replaying inside his head, "Wait! I'm sorry!" Maybe he should've stayed until they'd talked things through. This was why he didn't do relationships with women… he sucked at it.

The song on the radio changed, playing one of his favorites. He yawned.

A few more songs, and I'll head back.

COLE WOKE to a jingle in his ear and a dollop of slobber on his face.

"Gus! Ughh!" He sat up, wiping his face on his sleeve and wincing at the stiffness in his back.

Gus gave his head a shake, rattling his tags again, and leapt to the ground to sniff a few bushes before choosing one and lifting his leg to christen it. The sky glowed with the early-morning light.

"Oh, crud! I fell asleep!"

Cole jumped down and called for Gus, closing the tailgate. But the dog, who currently wasn't wearing his leash, was nowhere to be seen.

"Gus!" he called, followed by a whistle. "Gus! Here boy!"

He kicked himself for not keeping him on leash. Gus had been known to roam for an hour or more before returning home. He would come back in his own sweet time. Cole couldn't afford to wait around, knowing Brooke would be awake soon. He had to talk to her alone and set things straight. Gus would have to find his way back to the ranch house on his own.

Cole jumped in the truck and turned the key. But all he heard was a click. The next word he shouted would've had his mother washing his mouth out with vinegar.

Looks like I'm walking back.

AS THE DAWN light poked through the slats in the blinds, Brooke glanced over at the empty air mattress. This time, she'd gone too far. Why had she lashed out at him instead of giving him a chance to explain? He'd been nothing but kind to her for the past four months, yet she'd rewarded him with a rash accusation. Hadn't Nathan always told her she ought to keep her big fat mouth shut?

The fact that Cole hadn't returned all night could only mean one thing. He must've meant what he said when he suggested she leave. If not, he'd have come back by now and told her to stay. Was there even any chance to clear up their misunderstandings and go back to the way things were?

She crawled out of bed and scrubbed her face until it was raw, trying to wash away the memory of their horrible fight and the hurt in his eyes. Maybe it was for the best. They'd both known it was temporary from the start. But lately, she'd let herself pretend it was real. She'd imagined that he loved her and had committed to her for the rest of his life, like the words they'd both repeated during the bogus wedding ceremony. She'd known better than to let that dream take root. As she'd feared, it had grown like a weed no matter how many times she plucked it away, returning again, stronger every time.

She got dressed and padded through the silent house, intending to let Gus out. Then she saw the horrible truth. Cole was gone! He'd driven off in the truck and taken Gus with him. He was probably back at the apartment in Houston by now.

She couldn't even be angry at him for leaving. It was nothing but what she deserved. It was a sad ending to an amazing friendship, but she'd learned a lot. She owed Cole more than she could ever repay, but it wasn't too late to try. She still might be able to find some information about his birth mother. So far, her efforts had failed, but she hadn't given up. Maybe, if she could give him that gift, he would find it in his heart to forgive her.

Everything had changed, but she would find a way to survive. She had to. Her hands slid onto her protruding belly as her daughter reminded her of her presence with a kick.

Harper! Harper would know what to do!

Brooke slipped into the bedroom where her sister lay sleeping and patted her shoulder.

Her eyes popped open. "Brooke! What—"

Brooke put her hand over her sister's mouth. "Shhhh!" she whispered. "Mariah's in the next room. I don't want her to hear us."

"Why?" Harper whispered back, rubbing her eyes as she sat up and swung her legs off the bed. "What's going on?"

Brooke motioned for her to follow into the huge closet, lined in aromatic cedar, and filled with hanging racks of winter coats and sweaters. Even their breathing sounded muffled. When the door was shut behind them, Brooke said, "Cole left me."

"You can't be serious." Harper looked around the closet like she expected to find hidden cameras. "I thought you two were in love with each other. I expected you to stay married."

Brooke swallowed a lump the size of a watermelon. "I don't know why you thought that, but you were way off base. We've been clear from the beginning that the marriage was temporary. Now he's left me, and I need to get out of here before everyone wakes up."

"Hang on a minute." Harper compressed the sweaters, pushing them together down one side of the hanging rack to clear a space. "Let's sit and you can tell me what happened."

Brooke relayed the whole story, leaving nothing out, except the depth of depression that was threatening to descend. When she was done, Harper took a huge breath and blew it out like smoke.

"Are you sure he's gone?"

"He took the truck. And *Gus*. And he's been gone all night."

"What about his suitcase?"

"We don't take suitcases when we come here. We keep everything we need in both places."

"Wow. You must've really hurt his feelings for him to take off for Houston and leave you here. He left without even telling his family goodbye."

"I know." Her voice came out as small as she felt.

"What're you going to do?"

"If I can stay in Houston and keep working for six more weeks, I'll have my counseling hours finished. By then, I'll be thirty-six weeks pregnant. I guess I'll go back to *Nowhere*."

"If you're there, I'll call it Bellaire instead of Nowhere. And at least you'll get to eat Mom's cooking." Harper's chuckle was half-hearted. "What about money? It'll take a while to get your divorce settlement."

"I'm not taking his money. He's done enough already." Brooke sniffed, as tears flooded her eyes. "In fact, I intend to pay him back for everything he's spent on me."

"Oh my gosh, Brooke." Harper's mouth gaped open.

"What?"

"You *are* in love with him, aren't you?"

Her tight throat made it hard to breathe. She'd fought hard to hold back her attraction to Cole. But whether or not she was in love with him, everything was over now.

She pulled up her t-shirt to wipe her eyes. "No, I'm not."

"Then why are you crying?"

"Because I'm pregnant. That's pretty much all I've done since it happened."

"I guess that's true." Harper chuckled. "I think it's dumb for you to turn down the money, Brooke. He's got plenty. How are you going to get by without it?"

"I saved every dime I made the past four months, about $4,000. I just need food, clothes, and a place to stay for six weeks. After that, I'll be home."

"What about your car?"

"Cole got it fixed. It's out in the garage. I guess I'll take it, if I can find the keys." Brooke stood up, suddenly anxious to leave. "Will you help me pack a few things? It's six o'clock. People will probably be up in an hour."

"Shouldn't you wait to hear from Cole?"

"I don't want to have to be the one who explains it to our parents when they wake up."

"Cole's already gone. If you're not here, who's going to tell them?"

Brooke blinked sad eyes at Harper, letting her lower lip pooch. "I was hoping you would do it."

Harper squeezed her eyes shut and pinched the bridge of her nose. "No way."

"Please." Brooke used her best whiny voice. "I'll do anything you want."

One dark brow lifted in an ominous arch. "You have to give me all your Christmas candy for the next five years."

"Done."

Brooke jutted her hand forward, but Harper held back.

"And name the baby after me."

Brooke smiled as she shook her sister's hand. "It's a deal!"

CHAPTER 20

By Cole's best estimate, it would take just over an hour to walk home. He had no idea of the time, but the sun was well above the horizon when he started. Unfortunately, his only footwear was his cowboy boots, so running was out of the question. Gus caught up with him about the time he caught sight of the house and broke into a heavy jog.

"Oh. Decided to come back, huh? Maybe this time I won't let you inside the house."

Gus loped along beside him, tongue wagging. He could never stay mad at Gus, even though the dog had run away more times than he could count. He always returned, with a pleased look on his face.

When he reached the porch, he saw people sitting inside at the breakfast table. His hopes died. He'd wanted a chance to talk to Brooke before anyone else was awake. He took off his dirty boots and left them on the mat as he trudged inside, his eyes scanning the wide-eyed group at the dining table.

Relieved that Brooke wasn't there, he waved a casual hello, and headed toward the bedroom.

"Where have you been?" Mariah demanded, rising from the table to chase him across the family room.

"I'll explain later," he said, desperate to get away. As he scurried down the short hallway, he could feel her on his heels.

As his hand reached for the doorknob, she said, "If you're looking for Brooke, she's already gone."

"Gone?" He groped for the wall to keep his legs from folding. Gasping for air in the sudden vacuum, he said, "Where is she?"

Her sharp tone was replaced with a sympathetic one as she put her hand on his arm. "I'm sorry about the breakup. Harper told us."

"I don't understand." With his back against the wall, he slid to the floor. "We didn't break up. I just went for a drive."

"That's not what Brooke thought." Harper appeared in the hallway. "Did you or did you not leave and say, 'I'm outta here?'"

"I was mad," he choked, straining to look up at the two women. "I didn't think she would leave."

"Get off your butt, and go get her back," said Mariah.

"Don't you dare!" Harper scowled down at him, no longer resembling an adoring fan. "Don't go after her now and get her hopes up, just so you can dump her again in a few weeks."

"You make it sound like I've broken our agreement," he said, irritated at her accusing tone. "This was never about long-term. From day one, it was a short-term commitment, and I stuck to it. But after all this time, she still doesn't trust me. I don't know what she told you, but she accused me of lying to her."

"Yeah, I heard. You'll be happy to know she blames it all on herself," said Harper, with emphatic hand gestures. "The same thing she did every time Nathan walked out on her. He'd disappear for hours or days at a time. She never knew if or when she'd see him again. And every time, she'd apologize for making him angry, and he'd waltz back in like he was doing her a favor."

His righteous anger fizzled out like air from a balloon. "She never told me that."

"Would it have made a difference?" Mariah asked.

"I didn't mean to stay gone so long last night. I accidentally fell asleep, and the truck battery died."

He found no sympathy in his sister's eyes.

"Look, Cole," said Harper, "I was totally in favor of this relationship at the beginning, but I was wrong. My sister was on the rebound. You were too nice to her, and she couldn't help wanting more."

Wanting more? What does that mean?

"Now I'm in trouble for being too nice?" Cole banged the back of his head against the wall to accent his next words. "This. Isn't. Fair."

Harper sighed. "I know you didn't mean to, but you made her hope for things she can't have."

"Are you talking about marriage?" He gave an involuntary shudder. Even saying the word made him break out in a cold sweat. "Because I never said anything to make her think that was going to happen."

"Then let her go." Harper's jaw hardened. "She's already hurting. The more you drag it out, the worse it's going to be.

As it is, I'll never forgive myself for supporting this screwed up relationship in the first place."

How had this happened? They'd both known it was going to be temporary. When had Brooke changed her mind? Harper was right. He needed to let Brooke go before he hurt her any more. Why did he feel so empty?

Harper left, her sagging body language indicating she was almost as depressed as he was. Alone with Mariah, he cringed at the scary snake-eyed glare she sent his way.

"Tell me the truth, Cole. Are you in love with Brooke?"

"Me? In lo—" He choked, coughing into his hand. "No way. We're friends, and that's all."

"Like you and Bran and Finn and Jarrett?"

"Yes." Except for the physical attraction, but that was none of Mariah's business.

"So it won't bother you when Brooke gets married one day and her new husband adopts her baby girl?"

That was exactly what Brooke needed. Deserved. A man who would be a loving and supportive husband and father. Cole had known that from the start. Why did the idea suddenly make him feel like punching the wall?

Too bad I can't be that man for her.

"I have a different question for you... a rhetorical one." Mariah startled him out of his reverie. "What's the difference between *your* left arm and mine?"

"This is stupid—"

"Just answer the question." Mariah glared down her nose.

He would never understand his sister, but sometimes it was easier to go along with her. Or maybe *most of the time* it was easier. And right now, he'd rather talk about anything but Brooke.

"You were born with yours. Someone made mine."

"What else?"

What did she want him to say? "Yours works better than mine."

"Does it?" she asked, smirking as if she'd caught him in a lie.

"No, but I had to learn how to make mine work right."

"So did I. That's no different."

"You learned naturally, though, like I did with my right hand," he argued. "My left arm took a lot of work. It felt alien at first, but I practiced until it felt like part of me. I can't imagine my life without it."

A slow smile worked its way onto her lips.

"And what would you do if it broke? Would you throw it away?"

Where was she going with this? "Of course I wouldn't throw it away. It's irreplaceable. It cost a small fortune."

"So what would you do?" she asked again. "What if your arm broke? Would you toss it? Do without? Or maybe trade it in for a bright blue one?"

"What do you think I would do?" he asked, irritated with her questions. "I'd fix it."

"Exactly."

She turned on her heel and sauntered toward the kitchen.

"Mariah!"

"What?" she replied, without bothering to stop.

"What was that about?"

"Figure it out."

Her stride didn't falter as she turned the corner and disappeared.

"I FOUND a place to stay for the next six weeks." Brooke rotated in a slow circle, aiming her phone around the room to show her sister her new abode. She was proud of her find, especially since she'd managed to make all the arrangements online during her lunch break. "It's not great, but it's affordable. There's a mini-fridge and a microwave, and I pay by the week."

"I forbid you to stay there unless you buy your own sheets," said Harper in a horrified voice, obviously not impressed with her choice. "And you'd better not walk barefoot on that carpet. It looks like something died on it."

"Could be. There was yellow police tape all over the room when I checked in."

"Brooke! Get out of there, right now!"

"I'm just kidding." She was too drained to laugh at her own joke. "I went by Walmart and bought a set of sheets and some clothes."

"Oh, thank goodness," said Harper. "Speaking of clothes, your husband is pretty ticked that you didn't take yours with you. Have you talked to *Mr. Soul Killer* yet?"

Brooke rolled her eyes at Harper's new pet name for Cole. "I blocked him. It'll be too hard if I talk to him. It's better to make a clean break."

The sigh that blasted her ear lasted for twenty seconds. "He called an hour ago and made me promise to give you a message."

"I'd rather not hear it." Brooke paced from one side of the tiny room to the other and back again.

"It's about Nathan."

She stopped in mid-step, as her stomach revolted, almost sending back her recently-consumed microwave dinner. "Fine. I'm listening."

"Evidently Nathan knows you're pregnant. He must've seen pictures and figured out he might be the father."

Sinking onto the chair, she propped the phone up on the nightstand, noting the peeling wood veneer. "I was hoping he'd assume it was Cole's."

"Soul Killer's attorney told him Nathan's talking about his parental rights, although I can't see him doing anything about it. He's not going to want to pay child support."

"He's probably mad that I got pregnant when he swore I was sterile."

"Maybe he thinks you were secretly using birth control all along."

"He could be trying to blackmail Cole, hoping to get some money out of him."

"Whatever Nathan's up to, your husband said that's why he was talking about delaying the divorce."

Her paper house was falling down around her. But what had she expected?

"I've been hiding from my problems long enough. I need to grow up and take responsibility." She gritted her teeth in determination. "I'll call Nathan and tell him the truth. If I need to, I'll have a press conference and announce I'm filing for divorce and Cole isn't the father."

"What about your job?"

"If they fire me now, I'll find some way to finish my hours after the baby comes. I won't give up. Even if it takes another year to get them done."

"That's the spirit, sister! But aren't you worried you'll

hurt Soul Killer's public image?" Harper asked, with enough sarcasm to indicate she hoped it would happen.

"If I look despicable enough, he should get plenty of public sympathy." She felt her salivary glands working, the way they'd done in early pregnancy when she was about to throw up. "Your job is to keep me from finding out what they're saying about me on social media. I'm going to file those divorce papers, and I know the fans are going to start hating on me."

Harper chuckled. "That's nothing new. They've been hating on you ever since you stole their man away, along with their chance to watch him every week on Millionaire Matchup."

"You're not helping," Brooke said. "It's a good thing I don't watch television, since everyone despises me now."

"Not everyone. Some of us despise *Soul Killer* instead. I can't believe I used to crush on that guy."

"I know you're trying to be supportive, but I wish you wouldn't be so upset with Cole. He's been nothing but sweet to me. He didn't even desert me like I thought he had."

"He still broke your heart."

"Not on purpose. He's been the perfect gentleman."

"You're doing it again." Harper used her accusing tone. "You're taking all the blame, just like you did when you were married to Nathan."

"The blame for what? For the fact that I fell for him when I knew better? Is that his fault?"

"Maybe not, but I'm mad at him anyway."

Harper was as loyal as a sister could be, and Brooke loved her for it, no matter how misguided she was.

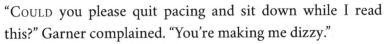

"Could you please quit pacing and sit down while I read this?" Garner complained. "You're making me dizzy."

Cole marched to Garner's desk and ripped the pages from his attorney's hands, shaking it in his face. "I don't think you understand the gravity of the situation. I've been served! Brooke filed for divorce."

How had it happened so quickly? Saturday had been an amazing day, with his sister pulling off a surprise shower that had brought Brooke to happy tears. By the next morning, Brooke had left him, driving off to Houston in her old junker of a car and giving him no information concerning her whereabouts. After several days, Mack had located her in a run-down motel in the worst part of town, and Cole had taken measures to ensure her safety. But he'd had no time to celebrate that victory before being served with divorce papers in his own office by a star-struck Sheriff's officer who asked for his autograph.

"I don't see the problem here," said Garner. "Isn't this divorce what you planned all along?"

"Not yet! You're the one who said we should wait until after the baby came." Cole flopped into the leather desk chair, the pages wadded in his grip.

"That's not what I said, but this is a moot point. We can't undo what's been done. And like I told you, the court may not grant the divorce until the baby's born, anyway. I'm hoping that document you both signed acknowledging that you aren't the baby's biological father will be enough for the divorce to proceed. That'll be the best way to get you out of this mess."

Cole finally understood the term *wanting to pull your hair out*. "You're not listening to me. I'm asking you how we can stop the divorce. Can't we contest it?"

Garner blinked a few times and gave his head a shake. "Did I hear you right? Did you just tell me you want to contest this divorce? The one you arranged months ago, before you ever got married?"

"Yes! That's exactly what I want."

"Excuse me..." Garner held up a finger as he opened his desk drawer and pulled out a large plastic container of fruit-flavored Tums. He opened the lid and popped a couple into his mouth. As he was returning the Tums to his drawer, he looked at Cole, then hastily dumped out a few more antacids, chewing them and washing them down with a long drink of water. He then folded his hands on the desk in front of him and leveled his gaze on Cole. "Why?"

"Why what?"

"Why do you want to contest the divorce?" he asked with a slightly crazed inflection, as if he might jump out the twenty-second story window if Cole gave him the wrong answer.

"Because..." Cole honestly didn't know the answer. "Because I want to protect Brooke and the baby from Nathan."

"So you just want to *delay* the divorce." Garner's chest deflated like he'd been holding his breath. "I thought you'd changed your mind altogether. It should be easy to delay things, and that works out well for you, money-wise."

"How so?"

"The quarter-million. Brooke won't get it until the

divorce is final. We can keep things tied up in the courts for quite a while if we play our cards right."

Obviously, Brooke needed that money as soon as possible. That's why she'd filed so quickly, despite Cole's warning about her ex.

"I'm issuing the settlement check today."

Garner pressed his fist against his chest. "You can't issue the settlement check before the divorce is final. The courts won't allow it."

"It's my money. If I want to give it to her now, who's going to stop me?"

"No one can stop you, Cole," said Garner, as he opened his desk drawer and pulled out the Tums container again. "You could write Brooke a partial check now, but you'll still have to pay the full $250,000 when the divorce is final."

"I don't think she'll take more than we agreed on. She's too proud. But I don't care if she does."

"Before you start throwing money at Brooke, you'd better remember that I still can't guarantee you won't end up paying child support." Garner ate a few more antacids and left the container out on his desk. "I'd make the check as small as possible, just in case."

"If you don't want to be involved, I can have Mack deliver it in cash."

"No, no, no!" Garner's face went pale, and he started writing on his legal pad. "Let me draw up a contract. I'll do an addendum to the prenup, based on funds paid in advance. It's worth a try. What amount are you going to pay early?"

"All of it." Cole chuckled when, once more, Garner reached for the antacids. "I believe that makes ten Tums you've eaten, now."

"Yes, I knew you were coming, so I had to be prepared. After much consideration, I stocked my desk with Tums calcium tablets, though the decision was difficult," Garner said, with a deadpan expression. "Perhaps cyanide would've been the better option."

∽

"Hello, Brooke."

Nathan popped the K sound, as he'd always done when he was talking down to her, which, come to think of it, had happened on a daily basis during their five-year marriage. Why hadn't she noticed that while she was living with him? Thank goodness she was having this conversation on the phone. In her present state of mind, she might have slapped the sneer right off his face.

"I'm surprised to hear from you," he continued. "I thought you were way too uppity to talk to commoners like me anymore."

She ignored his bait, weirdly numb to his words. "I'm calling to let you know you're the father of my baby."

"Ha! I'd have to see a DNA test to believe it. It's obvious you were sleeping around the whole time we were married. Any Joe out there could be the father."

She realized she didn't care one iota what he thought of her and wondered that his words had ever had the power to hurt her.

"It doesn't matter to me whether you believe it or not. I just thought you deserved to know, though maybe you don't."

"What do you want from me? Money? Doesn't your billionaire husband give you a big enough allowance?"

"Cole and I are getting a divorce." The lump in her throat made it hard to talk. It had only been a few days. Surely the rawness would go away. "Don't worry, though. I don't want anything from you. On the other hand, if you decide you want visitation rights, I will go after you for child support."

"You're not getting a dime from me, and I want nothing to do with that baby. My real son is due in two weeks."

"Yes. Congratulations, by the way. I hope the birth goes well." She was surprised she meant it.

"I bet the press would have a field day if they heard about this little conversation," Nathan said. "But I might be persuaded to keep my mouth shut about it… for the right amount."

Tired after all the stress and changes and a long week at work, she sat on top of the new Walmart comforter and flexed her swollen, aching feet. She missed her nightly foot rubs. Maybe, if she hired a massage therapist, she wouldn't feel the empty longing in her heart.

Who am I kidding? I miss Cole.

"Brooke? Are you there?"

"Sorry. I was thinking about something else." Brooke yawned and rubbed her eyes. "Go public, if you want to. I'm sure that'll have an effect on whether you get stuck with child support payments or not. I guess that's up to you."

"Right… well… uhm…"

"Bye, Nathan. Have a good life."

Brooke disconnected as the baby began some sort of calisthenics that distorted her belly, stretching one side as if she were trying to escape the confines of the womb. Brooke smiled, rubbing her tummy. She had her baby. Nothing else mattered.

It wasn't quite true, but she willed it to be so. Cole's actions, or lack of actions, since Sunday had solidified her decision to end the relationship early. Sure, she'd blocked his phone calls and he had no idea where she was living. But a part of her had hoped he would come galloping into Hayward Home on a white horse and carry her away to live with him, happily ever after.

That hadn't happened.

Instead, she'd received a visit from Cole's attorney at work Friday afternoon. He'd handed her a check for $250,000, along with a contract to sign, stating she had received the full amount of the settlement contracted in the prenuptial agreement. Her already broken heart ripped open, realizing that was all Cole was worried about, as if she would go after him for more money. Didn't he know her better than that after all the time they'd spent together?

Blinking her tears away, she'd signed the contract and waited until Garner left before tearing the check into the tiniest of shreds. She'd scooped the confetti into her hands and dropped it into the black metal wastebasket, watching it flutter down like snow on a dark night.

Cole didn't love her—that much was certain. The last of her hope shriveled and died, leaving a gaping hole in her soul.

CHAPTER 21

Two more weeks went by without another word from Cole. It was possible he'd tried to contact Harper, but she'd already blocked him, claiming solidarity or some such noble motivation. Meanwhile, the divorce had been delayed, as Cole's attorney had predicted.

Brooke had canceled her appointment with Dr. Harrison, fearing Cole might show up there. It seemed like a waste to find a new ob-gyn in Houston just in time to move to Oklahoma. As she read the thirty-third chapter in *Forty Weeks to a Brand New Life,* she wondered if Cole was reading the same thing, following the baby's progress. He might still care about the baby, but she was torn between wishing he would or hoping he wouldn't. Mostly, she was tired and lonely.

She missed everything about Cole, but she was surprised how much she missed Gus. They'd developed a nightly routine. She would feed Gus while Cole cooked their meal. After dinner, she'd put her feet up on the couch and Gus would lie on the floor where she could scratch behind his ears. Cole had teasingly complained that she was spoiling him, but being around the dog seemed to lower her blood pressure. Part of her wished she hadn't spent four months living with Cole and Gus so she wouldn't know what she was missing.

At least her accommodations had improved a bit. The changes were subtle, at first. Nothing to raise suspicion. Her next-door neighbors moved out, resulting in the absence of drunken brawling that had been her nightly companion when she was attempting to sleep. Some new shrubs appeared in the planter boxes. The parking lot seemed emptier. The putrid smell had vanished from her bathroom.

She'd been relieved when the management posted a note on the outside of every door to set up a schedule for maintenance and updates, to include new paint and carpet. She'd been too drained to consider how unlikely it was for even these small changes to be taking place at the decrepit motel. It wasn't until she stepped into the motel lobby to pay her fourth-week's rent that sirens went off in her head.

She couldn't see the face behind the newspaper, but the man's torso looked all too familiar. Arms folded over her chest, she tapped her foot on the tile floor in front of him. "You might as well give up. They don't make newspapers big enough to hide someone like you, Mack."

The paper came down, and Mack gave her a grin as big as his neck. "What would you say if I told you I'm here to see a friend?"

"I'd say I think you're lying." She rubbed her temples as the ramifications of Mack's presence sank in. "Will you give your boss a message for me?"

"Gladly." He ripped his phone out of his pocket. "If he doesn't fire me for getting caught."

"Would he really do that?" She was horrified to think of Mack losing his job because of her. "Just don't follow me anymore, and I promise he'll never find out from me."

"I'm afraid I can't do that. He's my boss, and besides, there's a witness." He tilted his head, his eyes darting toward the scroungy man at the lobby desk, who'd taken her check a few seconds prior. "That's one of our men, Phil Mackenzie. Phil, meet Mrs. Miller."

"Wait a minute. You work here. You're here every time I pick up my mail. How can you work for Mack, too?" She didn't mention he was so creepy-looking that she always kept one hand on the mace in her purse.

The greasy-headed Phil smiled, revealing horrible broken and decayed teeth. "Sorry for the subterfuge, Mrs. Miller. But I'm glad I don't have to wear these anymore." He removed the fake teeth, his white, perfectly-even ones appearing out of place on his grimy, unshaven face.

Cole had been spying on her, all this time, probably laughing at her efforts to get away from him.

"You tell your boss that—"

"Hold on!" Mack said, as he tapped on his phone screen and aimed it at her. "Now. Go ahead and speak your piece. This way, I won't have to repeat it."

She hesitated, a little intimidated to be recorded, but this was a great chance to let all her frustrations out.

"Listen to me, Cole Miller! I can't believe you have your security team here spying on me! You have no right to interfere in my life!"

It felt good to yell at Cole. So good that she took a deep

breath, preparing for another round. But his voice came from the phone's speaker, and her heart performed a double flip.

"Technically, I'm not spying on you. I'm simply protecting my property."

Mack flipped the phone, and Cole's face appeared on the screen. Her breath caught in her throat. She'd already forgotten how beguiling his eyes were. But she had to stick to her guns, no matter how good he looked.

With his eyebrows arched to his hairline, Mack stuck his phone in Brooke's trembling fingers. He jerked his chin toward Phil. "We'll go wait outside and give you two some privacy."

She stiffened, not willing to back down. "Married or not, I'm not your property."

"Yes, but the Starlight Motel is."

"You're bluffing." She wouldn't be fooled twice.

"Not this time. I bought it the week you moved in. You see, when we said our vows, I promised to protect you. Until the divorce is final, you're still my responsibility."

Being called his responsibility wasn't exactly flattering.

"Go back and watch the wedding video," she said. "You actually promised to *love, honor, and cherish* me, but I won't hold you to it." Particularly the love part. He'd done great on honoring and cherishing, if you counted cooking great food and giving fantastic foot rubs.

"Protecting is how I do those things." His chin jutted forward. "By the way, why haven't you cashed your check?"

"I don't need it, Cole." As exhaustion crept over her like a heavy blanket, she dropped onto Mack's vacated chair. "I don't want it."

"Was it so awful to be with me?" Hurt edged into his voice. "One minute, we're together, getting along well. The next minute, you're gone, you won't tell me where you are, my calls are blocked, you won't touch my money. I don't understand why you won't give us another chance."

His words tore at her, ripping at the scab she'd erected over her heart.

"A chance at what, Cole? A chance to be platonic friends for a few more weeks before I'm on my own again?"

"I miss you, and so does Gus. I wish you'd come home."

She turned the phone so he couldn't see the tears welling in her eyes. It sounded like pure torture. To have him around all the time, a constant reminder of everything she couldn't have.

"I hope you'll think about it," he said, "because Gus has quit eating."

"Why? Did you take him to the vet?"

"The vet checked him out. Everything's normal. He's fallen into a depression since you left. He lies on the floor and stares at the front door."

"He doesn't eat at all?" Gus' normal food consumption had been daunting. Her worry for Gus pushed her own troubles to a back burner.

"He'll eat a little, if I feed him by hand. The vet said it might be anxiety from the changes, but I think he's waiting for you to come home."

She could barely hold her stormy emotions in check. Poor Gus shouldn't have to suffer. He was completely innocent.

"Can you take the phone to him? Let me talk to him?"

"Sure, we can try."

The scene shifted as he moved through the house, and then Gus appeared on the screen, lying by the front door, as advertised. He barely lifted an eyebrow when Cole approached. Was he that weak?

"Hey, Gus! Hey, boy!" she called out.

Gus' head lifted, his ears perked. His nose sniffed the screen.

"I miss you, Gus. Have you been a good boy?"

He climbed to his feet, whining and pacing. He sniffed the screen again.

"I think he's looking for you," said Cole. "At least he's alert, for a change. Maybe he'll eat something."

Cole enticed him toward his food bowl, but he refused to come close, even though Brooke was calling to him also. A few minutes later, he returned to his place by the front door and collapsed, dropping his head to his feet.

"See what I mean?" Cole asked.

"I'm sorry," she said. "I was hoping he'd respond to my voice."

"I didn't think it would work. He doesn't even perk up when we go to the ranch."

Guilt niggled at her, and she knew it wouldn't go away. "I guess I could come over to see him."

"Would you?" Relief was written all over his face. "That'd be so good for him. Tomorrow's Saturday. Want to come over for dinner? I'll cook your favorite—shrimp enchiladas."

Her mouth watered. It sounded a lot better than her Healthy Foods frozen dinner. "Only if you promise to call off your security team."

"We'll talk about it tomorrow," he said, his eyes twinkling with excitement and something she didn't quite trust. "See you at five. Or you could come at noon and we'll grab lunch and catch a matinee in the afternoon. How does that sound?"

Lunch and a movie might be a better alternative to dinner. Less awkward time to fill. And she'd be home before he had time to offer a foot massage. "I like that idea."

"Great! I'll shop in the morning and have everything ready to go for the dinner, when we come back from the movie. We can take Gus along to lunch and drop him off at the Doggie Day Care right next to the cinema."

No way she could handle spending the entire day with him.

"But, Cole—"

"After the movie, I'll throw the enchiladas in the oven. And I'll make mango-habanero salsa for the chips."

She shushed her traitorous, growling stomach.

"Hold on, Cole. I thought—"

"Thanks for giving me a chance, Brooke." His earnest eyes locked with hers, wrenching her heart. "I promise you won't regret it."

"Okay."

Why did I say that?

"See ya at noon," he said, flashing his deep dimples. "Actually, you should come around eleven. Mack can give you a ride."

"I'm driving myself!" she said sternly.

"Okay, okay," he said, with a grin. "Whatever you say. I'll see you at eleven."

She hung up, proud of her victory. Until it hit her…

"Oh my goodness! I have the spine of a jellyfish."

"FINN, I just got your message about Brooke." Cole held the phone to his ear and lowered his voice so Brooke wouldn't hear. "She's here. She's in the other room."

"At your apartment? I thought you guys were split up for good. You know I've got money riding on this. You told me the marriage was only temporary."

"I talked her into spending the day with me. That's all," Cole murmured, checking around the corner where Brooke was sitting on the floor in the family room, encouraging Gus to eat. "We had lunch, went to a movie, and now I'm cooking dinner."

"You should snap a selfie together and make a media announcement. Imply that the marriage is doing great. It might calm down some of those crazies on social media."

"What kind of threats were they making? Do we know who they are?" Cole opened the pantry door, looking for a bag of tortilla chips, which were perched on the highest shelf.

"None were out-and-out threats. If they were, they'd have the FBI all over them. These posts are just stirring up emotions. Spouting a lot of hate. That's the kind of thing that sets off the true crazies, though. That's why I sent you a text. Just thought you might want to be extra cautious."

Hearing Finn speaking in such a dead-serious tone kicked Cole's pulse up a notch.

"I don't get it. Why are they in such an uproar today? As far as the public knows, we're still living together. We haven't announced the divorce."

"Oh, man! I thought you saw the news," Finn said. "As of today, everyone knows about the divorce. Brooke's ex gave an interview. Said some really nasty things. Mostly, he made

Brooke sound like she was sleeping around on him when they were married and doing the same thing to you, now."

Cole slammed the pantry door, wishing it was Nathan's head. "This is my fault. I pulled my men off Nathan two days ago when his son was born. Thought he'd be too busy for this kind of stunt."

"Probably did it for the money," said Finn. "Your guys couldn't have stopped him from going to the press."

"What should I do?"

"First of all, you should talk to Angie. She's been trying to respond on your social media accounts, but she can't really say anything of substance. Maybe let her post something about the baby. You could even announce the gender. Something to draw the attention away from Nathan."

"I shouldn't respond to Nathan's statements?"

"Right. Ignore him, like he's not worth acknowledging. Give evidence to counter his claims, though. And…" Finn's voice cut off as a female spoke in the background. "Just a second. Laurie's trying to tell me something. What?... Oh! Great idea! Laurie says to hire a photographer to take prenatal photos."

"What's that? Like ultrasound pictures?"

"No, no, no. It's this goofy thing where they pose you doing embarrassing stuff like talking to her stomach. It's kind of awkward to do, but women go gaga over those pictures."

"And you have to be more serious than Finn," Laurie shouted into the phone. "He cut up so much we only had one or two shots where we weren't bustin' a gut."

"If you can keep a straight face, those photos ought to tug

on the heartstrings of all your female fans," Finn said. "Maybe they'll stop hating on Brooke."

"It's not the female fans I'm worried about," Cole said, holding the phone on his shoulder as he chopped a red onion and bell pepper. "The *men* are more likely to be violent."

"Like that nut-job who shot your cows?"

"And the one who slashed my tires, although that could've been random."

"Yeah, not likely. Yours were the only ones slashed in the entire parking garage."

"What's this doing to our stock prices?" Cole cringed, waiting for the bad news.

"We're up," said Finn. "No such thing as negative publicity, right?"

"That's a relief." Cole added the chopped veggies to the mango and jalapeño. Chopped cilantro and lime juice were the finishing touches. "Don't think I'll share this with Brooke. She's really sensitive about this stuff. She can't stand the idea that someone hates her."

"She's bound to hear about it, since it was her ex who started—" A rustling noise interrupted, followed by Finn's shout. "Hey! Give me that!"

"Cole," Laurie's voice was in his ear. "You have Brooke at your house right now?"

"Yes, but—"

"Great! Whatever you do, don't screw this up. It may be your only chance to fix this relationship."

"You don't have to worry," Cole said. "I've got it all figured out. Mariah gave me some advice, and for once, I took it. I'm waiting for the right moment, and I'm going to lay everything out on the table."

"Really?" Laurie ladled so much sarcasm on the word that it dripped off like syrup. "Why don't you try it on me? Just to be sure you don't leave out any important points?"

"Fine." Truthfully, he was a little nervous. A practice run couldn't hurt. "Brooke, my sister told me our relationship is broken, but there's no reason we can't fix it."

"So far, so good," Laurie encouraged.

"She said the arm was working fine, but we can't turn it into a leg. That's why it broke."

"Yeah... no," said Laurie. "Let's go with something that makes sense."

"Let me try again." Cole took a breath. "When we were friends, we got along fine. It's what I'm good at. We were cruising along until we tried to make our relationship more than a friendship. If we go back to the way things were, we can be friends indefinitely."

Silence greeted him on the phone.

"Laurie? Are you still there?"

"Cole Miller..." He'd heard that inflection in his mom's tone when he wrecked her car as a sixteen-year-old. "So help me, if you speak a word of that malarkey to Brooke, I'm going to fly down there and ream you out until you don't know which way is up."

He shuddered, particularly glad she had a phobia of flying, though he knew better than to mention it.

"But Mariah said—"

"Forget Mariah," said Laurie. "You listen to me. If you say any of that to Brooke, she'll walk out of your life, and you'll never see her again. Is that what you want?"

"First of all, I think you're exaggerating her reaction." He carried the cutting board to the sink, fumes from the jalapeño juice making his eyes water. "But secondly, I'm not capable of committing to a real marriage, if that's what she's after. Not until I settle some issues in my head. I need answers from my birth mom."

"Cole," her voice softened. "I spent a lot of years wondering why my father made the choices he did, refusing to acknowledge me as his daughter."

"And you finally got your answer," Cole muttered. "That's what I need."

"So you know what I learned?" She didn't wait for his response. "I learned that I wasted all those years. I found out my parents were young. They were human. They made mistakes. And none of that stuff I was worried about mattered a bit. God had already provided me with everything I needed to be happy, and I almost threw it away in my search for the truth."

"But—"

"Do me a favor, and imagine the rest of your life without Brooke in it. Is that what you want?"

"Of course not. But I'm offering her friendship. It's what I'm good at."

Brooke's face appeared around the end wall, and he snapped his mouth shut.

"Who're you talking to?" she asked.

"No one." Cole disconnected the call, wondering how much she'd overheard. "It was work related."

She smiled, seemingly unperturbed. "Thought you might want to know Gus just finished his second bowl of food."

He sent up a prayer of thanks. It felt silly to pray for a dog, but that hadn't stopped him from doing it. Gus had been there for him, through thick and thin. He didn't know how he could go on without him. He'd become dependent on that dog. Easy to do, because dogs love unconditionally.

During dinner, he found himself watching Brooke eat, suddenly fascinated with the way her lips moved. Always proper, she chewed with her mouth closed and dabbed delicately with her napkin. But on occasion, her tongue would dart out and brush her lips, and his stomach would clench in response, remembering the times their lips had touched. He'd held himself at bay for almost five months. But her physical draw was even stronger than before, not diminished in the least by her pregnancy.

"Why are you watching me?" She paused, her hands folded in her lap, her scowl demanding an answer he couldn't give. "Do you think I'm eating too much? Am I gaining too much weight?"

"Not at all."

"Then why were you staring?"

"I was… uhm… thinking about your… uhm… your *safety*." Whew! He'd come up with that just in time.

"My *safety*? Is this some excuse for why you're spying on me?"

Appetite gone, he threw his napkin on the table. "I wasn't spying, Brooke. I'm watching out for you. Being associated with me means being exposed to all kinds of people. Like a while back, some guy figured out where my ranch was and shot some of my cattle with a rifle."

He deliberately avoided mentioning the anger that could be aimed directly at her. No use her worrying about something she couldn't control.

"That's awful! Who would do something like that?"

"Some folks are crazy, and I seem to attract them like flies to a cow patty. So unless you're willing to move back in with me, you have to let Mack do his job."

Her stiff posture crumpled. "Okay. I can't move back in, so I won't fight you."

He had an insane urge to rub his thumb across her forehead, to erase the frown lines marring her perfect face. "That'll make Mack's job easier."

"I don't like that you're wasting all that money on me. I'll never be able to pay you back."

"Don't you realize by now that money isn't a big deal to me?"

"Don't you realize for me it *is* a big deal?"

She wiped her mouth and pushed away from the table, shifting her weight awkwardly as she rose to her feet. She picked up her plate and reached for his. "I'll do the dishes, since you cooked."

He stood and took the dishes from her hands, placing them back on the table. "Leave those here. I'll do them later. Come sit down and let me give you a foot massage." He offered his left hand, not trusting himself if their flesh-and-blood fingers touched.

She didn't resist, as he'd expected, but she also didn't exhibit any enthusiasm. She allowed him to guide her to the couch as if she were resolved to some inevitable torment.

Once he had her stretched out on the couch, her head on a throw pillow, he sat on the opposite end and started in on her right foot. Rather than her customary sighs and moans of pleasure, she lay rigid and silent. Something had changed during their weeks apart… something intangible, but real. It was as if an invisible barrier had been erected between them.

He switched to the left foot, and this time he heard a

small sigh, though it stopped as abruptly as it started. *I'm getting to her. It's not too late. We can get back to where we were.*

She gasped. "Did you see that?"

"What?" He looked around the room, expecting to see a bug or a spider.

"The baby. She... Oh! Did you see it that time?"

"I missed it!" He dropped onto the floor and crawled down to sit by her end of the couch.

"Watch." She pointed at her t-shirt covered abdomen. "On the right side. There!"

Something moved.

"I saw it!" Without thinking he reached his right hand out to lay it on her rounded belly, but stopped himself at the last second. "Is this still okay? I don't know what the rules are anymore."

"I guess so."

He pressed his hand where he'd seen the last movement, and within a few seconds he felt a kick. He couldn't help laughing. "That was strong. I think she's trying to kick my hand away."

Shifting to get comfortable, he sat back and propped himself up with Shrek, his right hand still up on her belly. Brooke guided his hand to chase the kicks around her abdomen.

"She's training for the Olympics," Brooke said.

"I believe it," he said, as the next blow made his hand jump.

Somehow, he found himself leaning over to the side, his head sharing the edge of her throw pillow, while they both watched the acrobatics. As he caught a whiff of her intoxicating scent, he breathed in deeply, the baby's movements forgotten.

"I've missed the way your hair smells," he murmured. "In fact, I've missed everything about you."

Her head turned toward him, her eyes locking with his. "I've missed you, too." Her lower lip trembled, eyes glistening with unshed tears.

"Why are you crying?"

Her shoulders shrugged, and her hand came up to swipe across her eyes.

He climbed to his knees, and bent toward her, bracing Shrek on the arm of the couch. Cupping her cheek with his free hand, he traced her tear-streaked cheek with the pad of his thumb.

"What's wrong? Isn't it good that we missed each other?"

"It could be good, but I'm afraid it's not."

"I think it's good," he said. "*Really* good."

He slowly lowered his mouth toward her, waiting for her objection… but it never came. His lips brushed against her cheek, which tasted of salt. He moved his mouth along the edge of her jaw, and she lifted her chin, exposing her neck to him. In that moment, he felt the weight of her trust and vulnerability.

He couldn't let himself get carried away. Self-control must be his mantra. A chaste peck on the lips was as far as he should go.

He trailed his mouth up and pressed his lips to hers. But when she responded with hunger, his self-control went up in flames.

In that moment, he forgot all the rules. He forgot everything except Brooke... her face, her lips, her cheeks, her neck. The two of them, suspended in eternity. His hands tangled in her silky hair. He heard nothing but the sound of their labored breaths. He deepened the kiss, claiming her as his own. She couldn't leave him again. The two of them were meant to be together.

His heart stopped. *What am I thinking? We're supposed to be friends.*

Except what he was feeling for Brooke couldn't be classified as friendship... not by a long shot. What he was doing was wrong... just plain wrong.

He ripped his lips away and sat back, panting for breath. "Brooke, I have to tell you something."

"What?" she answered, breathless, her lips even more enticing in their swollen state.

"My sister gave me some advice, and I've been thinking about it. I've made a decision." He paused, waiting for his racing heart to slow.

"Okay..."

He stared into her wide eyes, dark and deep, filled with trust. If he abused that trust, he would be no better than her ex.

"I've decided... my sister is wrong. We can't be friends. I thought I could do it, but I can't. When you're around me... I lose control."

His fingers traced the frown line between her brows and moved across her soft skin to brush her hair off her face.

"I agree," she whispered, as if it hurt to speak louder. "It won't work."

"So what do we do?" he asked. "I've gotten used to having you in my life. I don't want to lose you."

"I don't want to lose you, either. But I don't think we have a choice. Unless…"

"Unless what?" He bent closer to hear, their lips only inches apart.

"Unless you *love* me."

Her gaze locked with his, the hope in her eyes tugging at his soul. But his heart was doing battle with his ribcage. If she'd asked for a forever friendship, he could've given it to her. But instead, she'd asked for the one thing he couldn't give… love.

"I care about you, Brooke. A lot. But love is bigger than four letters. It's—"

"Don't say any more." Her face turned away from him. "I understand. I get that you don't love me."

He couldn't let himself become dependent on her. What if she didn't really love him? Or what if she changed her mind? He refused to care so deeply that he'd be destroyed if he lost her.

"What's wrong with the way it is now? I'll admit I'm the one who keeps breaking the rules, but we could set some new boundaries. What if we don't touch each other at all? Keep a minimum distance between us. Say, three feet."

She shook her head. "I can't be with you, Cole. It hurts too much."

"Maybe you could keep your own place, and we could get together once a week. Gus needs you. He's been miserable since you left. Look how happy he is now."

On cue, Gus stuck his head between them, pushing his wet nose against her face. Brooke lifted her hand to caress his head. "I'll only be here three more weeks. Then I'm going back to stay with my parents."

She's leaving me!

He wanted to yell at her, "You can't go!" But instead, he asked, in as calm of a voice as he could muster, "Who's going to deliver the baby?"

"I'll have to find someone in Bellaire, or *Nowhere*, as my sister calls it."

How could she sound so calm?

He couldn't find a drop of saliva in his mouth. He'd come dangerously close to caring too much. *When did I lose control?*

Taking slow breaths and ignoring the blood pulsing in his ears, he tried to persuade her to at least stay close by.

"I'll make sure you have a safe place to live here in Houston. There's no need to move away and change doctors before you have the baby."

"I think I should go home. We need space, Cole."

How could she sound so calm?

"But, Harper calls your hometown *Nowhere*. That doesn't sound like a great alternative to me."

"Well, she calls you *Soul Killer*, so that's not any better."

His throat constricted. "Is that what I've done to you? Have I killed your soul?"

Her thick lashes blinked over glistening eyes, and she lifted her hand to his cheek.

"You didn't kill it, Cole. You brought it back to life. You were sweet and kind and caring. Yes, you made me want things I couldn't have, but at least now I know it's possible. You set the bar high for me. When I'm ready to date again, I'll hold out for someone who treats me like this."

Why did her words, so positive and affirming, tear through him like a jagged knife? He didn't want her to be with someone else.

She wiped her face with her hands and pushed herself to a sitting position, swinging her legs to the floor. She was going to walk out the door if he didn't act fast.

"If you stay here with me, you'll never have to worry about anything," he said. "You can count on me. I won't let you down."

"Cole, you're treating your soul like it's Shrek." Her chin trembled. "You're going through the motions and doing everything perfectly, but you're not feeling anything. I want more. It has to be real. Your foot rubs are amazing. But the fact that I can feel something so good means I can also feel pain. You can't have one without the other."

Her assessment was right on target. Over the years, he'd built and reinforced the protective barrier around his heart. It was safe. It was comfortable. Perhaps he hadn't experienced the emotional highs Bran and Finn had described, but he also hadn't suffered as they had.

"I'm sorry, Brooke. I wish I could give you what you want, but I can't." His eyes were as dry as his mouth. "I'm sorry I hurt you."

He perched beside her on the couch, dying to reach out and touch her. The inches between them stretched like miles.

"This isn't your fault. You've been honest from the start."

Had he? At the moment, his entire life felt like a lie.

She took a deep, shuddery breath. "I want you to know I've been allowed access to the archived records at Hayward Home. I don't know if I'll find your file or what will be in there if I get to read it. But if there's anything I can do to help you get answers without violating my ethics, I'll do it."

Why was she still trying to help him? He didn't deserve it.

"You don't have to do that."

"I know," she said. "You never asked me to, and I respect you for that. But you've done so much for me. I'm hoping I can find a way to pay you back."

His whole life, he'd blamed his lack of knowledge about the circumstances of his adoption for his inability to love. Yet Brooke had offered him a possible lead, and he wasn't even excited about it.

She stood up and smoothed her shirt. "I'm a little afraid, no matter what you learn, you'll find a way to twist it around and make it a judgment on who you are. I'm going to tell you something I say in counseling all the time… You are amazing and special. You matter. Other people's opinions don't. If anyone doesn't recognize how valuable you are, the problem is with that person, not with you."

It sounded like parting words. His heart hammered on his ribs.

I need to distract her.

"If you believe all that stuff you said, why would you get freaked out because some stranger said hateful things on social media?"

"Knowing it in my head and putting it into practice are two different things. I'm working on it, though. In fact, before I leave town, I plan to talk to the reporters and tell them I'm filing for divorce. I don't want you to lose any fans over this."

He cringed. "I think your ex-husband may have already spilled the beans. Evidently he made quite a stir today."

"Oh no!" She squeezed her eyes shut. "I didn't believe him when he threatened to do it. I'll make a statement or something. Somehow, I'll fix it."

"It's probably best to let it die down. But do me a favor and don't go anywhere without Mack."

She groaned. "Fine. I can handle having a Mack-sized shadow for three weeks, I guess."

He followed on her heels as she made her way to the door, snatching her purse from the entry table. Gus whined as he circled them, probably hoping for a walk.

"So this is it, then? You're leaving, and I'll never see you again?" He had to say something. Anything. Something to make her stay. But his head felt hollow. He couldn't even think.

"I'll call you if I have any information about your birth mom." A single tear rolled down her cheek, leaving a glistening track. "But yes, this is goodbye. Thank you for everything."

"We might run into each other," he said in desperation. "I still own your motel."

"It would probably be best if that didn't happen. Maybe we can communicate through Mack, since he's going to be around all the time."

She turned to leave, but he caught her arm.

"Brooke, I'm sorry," he said. "I'm sorry I couldn't give you what you want."

Her nostrils flared, and she stretched her lips into a trembling half-smile. "Don't be sorry. It was the best time of my life."

"Can I kiss you? One last time?"

The muscles in her throat convulsed, and she dropped her eyes.

"No."

With that whispered word, she turned and walked out,

the door closing behind her with a thunk that made him flinch.

Gus let out a mournful howl. Could he sense she was gone forever?

On wooden legs, Cole stumbled to the closest chair and dropped into it. The air in the room thickened, too congealed to pass into his lungs. Pain stabbed in his chest.

Deep inside, he knew this was the real reason he would never commit to a woman. It had nothing to do with what his birth mother might or might not have done, and everything to do with avoiding this inevitable agony.

If losing Brooke was this painful now, how excruciating would it have been if he'd let himself fall in love with her?

More than I could bear.

CHAPTER 22

"That's the last of them." Brooke pressed her hands into the small of her back, which had a habit of aching all the time for the past week or so.

Mack wedged the remaining gift bags into the back seat, along with the huge box that contained her brand-new Pack 'n Play. "Are you going to leave all this stuff in here when you drive back to Oklahoma tomorrow morning?"

"That was my plan. Cole already had my boxes shipped up there, so I only have a couple of suitcases left. Hopefully, they'll fit in the front seat."

She wasn't looking forward to the seven-hour drive. Her feet would be the size of watermelons by the time she got home.

"Are you going to miss this place?" Mack asked.

"Not the place, so much." She looked over her shoulder toward the long sidewalk that led to the Hayward Home entry doors. "But the people turned out to be pretty great, especially the ones who were nice to me before I married a billionaire. You know what I mean?"

"I do." His eyes crinkled as he smiled. "In my business, I get a feel for who's real and who's fakin' it."

"But I wasn't expecting the baby shower, so I'm kind of blown away by it."

Mack nodded, shifting on his feet. "Ms. Miller, I wish you'd let us drive you to Oklahoma. I don't think it's safe for you to drive alone, especially after you and Mr. Miller have your big press conference today. Some of those people are pretty riled up."

Her stomach probably would've lurched, if it'd had any room to move.

Mack must have noticed her anxious expression, because he hurried to add, "Don't worry too much about it. Most people didn't take your ex seriously. I think the press conference will be as smooth as glass."

She wasn't sure what made her more nervous... being on camera with all those reporters firing questions or seeing Cole for the first time in three weeks. Hopefully, Mack was right, and none of the people who'd been raging on social media would show up at the press conference.

Nathan—or Satan, as Harper now called him—had been spouting off, milking it for all he could get. Though many of his accusations were ridiculous, such as claiming she'd used the pregnancy to trick Cole into marrying her, the rumors had spread like wildfire on social media. Some had pointed out the rather obvious fact that he'd slept with his current wife while still married to Brooke, but he claimed Brooke's unfaithfulness had driven him to it.

"Once I get away from Houston, I'll be fine," Brooke told

Mack with more bravado than she felt. "Most people have better things to do with their time than to worry about some billionaire's ex-wife. Especially now that Nathan's quit running off at the mouth."

With one brow arched, she gave Mack *the eye*. Nathan had been inexplicably silent the last five days, a peculiarity that Mack claimed no knowledge of, though his smirk made her doubt the denial.

"I'd still feel better if a couple of us went along with you," Mack insisted. "Maybe we could drive with you as far as Dallas."

"We'll see," she said, too tired to argue. "For now, I'll follow you to the Phantom Enterprises building. I don't even know where it is."

Traffic was light at two p.m. and, in less than twenty minutes, they arrived at Cole's building, a mirrored high-rise with a parking lot on one side and a surprising amount of green space in front. Cole had told her the bottom was rented to a number of other businesses, but Phantom took up the top ten floors. As she entered the parking lot, she could see a small crowd of spectators gathered in the courtyard, with security holding a perimeter—a fact that made her heart race even more. She'd hoped the general public wouldn't have caught wind of the press conference.

Following Mack, she drove toward the front of the building and parked in an area marked off with yellow cones. With each passing day, her increasing girth made climbing out of the car more difficult, but she stubbornly refused to accept any vehicle Cole offered as a replacement. The past three weeks had been the most miserable of her life, as she finally acknowledged that their relationship would never turn into a real marriage.

Though she longed to see Cole again, she dreaded this encounter with every bone in her body. To stand so close to him and not be able to touch him. To have their last time together in front of a group of strangers who would be judging every nuance of their expressions. All with the knowledge that she would drive away and most likely never see him again.

According to Mack, Cole had been trying to reach her on her cell phone. But she'd blocked him once again. She couldn't risk a repeat of that last date. His kiss had awakened all the feelings she'd been trying to suppress. She'd been so foolish to let hope spring to life. She should've known he hadn't suddenly fallen in love with her—he was too closed off to his feelings.

Perhaps the clue, written on the sealed envelope inside her purse, would lead him to his birth mom and the answers he sought. Maybe then he could actually be in a committed relationship. But she knew better than to put her life on hold and hope, by some miracle, he would show up on her doorstep in Oklahoma to declare his undying love.

Mack took her elbow when they reached the steps, guiding her up to where Cole was waiting. With his suit coat laid aside somewhere, he'd rolled up the sleeves of his starched white shirt. In contrast, she was wishing she'd worn a sweater against the chill in the early November air. As usual, he wore the signature cowboy boots that she now could've picked out of a line-up.

Why did he have to look so good? Those eyes... that broad jaw... that perfect body—she understood why so many women thought they were in love with him, and they hadn't even experienced one of his foot massages.

When she arrived at his side, he turned, wrapping his arms around her in an embrace so tender she almost cried.

"You're shaking," he whispered in her ear. "Are you okay?"

"I'm just nervous. But we can't do this. Everyone's waiting."

"Let them wait." His arms tightened. "Can you stand up for this? Do you need a chair?"

His breath in her ear sent shivers down her spine, which only encouraged him to hold her tighter. Her cheeks heated as a hundred pairs of eyes observed their encounter, lights flashing and cameras running.

"Let's get this over with," she rasped.

He nodded, exchanging the hug for an arm around her shoulder that assured she was tucked against his side. Unyielding, he moved her with him toward the microphone.

"Ladies and gentlemen, thank you for coming." He addressed the reporters and camera operators gathered on the steps below, though he nodded acknowledgement to the spectators in the courtyard. "Since it seems certain people are intent on spreading rumors and lies about our private lives, Brooke and I are here to set the record straight. I'll make a statement, and then we'll answer a few questions, although we may deem some information too private to share."

Brooke should've known Cole would protect her from probing questions. She would've relaxed completely, if she hadn't been so self-conscious about having his arm around her. They had to be wondering why he was acting so affectionate when they were getting a divorce. For that matter, she wondered the same thing. He'd better not try to talk her into staying with him. She would probably dissolve into a puddle of tears right where she stood.

"First of all, let me put one particularly nasty rumor to rest," said Cole. "Brooke did not *trick* or *trap* me into marriage. I had to beg her to marry me, and I did so, knowing full well that she was pregnant."

His eyes darted toward Brooke, and she gave a confirming nod.

"Also, as you can see, Brooke and I are on good terms. We care deeply for each other. There's no animosity between us."

On her shoulder, his hand gave a little squeeze, and she looked up, noting a hard glint in his eye.

"And finally, let me say that I want the best for Brooke and her daughter. Even after the divorce is final, I will consider her under my protection."

Her breathing was easier, though her knees were still trembling. She might not have to talk at all.

Hands shot into the air, "Mr. Miller! Mr. Miller!"

"Yes." Cole pointed to a woman on the front row.

"Mr. Miller, whose name will be on the birth certificate as the father?"

He didn't even glance Brooke's way before answering. "I'm afraid that's private."

"Mr. Miller, when will the divorce be final?"

"We're not sure. There've been some delays. I expect it will happen after the baby comes."

"How much is the divorce settlement?"

"Brooke doesn't have a lot of assets, so she's only going to fork up fifteen hundred dollars."

The crowd laughed and Cole winked at Brooke.

"We have a prenup, of course. But let's just say I intend to make sure Brooke and her daughter are taken care of, though Brooke will soon have her counseling license and will probably start her own practice." On her shoulder, his hand gave her a little shake for emphasis. "No doubt, she'll be successful."

He'd made sure of it, with that free plug. That he was still so thoughtful made it even harder to understand why he couldn't bring himself to love her. He was obviously capable. There had to be something wrong with her. Was she too needy? Or too strong-willed?

"Mr. Miller, it seems like the two of you get along better than most married couples. Why are you getting divorced?"

For the first time, Cole hesitated, looking uneasy.

"I can't answer that question, Rick. But I can tell you it has nothing to do with the baby."

"When is the baby due?" asked a woman wearing a bright red blouse. "And will you be present at the birth?"

Brooke wriggled out of his grasp and moved to the microphone, pointing it downward. "She's due on December fourth, and yes, I intend to be at the birth."

This produced another round of laughter, and Brooke stepped back, pleased with herself. The way Cole smirked, he must've been equally pleased.

"Mrs. Miller," someone called out. "What do you say to the rumors that you've had multiple affairs since you and Cole got married on the first of June?"

Her face burned. She opened her mouth to answer, but Cole beat her to it. "It's a bald-faced lie! Brooke has not only been faithful to me, but was also faithful to her ex-husband,

Nathan Riggs. And if I'm not mistaken, he'll be confirming that in a statement later today."

How had Cole pulled that off? She imagined Mack lifting Nathan in the air, his feet dangling above the ground, the front of his shirt bunched in one of Mack's huge hands. She clamped on her lips to keep from smiling.

"Mr. Miller!" "Mr. Miller!"

Cole cut off the questions, ignoring the protests. "That's all for today, other than my written statement. Thank you for coming."

Off on the courtyard lawn, voices were shouting for attention. Most sounded like excited fans, but a few were angry, evidently not appeased by their explanations. Brooke worried a little about leaving Cole in Houston to deal with it, but hopefully her final departure would dissipate the emotions.

Her own feelings were in turmoil, simply from being in close proximity to Cole. His touch was still charged, though she knew there was no love behind it. Her greatest fear for him now was knowing how easily he could find a woman willing to enter into a loveless marriage, simply for the sake of his money. Was that what she'd awakened in him? A desire for the stability of marriage without emotional involvement?

I'm going to be a terrible counselor.

A man in a suit pulled Cole aside for a deep conversation, and Brooke saw her chance to escape. Waddling as fast as she could, she headed for her car. As she opened the door and glanced at the back seat, packed with presents from the shower, she realized she'd hardly had time to get excited about the baby. Maybe now that she could put all this business with Cole behind her, she would have time to concentrate on her baby girl. She hadn't even chosen a name. She intended to keep her promise to her sister, but she would probably use Harper as the middle name.

"You weren't trying to give me the slip, were you?"

She jumped at Cole's voice behind her.

"No." She slid into the safety of her car, though he leaned against it, blocking the door from closing. "But you were busy, and I'm headed back to pack my suitcases."

"You're leaving in the morning, huh?"

"Yep. Long drive."

She started the car, but Cole didn't take the hint. He kept standing there, while the car dinged, protesting the open door.

"Have you changed your mind about letting Mack or one of his men travel along with you?"

Struggling to keep her frazzled emotions in check, she was willing to do anything to get away from Cole. Already, some cameras appeared to be pointing their direction. Any minute the tears would start pouring out, and her snotty, red-faced image would end up plastered all over the media.

"Sure. Whatever. I don't care if someone drives along with me."

"Can I buy you dinner tonight? We'll go someplace public, so you don't have to worry about me breaking any rules."

"I don't think so."

"So you're saying it's a possibility?"

He winked at her, and she laughed, in spite of her anxiety. How did he always manage to do that? She knew it was a bad idea, but she was tempted to say yes, just so he would let her leave the parking lot.

"I don't think we can, because we'd be breaking your one-and-done rule."

Was the door alarm dinging louder with each passing second?

"Technically, this might be our first real date where I pick you up at your door and drive you somewhere."

She groaned. "You are the master at finding a way around the rules, aren't you?"

"That's me." He puffed out his chest and pointed both thumbs at himself.

"Seriously, Cole. I think it would be too hard."

"I need this, Brooke. I have things to say to you. If you don't agree to dinner, I'll have to say them right now."

He jerked his chin over his shoulder, indicating the group of reporters who'd moved down, probably hoping to eavesdrop.

"Fine. I'll do dinner if you'll let me leave."

"Great. I'll pick you up at seven thirty." He tipped his hat and closed her door. Then he pointed behind her, calling out, "Mack's right there, waiting to follow you home."

Brooke knew dinner was going to be torturous, but she hadn't seen another way to get rid of Cole. She backed out and followed the curved lane until she reached the exit to the main street. As she waited for a break to turn right in the heavy traffic, she heard the roar of an engine and caught a glimpse of movement on her left.

The world exploded in her face.

With her ears ringing, she tried to make sense of her surroundings. The air smelled like gunpowder, and her arms were stinging. She became aware of the powder covering everything and the deflated airbag in her lap. Was she injured?

Her car door was crumpled against her, the window shattered, glass fragments everywhere.

Her ribs were sore on the left side, especially if she took a deep breath, but none of her limbs hurt terribly.

I'm alive and nothing's broken!

Someone was screaming, pounding on the passenger window. Cole.

"Brooke! Brooke! Are you okay? Brooke! Unlock the door!"

She groped for the switches on her crumpled door panel. But when she pressed the toggle, nothing happened. She tried again, pushing every toggle, with no results.

"I can't open it!" As she yelled, a sharp pain tore through her abdomen. She cried out in pain, fumbling under the airbag to press her hands on her belly. She felt warm moisture between her legs. "The baby! Help me! The baby's coming!"

"I'm getting you out, right now." Cole's mesmerizing hazel eyes locked with hers, and she felt an eerie calm. He was going to take care of her. "I'm breaking this window."

It took several blows before he hit the window just right with some part of Shrek and shattered the glass. Then he cleared an opening and reached in to unlock the door. In a flash he was inside, his hands unlatching her seatbelt.

"Is anything broken? Does your back hurt?"

"Just my belly." She panted to control the intense pain.

"Labor pains?"

"Yes, but it doesn't stop." She tried to hold her composure. If this was labor, the pain was going to get a lot worse by the end. "It's contracting, and it feels like someone is stabbing me."

"The ambulance is on the way. I'm going to get you out of here."

The sirens were getting louder but didn't sound that close. Then again, her ears were still ringing and everything sounded muffled. Outside, she could hear more shouts.

Mack stuck his head in the open door. "Is she hurt?"

"She's in labor," Cole answered. Then he covered her hand with his and caught her gaze. "You're going to be okay. I'm not leaving you."

She nodded, grimacing from the pain.

He carefully brushed away the safety glass fragments and pushed up on the airbag, clearing it off her lap.

And she saw it… blood.

A *lot* of blood.

"I'm bleeding, Cole! Please, God! Don't let me lose the baby!"

"You're going to be fine. You're both going to be fine."

Cole's voice was calm, completely in control, but she saw tears rolling down his face. She'd never seen him afraid before, and it scared her even more. Her heart raced, out of control.

He scooped his arms under her and hefted her across to the passenger's seat, her legs dragging awkwardly over the center console. Every bone in her body hurt, but the pain in her abdomen was so severe she couldn't help sobbing. She ended up in Cole's lap, and she was horrified that she was bleeding on him.

"I'm so sorry," she said, fighting a wash of vertigo. "I'm ruining your suit."

His words came out angry and strangled, like he was talking between his teeth. "I don't give a flip about the suit, Brooke. All I care about is you!"

The sirens were louder. Closer. More shouting. Hands grabbing her.

Her vision narrowed.

Why does it hurt so bad?

Cole's voice in her ear. "Shhh… I'm right here. Shhh… I'm right here…"

And then nothing.

CHAPTER 23

"Finn and I are already on our way. We'll be in the air in twenty minutes. Jarrett's taking off as we speak. He's only two and a half hours away."

"It's all my fault, Bran. I might as well have been driving the car that hit her." Cole's throat cramped, making it hard to speak.

"You need to calm down. You aren't helping anyone by panicking." Bran's voice in his ear should've been soothing, but Cole found himself gripping the phone so hard his hand was shaking.

"They sent me out of the room," he said, not caring that his voice broke. "I told her I wouldn't leave her, but they made me. What if she wakes up and I'm not there?"

"She'll understand. You can explain it when you see her."

People were staring at him with wide eyes. Maybe they recognized him. Or maybe they were afraid of the blood-soaked, deranged-looking man who paced relentlessly from one side of the emergency waiting room to the other. Mack had stayed behind to talk to the police, which meant Cole was alone and feeling as desperate as he probably looked.

"There was so much blood." He choked. "So much blood."

"But she's in good hands now. The doctors know what to do. They'll take care of her."

"I don't know." As he strode across the room, he kept one eye on the forbidding double-doors, marked with the sign, *Hospital Staff Only*. "They were all yelling and running around and grabbing things. Then a man in scrubs just shoved me out the door. I tried to look through the glass window, but they shut the blinds."

"Didn't they come out and explain what was going on?"

"After a few minutes a doctor came out and made me sign something saying they could do whatever was necessary to save her life, including surgery."

"What kind of surgery?"

"I don't know. She said something about blood loss and oxygen levels. Then she told me someone would come out and talk to me, but that was fifteen minutes ago." Cole had a crazy urge to punch a hole in the wall, right under the sign that said, MAKING HOUSTON HEALTHIER, ONE PATIENT AT A TIME.

"She must've said something else," Bran urged. "Something that would give us a clue what's going on."

"She talked so fast," Cole said. "And I signed a paper saying I was aware that Brooke might die and the baby might die. How am I supposed to be sane after signing that?"

A voice called from a cubical on the side of the room. "Mr. Miller?"

"I've gotta go! They're calling me." Tucking his phone

away, he trotted to the sign-in desk, tucked behind a privacy wall.

The woman behind the counter barely glanced up from her computer as she pushed a clipboard toward Cole. She tucked a strawberry-blond curl behind her ear. "I'll need you to fill out this paperwork, please. Be sure to sign or initial where you see a red X."

His heart pounded behind his forehead, every muscle fiber trembling, as he put both hands on the counter and leaned over it. "Trudy," he read from her name tag—*Trudy Cordle, Patient Coordinator*—"I'm not filling out a single page until someone tells me what's happening to my wife."

He was proud that he hadn't shouted. But his mannerisms must've been threatening, because her eyes looked like green dinner plates.

"I'm only an intake clerk," she said, with a trembling voice. "I don't know anything about the patient's treatment."

Her gaze dropped down from his eyes, and her mouth hung open—she'd probably noticed his green hand. Cole glanced at Shrek and realized his fingers were bloody. In fact, a coating of mostly-dried blood covered both his hands. He clenched them into fists.

"Then go find someone who does," Cole growled, ignoring the fact that he was taking out his frustration on an innocent bystander.

"I'm sorry." She gulped, visibly. "But I can't go into the emergency ward and—"

"Now! I want to know something now!" He slammed Shrek's bloodied hand onto the counter with a loud clank.

Trudy jumped up from her chair and took a few steps back. But he was blocking the only way in or out of the small cubical. At least a foot shorter than him, she shrank away and he drowned in sudden guilt. "I'm sorry, Trudy. I—"

Cole felt a hand on his shoulder and reacted by reflex, grasping the wrist and twisting as he turned.

"Ow!" The hand's owner was bent over at the waist, his arm wrested behind him.

"Dave!" Cole released him and helped him straighten. "Sorry. I didn't know it was you."

"I'm okay, I think." Dave rubbed his arm gingerly. "I got here as soon as I could, but I had to change into scrubs. Tell me what happened."

Cole let his friend lead him away from the frightened clerk, who probably contacted security the moment he left. He related the details of the accident to Dave, his pulse rising even higher as he read the concern on his friend's face.

"Sounds like a placental abruption," Dave said.

"Meaning what?"

"Meaning the placenta that attaches the baby to the uterus was torn, to some unknown extent." Dave reached in his pocket and pulled out an ID, attaching it to his scrub top. Then he aimed his gaze at Cole's bloodstained pants. "And all that came from Brooke?"

"Yes." He swallowed at the inference of the question. "Will she be okay? And the baby?"

"If they got here fast enough." Dave headed to the double doors and punched a number into the keypad. The doors swung open. "Let me see what I can find out. I'll be—"

"*Please*," Cole begged in a ragged voice. Dave's image rippled in his watery eyes. "Please, take me with you."

"It might be best for you to wait here."

"I can't! You saw me—I'm going crazy! I told her I

wouldn't leave her, and she's in there all alone." He swiped his eyes with the back of his hand. "Please, Dave. If our friendship means anything."

Dave's hand gripped his arm like a vise. "If it's bad, can you hold yourself together?"

Cole nodded, swallowing the rock in his throat.

"Okay." Dave's eyes darted over his shoulder down the long corridor. No one seemed to pay them any attention. "But you have to stop in the restroom and wash the blood off your hands... and your *face*."

FRESHLY WASHED and looking less like an actor in a horror movie, Cole sat on a hard metal chair against the wall in the hallway, his boot tapping a nervous rhythm on the tile floor. Every minute lasted an eternity as he waited for a report on Brooke's condition. Dave came around the corner. Cole stood up, trying to read his friend's face. All he could see was worry.

"They're both alive," Dave said, pushing his fingers through his hair.

"Both? Meaning the baby is here?"

Dave nodded. "They had to take the baby via C-section. They didn't have a choice—Brooke had lost too much blood and the baby was in distress."

"She was only thirty-six weeks along," Cole said, his mouth so dry he could barely make his tongue work.

Dave moved to put a hand on Cole's shoulder. "Thirty-six weeks is considered late pre-term. The health risks are significantly lower now than if this had happened even a week ago. And this hospital has one of the top neonatal units in the country."

"But what about Brooke?" Cole asked.

"She lost so much blood they started a transfusion. That's going to take a couple of hours." Dave tightened his grip on Cole's shoulder. "She's not out of the woods yet. She could have other internal injuries. She could go septic. Hopefully, everything will be good, and she'll move to a regular room when she regains consciousness. But they haven't ruled out critical care."

"She didn't break any bones, though?"

"Dr. Garcia found heavy bruising and gashes on her left side. She expects to find broken ribs, at the very least. Probably some whiplash. They're watching closely, looking for internal bleeding."

"If that parking lot had been any wider, the car would've been going a lot faster when it hit her." An involuntary shudder rocked through his body. He'd come so close to losing her. "I need to see her, Dave."

"You can't, yet. But you can see the baby now, if you want."

How could he steal that moment from Brooke—to be the first to see her daughter outside the womb? Because of him, she and the baby had almost died, and Brooke had missed the joy of giving birth. Hadn't he done enough damage?

"No." Cole spoke louder than he meant to, and Dave regarded him warily. Cole lowered his voice. "Brooke should see the baby first. It wouldn't be fair if I saw her while Brooke was still unconscious."

Frowning, Dave took a step back and folded his arms.

"Two weeks ago, you told me you two were getting a divorce. Has that changed?"

Cole took a deep breath, the acrid smell of disinfectants burning his sinuses. When he'd come to the press conference that afternoon, divorce seemed inevitable. His goal had been to persuade Brooke to keep their communication channels open. But now the truth lay before him, as plain as if it had been engraved on his hands. He couldn't live without Brooke in his life.

"I really don't know," Cole said, "but you have to let me see her. Can't I just look in the door?"

"You're killing me, Cole." Dave's head shook slowly. "Fine. I'll get you in there. But only for a few minutes. Then you've got a ton of paperwork to fill out."

"And someone to apologize to, if she hasn't already quit her job." Cole grimaced. "I was a little impatient with the intake clerk."

"You were mean to *Trudy*? What's with you, Cole? She's like the sweetest person on the planet."

"This hasn't been my best day."

COLE HAD GIVEN the hospital administration permission to make a statement to the press, describing Brooke's condition as stable, with no mention of the baby's delivery. Meanwhile, Mack was working with the hospital security to keep the reporters at bay.

Jarrett showed up about the time the police finished taking Cole's statement. He barely kept his emotions at bay when Jarrett embraced him in the hospital lobby.

"Thank you so much! You're the first person to make it here." Cole clamped his jaw tight as he swallowed. "I can't believe you dropped everything to come."

"Like you haven't done the same for me, more than once," Jarrett said, slapping his back as he released him. "Of course I came."

"She's finally awake. They're moving her to a room."

"Thank God," said Jarrett.

"Walk with me. I'm headed to that flower shop." He pointed across the lobby.

"Have you seen her yet?" Jarrett asked.

"Just for a second." Cole's chest went tight. "She looks like she's been in a war zone. This is all my fault. I almost killed her."

"You know that's not true." Jarrett put an arm around his shoulder. "That guy was crazy. Literally. The news reports said he tried to burn down his ex-wife's house."

"But I'm the one who exposed her to that. When I think what could've happened, I can't even breathe."

"I hope this is a wake-up call for you."

"Believe me, it is." Cole stopped outside the store. "I've been struggling with what this means and what I should do. All I really want is to keep her with me. To never let her out of my sight. But I know I'm being selfish. As long as she's with me, she'll be in danger like this. I ought to let her go."

He started to walk into the store, but Jarrett grabbed Shrek's elbow and dragged him back, his expression dark. "I know you've been through a lot today, but I'm not going to stand by and let you throw away your chance at happiness. It's time you admit you're in love with Brooke."

"I admit it," Cole fired back, jerking free of his grasp.

"Okay? Are you happy? Because I'm not. I'm miserable! I've had a great life living above all that. I didn't need anyone's love and approval, only my own. I didn't care who liked me or hated me, except for how it affected our stock prices. But *now*... Now, I'm a wreck!"

"You have a chance with Brooke. A chance for something real. A chance to build a life together. Maybe your life was easy before, with that stupid one-and-done dating rule, but it was empty."

"Better empty than agony." Cole shoved past him and stomped into the gift shop, heading straight to the cooler with a variety of flower arrangements.

"That's like saying you'd rather be dead than go through chemo to stay alive."

Leave it to Jarrett to use cancer to make his point. How could he argue against that? Cole gripped the handle of the cooler, staring unseeing at the flowers behind the glass. "I'd gladly go through chemo if I *knew for sure* it would..." He stopped, realizing Jarrett's trap.

"That's right. There's no way to know for sure. You have to take a chance."

Cole knew Jarrett was smirking. He could hear it in his voice.

"What if I can't do it?" Cole glanced around, glad to find the tiny store virtually empty at six thirty. At least there were no shoppers to eavesdrop on their conversation.

"You *have* to," Jarrett said, his voice deathly quiet. "You have the chance to be with the woman you love. I never had that chance, and I'm not going to let you throw yours away."

Jarrett didn't talk about his love life. Ever. The four friends had a tacit agreement to never mention it. Back in college he'd told them he'd only ever loved one woman in all his life, but she'd married another man. That Jarrett would bring it up now was huge. And the pain in his expression, as wounded and raw as ever, was a chilling testimony.

"Even if you don't care about your own life," Jarrett said, "do you want Brooke to hurt like this?"

"You know I don't." Cole's shoulders sagged, exhaustion drenching him like an ocean wave. "But I've got all these crazy followers. Brooke will never be safe with me."

"You've been in the limelight for ten years. Maybe it's time to step out of it," said Jarrett. "Finn did it. No one's interested in his private life since he's happily married. You could do the same thing."

"But our stock values might drop."

"We'll be fine without our green-armed cowboy making the news all the time." Jarrett rolled his eyes. "This week, Finn ramped up the noise about the voice command climate control. Bran's developing a new line of video games for sighted players, using blind gaming protocol. Parts of the game, the screen goes black, and the gamer operates by audio cues only. The website hits are already off the charts."

Cole knew his argument was lame. He'd enjoyed the fame for himself as much as for what it did for Phantom Enterprises. Could he give it up?

His watch beeped with an incoming message. Mack had brought in three more of his security team in a vain attempt to keep the press outside.

"You know what? I think you're right." Cole said. "I might like having some privacy. That's probably why I spend every weekend at the ranch."

Jarrett smiled and clapped him on the back. "Don't you have some flowers to buy?"

Cole reached into the cooler and took out the two largest arrangements, carrying them to the front of the shop. "Sherry," he asked the middle-aged woman behind the counter, "would you mind trading some flowers between these two arrangements for me? I want to switch all the pink flowers out of this one for the red roses in the other one."

"Sure, Mr. Miller." Her hands trembled as she worked. "I'm sorry about your wife. My whole Bible study group is praying for her. They aren't going to believe I saw you in person."

"Thank you, Sherry," he said, ignoring Jarrett who elbowed him in the ribs.

When he'd paid, he handed her a rose and made Jarrett take a picture of them together on her cell phone.

Jarrett laughed as they left the shop. "She didn't even recognize me. She probably thinks I'm your bodyguard."

Cole made a detour through the emergency waiting room and interrupted Trudy's consultation.

"Excuse me, but this'll only take a second. Trudy, I'm sorry for behaving so badly earlier today." He presented her with the bouquet that included the pink flowers. "I hope you'll forgive me."

"That's okay, Mr. Miller." Her face bloomed red as she eyed the huge arrangement on the low counter. "I heard what happened, and I'm so sorry. I don't blame you for being upset."

"Yeah," the grey-haired man at her desk piped in. "That was horrible! I hope they hog-tie that guy and lock him up forever."

"I heard they took him to Central Hospital," said Trudy. "I'm glad they didn't bring him here."

"You be nice to Trudy," Cole warned the man. "She's had a rough day."

"I promise." The man nodded solemnly.

Another text came in on Cole's watch, this one with Brooke's new room number. His heart thrummed against his breastbone. "I'm going up," he told Jarrett. "I hope I don't say the wrong thing."

"Ha! That's inevitable with you." Jarrett gave his shoulder a friendly shake.

"Thanks for the vote of confidence."

"If I'm right—and I usually am—she'll love you anyway. You're a lucky man, Cole. Go convince her she's a lucky woman."

He expanded his lungs to full capacity, working up his courage.

"And Cole," Jarrett added. "Congratulations! You'll be a great dad!"

CHAPTER 24

White acoustic tiles whipped past overhead, too fast for Brooke to count. Around corners, down hallways, onto the elevator. Every part of her body was hurting, like she'd been dropped from two stories up onto a pile of sharp metal. But her belly hurt the most. Whatever drugs they had given her were wearing off, fast.

Her hands slid down, missing the firm roundness that meant her baby was safe inside her. Though some stranger with *M.D.* on his tag had informed her they had safely delivered her daughter, she sensed something was wrong. She'd begged to see her baby, but it hadn't happened. Surely, if the baby had been alive and healthy, they would've brought the infant to her. Who cared if her blood pressure was still low? She *had* to see her baby... to know the truth!

The orderly shot a glance her direction before checking his cell phone and tapping on his screen. The bell dinged and the doors opened. Gliding down another maze of hallways, she read a sign as they passed, *Surgical Recovery Unit.* Why wasn't she in the maternity ward? Women who had C-sections didn't go to the surgical wing, did they? Not if their baby was born alive?

Tears leaked from her eyes.

Where was Cole?

She wanted to talk to her sister. And her mom. Did they even know what had happened to her?

At last, the bed glided through a doorway into a room. Two more women came into the room and lifted the sheet underneath her, hefting her onto another bed. She clenched her teeth against the agony, refusing to cry out. She felt like she was dying. Maybe she was. If her baby was dead, she didn't want to live anyway,

"Hi, Brooke. I'm Tessa. I'll be your nurse until the night shift."

Tessa jostled her around on the bed and stuck a scanning device against her forehead. As Tessa wrapped a blood pressure cuff around Brooke's arm and pressed her fingers against her wrist, she chatted inanely about her vital signs improving, as if Brooke cared.

"I want to see my baby," Brooke croaked.

"I'll check on that for you," said Tessa, in a casual tone that didn't fool Brooke. Tessa's gaze darted back and forth across the computer screen. "All I can see here is that you had a live birth. But here are your doctor's orders. Let's see... it looks like she wants to keep you on fluids."

"Where is my baby?" Brooke said, with a little more force.

Tessa's eyebrows arched high as she tapped on the computer keyboard. "Your temperature is above a hundred. I'll need to contact the doctor."

"Why won't someone tell me the truth?" Brooke sobbed,

wincing at the pain in her side. "What happened to my baby?"

Wide-eyed, Tessa backed out the door. "I don't know. I'll be right back."

The room fell silent, but for the click of the second hand on the wall clock. Brooke followed its path around the circle of numbers, from twelve around to six and back, only to repeat the same thing over and over again. As meaningless as her life.

Brooke knew the answer long before anyone walked through the door to give her the bad news about the baby. The only question was why Brooke had survived the crash. If her baby had to die, it would've been better if they'd gone together. She welcomed the pain of her sliced and stitched belly. Focused on it. Anything was better than the agony of losing the baby.

The door rattled and swung open, and she steeled herself for the blow. But instead of Tessa's stricken face, a huge bouquet of flowers appeared to float into the room of their own volition. Was this how the hospital broke bad news to a patient? Her tears flowed, wetting her pillow.

The flowers deposited themselves on her bedside table, and Cole's face peeked from behind them.

"How are you feeling?"

His wobbly smile further confirmed her deduction. She let out a moan, unable to slow the flood of tears.

He moved beside her, his hand cupping her face. "I'm sorry! I'm so sorry! It's all my fault!"

She could barely breathe, much less speak.

"Are you hurting?" he asked.

She shook her head no, the tenderness of his touch

tearing at her already-broken heart. Though well intentioned, his kindness and sympathy was a mockery to the love she'd practically begged him for.

"If I could, I'd take your place."

His expression was so earnest, she believed him. She gave him a nod.

"Can you ever forgive me?"

His face mirrored her agony. He'd had no actual fault, but she could tell he would only be satisfied when she spoke his pardon. Her peace had been forever stolen, but she held the power to grant his. She gave it. How could she not? She still loved this man who'd admitted he would never return the feeling. He'd been there for her when she was at her lowest, and treated her with respect. She owed him for that, if nothing else.

"I forgive you," she whispered.

"I love you," he said.

"You don't have to do this." Her eyes shut tight. "I don't expect anything from you. Nothing's changed between us."

"Everything's changed. Because I'm admitting what I felt all along."

"Don't, Cole. Don't tell me you love me now." She peered through her wet lashes. "What you're feeling is guilt, because you think you're to blame and you aren't. And you're feeling pity because the baby is gone, but that's not your fault, either."

"What do you mean?" His hand grabbed her arm and shook until her eyes flew open. "What do you mean, the baby's gone?"

"She's dead," Brooke sobbed. "But I still want to see her. I deserve to see my baby."

Cole's face went flour white, and he stumbled backward. Then he turned and raced out of the room.

Alone again, Brooke lay awash in pain, wishing she'd asked for medication. Perhaps she could escape into a narcotic-induced coma, where her thoughts couldn't invade. Women lost babies every day. How did they endure? How did they find the strength to get out of bed and go on with their lives?

She gradually became aware of voices shouting in the distance. As the clamor drew closer, she recognized Cole's shouts among the others.

"I can't understand how something like this could happen!"

"It was a simple misunderstanding, Mr. Miller," a man answered. "No one told her the baby was dead!"

"She's been awake for over an hour!" he yelled. "Over an hour! You promised you would personally bring the baby to her the minute she was fully awake. You told me holding the baby would help her heal. You gave me this whole spiel about the uterus contracting and hormones and trauma and whatnot. You swore you'd do it immediately!"

A wail broke out... a tiny newborn cry. Brooke's heart leapt out of her chest.

"I'm sorry, Mr. Miller, but Brooke isn't the only patient in this hospital. I was called into surgery before I got a chance."

The wail got louder. Her baby was alive! Right outside her room.

"Then someone else should've taken care of it," Cole growled. "Your nurse said her hands were tied because of your stupid orders."

"What are you doing?" the man protested. "That's against

protocol. You can't take the baby out of there. You don't have a hospital tag."

"I'm her father." Cole's tone was as hard as granite. "I'm picking my daughter up, and I'm carrying her into the room so my wife can hold her. Call security if you want to."

The baby's cries calmed as Cole's deep voice shushed her. The door opened, and Cole came inside, his eyes shining as he held the baby, swaddled like a tiny burrito and wearing a soft pink cap.

Brooke's pain moved to the background when the baby nestled in the crook of her arm.

My baby! I have a baby... a tiny human.

"She's beautiful," he said, "like her mother."

"I can't believe it." Marveling at her tiny features, Brookes heart swelled so big it pressed against her throat. "She's perfect."

"I'm so sorry you thought she died. It's just one more way I failed you."

He bent to brush a tear from her cheek. "You're still crying."

"Happy tears now," she said. "That and hormones galore."

"Dave says the baby's really strong." Cole lifted his chin, as if her strength somehow reflected on him. "They didn't have to put her in the neonatal unit. Her lungs were fully developed at thirty-six weeks."

"How much does she weigh?" Brooke asked. It seemed impossible that a few hours earlier, the baby had been inside her. How did she fit?

A sheepish smile crept onto his face. "I don't know. It's written on the outside of her bed. But I think it's out in the hallway—they were afraid to come inside after I yelled at them."

"You do have a problem with your temper," she teased.

"I wonder if Dr. Black likes flowers."

"An apology would probably do," Brooke suggested. "But you should wait until you're genuinely sorry."

"I am genuinely sorry," Cole said, "but not for that. I'm genuinely sorry I brought all this on you. Thanks to me, you almost died and you almost lost the baby. Not to mention how I hurt you."

"It doesn't matter," she said, gazing at the baby in her arms. "Nothing else matters now."

"I love you, Brooke. Do you believe me?"

Her chest clenched around her heart. "Cole, I know you mean well, but you don't really love me. This is you feeling guilty for something that wasn't even your fault. You can't help that there are crazy people out there. I'm alive. The baby's alive. You're not responsible."

He pulled a chair next to the bed and sat down at eye level, gently resting his hand on her arm, wrapped around the squirming baby.

"Jarrett says I'll mess this up, so I need you to listen with your heart." He swallowed hard. "When I say I love you, I'm not just throwing words around. I haven't said that to anyone since... well, since *ever*. Not counting my mom and my sister."

She wanted to believe it, but she couldn't stand going through that heartache again.

"You can't suddenly decide you're in love when you weren't in love before. Love isn't something you can turn off and on."

"Before I met you, I was like Shrek." He lifted the green prosthetic arm. "I performed well, but I had no feeling. But you brought me to life! For the first time, I can *feel*. It's scary, because I can feel the good stuff and the awful stuff. The point is, now that I can feel, I can never go back. Even if I wanted to."

"Cole, it sounds good. But you're making an emotional decision. You didn't love me three weeks ago. We haven't spent five minutes together and suddenly you love me? How am I supposed to trust you?"

"It's okay if you don't believe I love you." His eyes softened, his pupils so dilated she could've fallen into them. "All I'm asking for is a chance to prove it to you... today, tomorrow, and every day for the rest of our lives."

He'd said the words she'd longed to hear. Why couldn't she believe him?

"How can I know for sure, Cole? I've been hurting for so long. I was ready to get on with my life and try to forget you ever existed. I don't want to take a risk that I'll have to start all over again."

His brows furrowed, and he stood up, pacing in the small space like a caged lion. Then he froze and turned to her, enthusiasm etching dimples into his face.

"I've got it!" He lifted a finger in the air. "Didn't you tell me you'd found a name for me? A lead that might help me find my birth mom?"

"Yes, I forgot all about it. I had it with me today. It's in my purse, wherever that ended up."

He crossed his arms and huffed out a long, slow breath, like he was trying to work up his courage. "Throw it away," he said, with a sharp nod. "I don't want it anymore. I don't need it."

"Why not?" She patted her squirming baby as she made little grunting noises.

"Because it doesn't matter why the woman who gave birth to me chose to give me up for adoption. It doesn't even matter if she tried to abort me and messed up my arm."

He was practically dancing in his boots, but she still didn't get it. "Why not?"

"Don't you see? Every single thing that happened in my life brought me to the point where I walked into that coffee shop and spilled my coffee on you." He gestured in the air. "If I hadn't been adopted... if I hadn't had this arm... we never would've met! I was praying for answers, and the answer was *you*."

Something like a crusty shell crumbled and fell from around her heart.

"You really love me?" she asked, wanting to hear it one more time, just to be sure she wasn't dreaming.

"You're so lovely. So beautiful. Inside and out." His hand reached out, knuckles brushing along her cheek. "How could I not love you?"

Her eyes filled with tears. "No one's ever said anything like that to me before."

"And what about you?" A crease formed between his brows. "Do you still love me? Please tell me I didn't wait too long."

"I do." She sniffed, blinking the moisture out of her eyes. "I love you with every stubborn, foolish, hopelessly romantic part of me that somehow refused to die no matter how many times I tried to kill it."

"I want you to know," he said, his voice unsteady, "you just made me the richest man on earth."

His eyes fell on the sweet, sleeping baby in the crook of her arm. She could see his throat working as he swallowed.

"I don't know how to explain it," he said, "but I love her, too. I barely know her, but I love her. Both of you. It's… it's… I don't know how to explain it."

She kissed the top of her baby's head. Her heart was so full it was going to burst.

"It's *fierce*. That's what it is." He reached for her hand. "I love you, *fiercely*. Like if anyone tried to hurt you, I'd defend you with my life."

"Let's hope it never comes to that." She squeezed his fingers. "I'd hate to see what you did to the other guy."

He grinned as he bent to place the tenderest of kisses on her lips, so soft and tempting she tried to cling to him, wanting more.

"Ow!" The incision in her abdomen protested her efforts.

His mouth dropped open. "Are you okay? Did I hurt you?"

"I'm fine," she said, as her forgotten pains worked their way back into the foreground. "I might need some pain medication."

A tentative knock sounded on the door, and a woman walked in, fidgeting with the booklets in her hand.

"Hi, I'm Jennifer, your lactation specialist. I can come back later if now's not a good time."

"I need you now," Brooke hurried to say, relieved she was going to have help. Cole, on the other hand, was as red as a cherry tomato. "But if you don't mind waiting outside for just a second, I need to talk to my husband."

Though they'd been married for over five months, it was the first time she'd really thought of him as her husband.

"I can leave," he offered, when they were alone. "I know this is totally awkward. I mean, she has no idea we've never... uhm... Although, I guess we will be now. Right? We didn't talk about it, but I was assuming we would. Not right away, of course. But I guess I can stay and learn about this stuff, in case husbands help with this sort of—"

"Cole," she interrupted. "I won't make you stay and watch right now."

Air blew between his loose lips. "Thank you."

"But the answer to your question is *yes*." She waited until her message sank in and a slow smile smoldered on his face. "Although I wouldn't hold my breath, if I were you. Every part of my body hurts right now. It may be months before I'm healed."

With his hands on her pillow on either side of her head, he lowered his mouth toward hers with excruciating deliberateness. Her pulse quickened. She hoped the various wires on her body weren't keeping a record of her temperature, which must've spiked by two or three degrees. By the time his lips pressed against hers, the opiate-effect of his kiss had drugged every nerve ending, eclipsing her pain. Dizzy with bliss, she blinked her eyes into focus.

"I can wait as long as we need to." His half-lidded eyes regarded her from inches away, with a sizzling combination of tenderness and hunger. "After all, I've been waiting for you my whole life."

EPILOGUE

(Two months later)

"Heel, Gus!" Cole tugged on the dog's collar, but he was intent on sniffing Garner's shoes, which, unfortunately, left a trail of slobber on the silk suit pants. "Sorry about that. He's not usually like that with strangers. Please add the dry cleaning to my bill."

"Perhaps he was drawn to the houndstooth," Garner said, sarcastically, as he backed behind the safety of his desk. He swept his hand toward the leather, client chairs. "Please, have a seat."

"Thanks for seeing us on such short notice," Cole said.

"When you said you were stopping by, I thought you were coming alone." Garner looked pointedly at Brooke, who was carrying the baby against her in a mile-long wrap that had taken twenty minutes and two You-Tube videos to decipher.

"I'm sorry. I should've introduced you. This is Nicole Harper Miller, and she's two months old, today." Cole

EPILOGUE

beamed, as he always did when he talked about his daughter. Her cheeks, rosy from the cold air, matched her perfect lips. The pink sweater cap she wore covered the short, dark hair on her head. She already looked like a miniature version of her mother, so much so that he worried how he would keep the boys away from her when she grew up.

"Congratulations. You have a lovely baby," he said wearing a smile that seemed to cause a great deal of pain. "I suppose you're here to ask about the divorce. If you'll both sign the agreed divorce decree, we can expedite this thing. Now that a child's involved, Brooke will need to appear before the judge for the final hearing, but that'll just be a formality."

Cole exchanged a glance with Brooke, whose hand was covering her mouth. From the crinkle of her eyes, he suspected she was stifling a laugh.

Cole cleared his throat. "I thought I called to cancel that."

Garner sat deathly still in the silence that followed. Not even a blink to indicate he was still alive. When he spoke at last, Cole had to strain to hear him.

"Cancel?" Garner's left eye twitched.

"It must've slipped my mind." Cole rubbed the back of his head. "We've been so busy, with the car wreck and near-death and the baby and the hospital. Then there's all the company. We've had one set of in-laws or the other, almost non-stop. Not to mention both our sisters, plus the Phantom guys. We've just been swamped. And we've been staying out at the ranch, trying to fly under the radar, so to speak."

"Slipped your mind?" Both eyes were twitching now.

"Uh, yes. But did you hear all that other stuff I said after that? Brooke almost—"

EPILOGUE

"Are you telling me the two of you decided you no longer intend to go through with the divorce?" With his eyes bulging and the veins standing out on his neck, Garner looked like he might explode. "The divorce that you planned before the marriage? The one that started out as agreed? The one I thought I was simply delaying when I filed an answer with the court and then filed interrogatories? Is that the divorce you're talking about? Is that the divorce that *slipped your mind?*"

"Nah! I'm talking about the *other* divorce."

Cole chuckled, but Garner didn't seem amused. He reached in his desk drawer and pulled out a prescription bottle, popping a pill in his mouth and downing it with a drink from a thermal tumbler.

"Using prescription antacids now? Tums aren't cutting it anymore?"

"These aren't antacids." Garner shook the pill bottle as he spoke between gritted teeth. "This is Xanax. But I only take them when I'm *extremely* agitated."

"No need to be upset," Cole said. "I'll still pay your hourly rate."

"Please don't speak." Garner held up his hand to shush him, then lowered it into his lap. Swaying slightly in his chair, he stared at the wall behind them, his eyes unfocused. "I need to meditate now," he said in a calm tone, like Mr. Rogers.

"We actually stopped by because we wanted you to draw up a will," said Cole.

Garner closed his eyes and made a humming noise through his nose.

EPILOGUE

"Oh, and we want to do away with that prenuptial agreement, too."

The humming noise got louder, pausing only when he stopped to take a breath.

"Maybe we should go," Brooke whispered. "I think Nicole is getting hungry."

Cole helped her stand up, the baby still safely nestled in the wrap. "Should we do anything about him? You think he's okay?"

Brooke shrugged and circled her finger at her temple, making the *crazy* sign. "He seems really stressed."

"Maybe he needs counseling." Cole wagged his eyebrows. "You should leave him one of your new cards."

∼

(Ten months later)

"May I have this dance, Mrs. Miller?" Cole bowed, gallantly holding out his hand.

"Why yes, Mr. Miller, I'd love to dance." Brooke relaxed in Cole's confident arms as he led her around the dance floor in a two-step. He looked amazing, as he always did in his tuxedo, custom cut to allow for his broad shoulders and narrow hips. When the music slowed, he pulled her close, and she let her left hand rest on the hard planes of his chest.

"I can't believe it's been a year and a half since we got married in Vegas," he said, bending to nuzzle her neck, an act which never failed to send chills down her spine.

"Mmmm... You'd better stop that or I'm not going to want to stay until they leave in the limo."

EPILOGUE

"Great idea! They'll never miss us." Cole nibbled on her ear. "Jarrett hasn't taken his eyes off his bride since he got here."

She gave him a playful slap on his arm. "Everyone else will miss us. We can't go upstairs early."

"We only have one night away from Nicole. We need to take advantage of every minute."

She pushed her lip out. "Don't you miss your daughter?"

"You know I do." He squeezed her with his arms and bent his back to lift her off the floor and twirl in a circle, leaving her laughing and breathless. "I'm the one who watched the video your mom sent, three times during dinner. She's walking so well, she'll probably be running by the time we get home."

"Do you ever regret staying married to me?"

It was a game, and Cole knew the rules.

"Not usually. Most of the time, you're a pretty incredible wife."

"Most of the time?" She feigned anger. "What about the rest of the time?"

"When you're not incredible, you're perfect, and that's a problem."

"You don't think you're lucky, having a perfect wife?"

"There's such a thing as being too perfect," he said. "It's intimidating. A guy like me needs a woman who worships at his feet."

"But I do. Who could resist worshiping those boots? They're almost older than I am."

"Well, then... I suppose I don't regret staying married to you, after all. Though I have to say, I wouldn't want to repeat those first five months. Like the night I slept next to you and couldn't touch you. That was about the worst torture I've ever endured. Worse than when I tripped and landed butt-first on that cactus."

She chuckled and rested her head on his shoulder as they swayed together. Everything felt right with the world.

"Cole, you know how we talked about how many kids you want to have? And you said four, and I said two at the most?"

"Yes." He kissed her cheek. "But I was only teasing. I'll be happy with however many you want."

"Well, I've decided three is a good compromise."

"I already offered to let you drag me off to our room early." He grinned, his delicious dimples winking at her. "Did you want to start that second one tonight?"

"Actually, that second one started about six weeks ago."

He froze, mouth dropping open. "Are you serious?"

She nodded. "It's early, so don't—"

He swallowed her objections with a kiss that curled her toes. Laughing like a wild man, he lifted her again to spin in a circle. Then, he froze and let her slide to the floor.

"Did that hurt you? Or the baby?" he whispered, his brows bunched in a knot.

"No. I love it." She giggled. "I love *you*."

"Brooke, I love you so much. You brought me to life, and I'll never regret a day we spend together." He kissed her, melting her knees from under her. But his strong arms held her up, like always. He would never let her fall.

"And that's not temporary," he murmured. "That's *forever*."

THE END

ABOUT THE AUTHOR

Tamie Dearen lives in Texas with her incredibly romantic husband and two dogs. She loves anything musical or artistic, but hates dusting and exercising. When she's not writing books, you might find her playing with her grandkids or drilling on someone's tooth.

ACKNOWLEDGMENTS

First, I'd like to thank Donna Weaver, fabulous author and friend, who's given me feedback and encouragement throughout this writing process.

Thanks to my great team of ARC and beta readers. I couldn't have done it without you! And a special thanks to Tamie Dearen's Remarkable Romance Readers: Wanda Liendro, Jessica Dismukes, Nadine Peterse-Vrijhof, Trudy Dapprich, Rennae McIntosh, Lisa Stillman, Clare Rauch Drexel, Sue Stinnett, Loriann Peterson Merritt, Linda Wesson, Caroline Lemke Frost, Jennifer Chastain, Melissa Ann Medell Hayford, Barbara Gill, Dana McCall Michael, Jennifer Chastain, Teresa Brown, Caroline Frost, Misty Goan, Patti Ferrin, Victoria Higham Thomley. This team is my sounding board and cheer squad. I love you guys!

Thanks to my fabulous editor, Laurie Penner, and my proofreader, Tabitha Kocsis! You're the best!

Thanks to my family and friends who put up with my stress and crazy schedule.

And last, but not least, thank you, sweet hubby, for being the most romantic and supportive husband in the universe!

ALSO BY TAMIE DEAREN

Sweet Romance

The Best Girls Series:

Her Best Match

Best Dating Rules

Best Foot Forward

Best Laid Plans

Best Intentions

Sweet Romance

A Rose in Bloom

Restoring Romance

Wrangled by the Watchful Cowboy

Sweet Adventure

Love, Snow, and Mistletoe

Sweet Inspirational Romance

The Billionaire's Secret Marriage

The Billionaire's Reckless Marriage

The Billionaire's Temporary Marriage

The Billionaire's Alternate Marriage (November 2019)

Christian Romance

Noelle's Golden Christmas

Haley's Hangdog Holiday

Shara's Happy Newfoundland Year

Holiday, Inc. Boxed Set

The Alora Series

YA/Fantasy

Alora: The Wander-Jewel

Alora: The Portal

Alora: The Maladorn Scroll

Subscribe to TamieDearen.com and get your free books!

Follow on Facebook: Tamie Dearen Author

Follow on Twitter: @TamieDearen

Made in the USA
Coppell, TX
27 March 2020